TIDES OF ATTRACTION

EMILY HAWTHORNE

Copyright © 2024 by Emily Hawthorne

All rights reserved.

No portion of this book may be reproduced in any form without written permission from the publisher or author, except as permitted by U.S. copyright law.

Contents

1. Prologue — 1
2. Chapter 1 — 3
3. Chapter 2 — 14
4. Chapter 3 — 26
5. Chapter 4 — 36
6. Chapter 5 — 46
7. Chapter 6 — 58
8. Chapter 7 — 70
9. Chapter 8 — 80
10. Chapter 9 — 90
11. Chapter 10 — 99
12. Chapter 11 — 109
13. Chapter 12 — 120
14. Chapter 13 — 132
15. Chapter 14 — 142

16.	Chapter 15	152
17.	Chapter 16	162
18.	Chapter 17	170
19.	Chapter 18	179
20.	Chapter 19	193
21.	Chapter 20	207
22.	Chapter 21	218
23.	Chapter 22	229
24.	Chapter 23	238
25.	Chapter 24	250
26.	Epilogue	261

PROLOGUE

I stood before the grand doors of Cambridge University, my heart pounding with a cocktail of excitement and trepidation. This was it—my fresh start, a chance to escape the shadows of high school and immerse myself in the promise of a new beginning. The air was crisp, filled with the scent of freshly cut grass and the distant murmur of eager students. I took a deep breath, trying to steady my nerves as I pushed through the imposing entrance.

The campus was every bit as magnificent as I'd imagined, with its sprawling courtyards and ancient stone buildings whispering tales of scholars long past. I was determined to focus solely on my studies, to leave behind the drama and distractions that had marked my teenage years. This was my chance to reinvent myself, to carve out a future defined by my own ambitions rather than the conflicts that had once consumed me.

Little did I know that fate had a different plan. As I approached the door to my dorm room, I felt a flutter of anticipation. I was ready to embrace my new life, to meet new people and start fresh. But when I swung open the door, the sight before me stopped me dead in my tracks. There, with his familiar smug grin, was Kylian—my worst enemy from high school.

The shock was immediate and overwhelming. Kylian, the very person I had hoped to leave behind, stood in my new world like a ghost from my past. His presence was a jarring reminder that no matter how far I tried to run, some things were simply beyond my control. As I struggled to process the situation, I realized that my journey at Cambridge was about to take an unexpected turn, one that would challenge everything I thought I knew about myself and him.

And so began the unlikely cohabitation between two people who had once clashed at every turn. What lay ahead was a story neither of us could have anticipated, unfolding against the backdrop of one of the world's most prestigious institutions.

Chapter 1

I'm Kathleen, and as I stood on the brink of a new adventure, my life felt like a sitcom episode waiting to happen. Here I was, stuffing the last of my belongings into an overstuffed suitcase that seemed determined to mock my attempt at organized packing. The mission was clear: leave behind my high school drama and head off to Cambridge University, where the only thing I hoped to confront was the challenge of advanced calculus.

But packing—oh, packing was a whole different beast. It's amazing how many seemingly essential items one can accumulate over the years. I pulled out a box labeled "Sentimental Crap" that I'd been meaning to sort through for months. Why did I need a tattered teddy bear from kindergarten or a collection of outdated concert tickets? I'm sure future me will appreciate the sentimental value of a 2009 Blink-182 ticket. Or maybe not.

As I wrestled with the suitcase's stubborn zipper, I glanced around my room. It was filled with posters of bands I swore I'd outgrow, stacks of textbooks that looked suspiciously like they hadn't been touched in a while, and enough clothes to clothe an entire army. I sighed and muttered to no one in particular, "I'm starting to think this suitcase might be sentient and actively trying to prevent my departure."

My mom, bless her heart, was hovering nearby with a mixture of pride and worry etched on her face. "Are you sure you don't want to bring your lucky socks? You know, the ones you haven't washed since sophomore year?"

I shot her a look that could only be described as "mother, please." "I'm sure, Mom. I'm trying to start fresh here, not drag my old bad habits along with me."

With one final heave, I managed to wrestle the suitcase shut. I looked at it, victorious, as if I'd just conquered Everest. And then came the reality check: I still had to fit in my favorite books, my old comfort food snacks, and, most importantly, my prized collection of mismatched socks.

As I prepared to leave, a pang of sadness tugged at my heart. It wasn't just about leaving home; it was about stepping into the unknown. Cambridge was a world of ancient libraries and esteemed professors, a place where the next chapter of my life was waiting to be written. I couldn't help but think about the high school dramas I was leaving behind and how they might just be waiting for me in the form of an unexpected roommate or a surprise plot twist.

With one last look at my now comically overpacked suitcase, I took a deep breath. I was ready to face whatever came next, even if it meant stumbling through a new world with nothing more than a suitcase full of mismatched socks and an optimistic smile. Here's to new beginnings and hoping that my future self would forgive me for the questionable packing choices of my past.

Leaving the house was a bittersweet affair. My mom stood on the porch, waving with that look that said, "I'm proud, but also secretly terrified you're going to stumble into a series of unfortunate events." I gave her a thumbs-up, trying to mask my own nerves with an overly enthusiastic grin. I could almost hear her muttering, "Don't forget your umbrella!" even though it was sunny.

The drive to the airport was uneventful, save for the minor mishap of accidentally spilling coffee on my favorite travel mug. Somehow, the universe had decided that my pre-departure rituals needed a touch of chaos. The airport, in contrast, was a bustling hive of activity. I navigated through the check-in counters, security, and the endless sea of people with a kind of grim determination that only comes from having too much caffeine and too little sleep.

Once I finally reached my gate, I plopped down in my assigned seat, feeling a mix of relief and anticipation. I pulled out a tourist map of the United Kingdom, determined to plan out every possible sightseeing opportunity between lectures. As I was engrossed in deciphering the mysteries of London's tube system, a voice cut through my concentration with the subtlety of a foghorn.

"Is that the map to the tourist trap section?" the voice sneered. I looked up, and there he was: Kylian Rivera.

Kylian Rivera was the very definition of high school annoyance. He had this knack for turning even the simplest of tasks into an opportunity for mocking others. With his perfectly styled hair and an arrogant grin, he had been the bane of my academic existence. He thrived on making everyone else feel inferior, and I was his favorite target. I had hoped that leaving for Cambridge would mean leaving behind his smirking face and his endless supply of condescending remarks. Apparently, life had a different sense of humor.

"What's wrong, Kathleen? Not sure if you're heading to an Ivy League or just another amusement park?" he quipped.

I rolled my eyes, already feeling my patience wear thin. "Oh, Kylian. I didn't realize they allowed failed comedians into prestigious universities."

His grin widened, clearly pleased with his own wit. "Well, it seems I've managed to get in despite the odds. Maybe you'll find that Cambridge has a sense of humor after all."

As if that wasn't enough, Kylian casually strode toward his seat, only to "accidentally" swing his oversized travel bag in my direction. It connected with my shoulder in a way that could only be described as a "well-placed accident." I glared at him, incredulous. How in the world had this guy been admitted here?

He settled into the seat next to mine, still wearing that irritatingly smug expression. I had hoped that the vastness of the university would keep us from crossing paths, but it seemed fate was not on my side. We were now destined to share an airplane ride, and, apparently, part of our university experience.

As we both settled in, I tried to ignore the way his presence seemed to loom over my newfound adventure. The universe might have a twisted sense of humor, but I was determined not to let Kylian ruin my excitement. After all, if I was going to survive Cambridge, I'd have to be prepared for a few unexpected twists—and maybe, just maybe, figure out a way to avoid bumping into him too often.

Sitting next to Kylian for a six-hour flight was nothing short of torture. Each time I stole a glance at him, my irritation grew. There he was, lounging comfortably, headphones on, seemingly oblivious to the world. Kylian was a professional swimmer, and it showed. His athletic physique was practically on display, and he knew it. With his flawless hair and self-assured grin, he was the sort of guy who made you wonder if he'd ever faced a day of normalcy.

But the worst part? He had the audacity to act as though he was completely engrossed in his music, as if the rest of us didn't exist. The plane was packed, and though I had managed to get a window seat originally, I had foolishly agreed to switch to the middle seat when it became clear that Kylian's spot was the only one left next to mine.

Now, with only two hours left of this flying nightmare, nature decided to make its presence known. The pressure on my bladder was becoming unbearable. I glanced at Kylian, hoping he might take pity on me and move, but no. He was blissfully unaware—or pretending to be—buried in his music.

"Excuse me," I said, leaning over and giving him a gentle nudge. "Can you please move? I need to get to the bathroom."

Kylian didn't budge. I repeated my request, raising my voice slightly. Still nothing. It was as if he was in his own private concert, and my pleas were just background noise.

Frustration mounting, I shifted uncomfortably, crossing and uncrossing my legs in a desperate attempt to relieve the pressure. I tried to think of anything else, but the thought of how my predicament was entirely due to my bad luck and the fact that Kylian was too absorbed in his own world to notice me was maddening.

Finally, with a sigh of resignation, I resolved to endure the rest of the flight with my discomfort. I watched the clock tick slowly, each minute feeling like an eternity. When the plane finally landed, I scrambled to my feet, more than ready to escape both the flight and Kylian's infuriating presence.

As I disembarked, I vowed that the next few years at Cambridge would be spent avoiding him as much as possible. After all, if I had to share more moments with him, I'd prefer them to be in a setting where I didn't have to beg him to move so I could pee.

As I stood at the baggage claim, anxiously scanning the conveyor belt for my suitcase, Kylian hovered uncomfortably close. His presence was a reminder that the universe truly had a twisted sense of humor. I was fuming, the discomfort of the flight still fresh in my mind.

Kylian, clearly enjoying my frustration, leaned in with that infuriating smirk plastered on his face. "So, did you finally manage to make it to the bathroom, or did you have to hold it all the way?"

I shot him a glare that could have frozen lava. "Oh, very funny, Kylian. It's not like I had a choice with you ignoring my requests. Some people actually have basic manners."

He chuckled, clearly delighted by my irritation. "Hey, I was just enjoying some music. Didn't realize my playlist was also supposed to include bathroom breaks for my seatmates."

I wanted to retort further, but the sight of my suitcase finally emerging on the conveyor belt distracted me. I grabbed it quickly, my frustration still simmering as I prepared to head to the exit.

Kylian gave me one last, smug look before grabbing his own bags and walking off. His laughter echoed behind him, a reminder that no matter how far I tried to distance myself from him, Kylian was always going to be a thorn in my side.

With a resigned sigh, I took a deep breath, reminding myself that this was just the beginning of a new chapter. If I could survive six hours of discomfort next to Kylian, I could handle whatever Cambridge threw my way.

The drive to the university was smooth, and as I arrived on campus, the grandeur of the buildings took my breath away. I gazed out of the window, marveling at the historic architecture and the sprawling greenery. It was hard to believe I was finally here, ready to start this new chapter of my life.

With a determined stride, I hauled my heavy suitcases toward the student housing. Each step felt like a small victory as I navigated the maze of corridors, memorizing the number of my room to avoid getting lost. I couldn't wait to meet my new roommate and find out what she was like. Would she be friendly? Quiet? Or perhaps a complete opposite of me?

When I finally reached my door, I took a deep breath and turned the handle, eager to see my new living space. As I stepped inside, the room was empty except for a few bags on one of the beds. I noted the absence of my roommate and, feeling a little like a kid at a sleepover, picked the bed closest to the window.

I was about to start unpacking when I noticed a logo on one of the bags—an emblem for the swim team.

My heart sank. Was my roommate a swimmer? Please, not another Kylian. I desperately hoped she wouldn't be as unbearable as him.

Just as I was about to put my first book on the desk, I heard the bathroom door creak open. Excitement bubbled up inside me. Finally, I'd get to meet her. I turned around and froze. Out of the bathroom stepped none other than Kylian Rivera, looking as smug as ever.

"What the hell?" I blurted out, my voice echoing in the small room. "What are you doing here?"

Kylian's smirk grew wider. "Looks like we're not just seatmates on the plane, Kathleen. We're dorm mates too."

I stared at him in disbelief. "You've got to be kidding me. This is the worst luck ever. What are you even doing here?"

Kylian shrugged nonchalantly, as if the universe had handed him the ultimate prize. "I'm here for swimming, obviously. And it seems fate has a wicked sense of humor. Maybe you should've paid more attention to your seatmate's details."

"You're an absolute nightmare," I snapped. "I can't believe this. First, you ignore me on the plane, and now you're my roommate? Is there no escape from you?"

He took a step closer, our faces inches apart. The proximity made me shiver, and my breath hitched. Kylian's eyes locked onto mine, and his voice dropped to a conspiratorial whisper. "Listen, if you want to make the best of this situation, you should go see the administration. There's a mix-up that needs fixing."

I was taken aback by his sudden shift in demeanor, but I wasn't about to be swayed by his charm. "Oh, so now you're playing the helpful guy? What's next, offering me a welcome basket?"

Before I could react, Kylian snatched my glasses off my face. "You'll need these to see clearly," he said, his tone dripping with sarcasm.

"Give those back!" I shouted, snatching the glasses from his hands with a fierce tug. "You're such an ass!"

I stormed out of the room, my frustration and confusion boiling over. My heart pounded as I made my way to the administration office, hoping they could sort out this mess and, hopefully, get me away from Kylian for a while.

I trudged back to the administration office, trying to keep my frustration in check. The clerk behind the desk looked up with a sympathetic smile as I approached.

"We've confirmed that there was indeed a mix-up," she said, her voice tinged with regret. "However, all the dorms are currently full. We don't have any available rooms at the moment. You'll need to wait for about four months for a new assignment."

Four months? My jaw dropped. "You've got to be kidding me. I can't stay here for four months!"

She gave me a small, apologetic smile. "I'm really sorry, but that's the earliest we can offer. In the meantime, we'll make sure you're on the top of the list for the next available room."

I forced a smile, my mind racing as I left the office. Four months with Kylian was the last thing I wanted. I made my way back to the dorm, my steps feeling heavier with each passing moment.

When I returned to the room, Kylian was already settled in, his belongings neatly arranged and a faint smell of his cologne lingering in the air. He looked up as I entered, his expression a mix of curiosity and amusement.

"So, what did they say?" he asked, casually stretching out on his bed.

I took a deep breath, trying to keep my irritation in check. "There was a mix-up. Apparently, all the dorms are full, so I have to wait about four months for a new room."

Kylian raised an eyebrow, clearly not thrilled by the news. "Four months? That's rough. I guess we're stuck together for a while."

"Yeah, stuck together," I echoed, my voice dripping with sarcasm. "Lucky me."

Kylian chuckled, "Well, at least you're with me. Plenty of girls would kill to be in your position."

I narrowed my eyes at him. "Oh, really? And why would they want to be with you? Just because you're a swimmer doesn't mean you're some kind of prize."

He shrugged, his grin never faltering. "I'm just saying, you could do worse. And if we're going to be stuck together, it might be better if we figure out how to make it work."

I threw my hands up in exasperation. "Make it work? This isn't some kind of reality show. I just want a space where I can breathe without having to deal with your attitude."

Kylian rolled his eyes. "Look, I get it. This situation sucks for both of us. But for the next four months, let's just agree to keep our distance. You do your thing, I'll do mine. It'll be less painful for both of us."

I took a deep breath, trying to calm down. "Fine. I can deal with that. But don't think for a second that I'm going to make this easy for you."

"Wouldn't dream of it," Kylian said with a smirk. "Just try not to let your frustration spill over too often. I like my space as much as you do."

I shook my head, muttering under my breath as I began to unpack my things. It wasn't ideal, but if keeping my distance from Kylian was the key to surviving the next few months, then that was exactly what I'd do.

Chapter 2

I opened the windows wide, hoping to flush out the cloying scent of Kylian's cologne that seemed to cling to every corner of the room. The smell was overpowering, a mix of musky undertones and something that I could only describe as "trying-too-hard."

Kylian looked up from his spot on the bed, his brow furrowing in confusion. "What are you doing?"

I shrugged, trying to keep my voice neutral. "Just airing out the room. Your cologne is a bit much."

He gave me a bemused look but didn't press further, opting instead to return to his own business. As evening fell, the room fell into an uneasy silence. Kylian was in his corner, and I was in mine, each of us ensconced in our own activities.

From where I sat, I watched him move about. He was engrossed in his phone, occasionally glancing up at the ceiling as if pondering some great mystery. Every so often, he would stretch, his muscles rippling under his shirt—a reminder of his status as a professional swimmer. His dark hair fell into place with a casual ease that somehow seemed to enhance his already perfect appearance. His blue eyes, though frustratingly handsome, were just another reminder of how undeserving he was of all the attention he got.

As I looked at him, I couldn't help but wonder how on earth anyone could fall for someone so self-assured and annoyingly attractive. Sure, he was tall, with dark hair and striking blue eyes, but in my opinion, his charm was more about confidence than actual substance.

The day had been a whirlwind of unpacking and organizing my belongings. I'd managed to get my things sorted out and had finally learned my class schedule, which was a small victory in itself. The sense of accomplishment was overshadowed by the frustration of having to share a space with someone I found insufferable.

Kylian, for his part, seemed to be perfectly content. Occasionally, I would hear the muffled sounds of him laughing at something on his phone or chatting with friends. It was clear he was used to being the center of attention and had no intention of letting the change in scenery affect him.

As I tried to focus on my own tasks, the dissonance between our worlds was glaring. I was here to focus on my studies and make a fresh start, while Kylian seemed to float through life with effortless charm. The more I observed him, the more I felt the weight of the four months ahead.

The silence in the room was a stark contrast to the chaos I had felt earlier, and as the evening wore on, I settled into a routine of trying to ignore Kylian's presence. It wasn't easy, but it was clear that if I wanted to survive this, I'd have to master the art of coexistence.

I opened the windows wide, hoping to flush out the cloying scent of Kylian's cologne that seemed to cling to every corner of the room. The smell was overpowering, a mix of musky undertones and something that I could only describe as "trying-too-hard."

Kylian looked up from his spot on the bed, his brow furrowing in confusion. "What are you doing?"

I shrugged, trying to keep my voice neutral. "Just airing out the room. Your cologne is a bit much."

He gave me a bemused look but didn't press further, opting instead to return to his own business. As evening fell, the room fell into an uneasy silence. Kylian was in his corner, and I was in mine, each of us ensconced in our own activities.

From where I sat, I watched him move about. He was engrossed in his phone, occasionally glancing up at the ceiling as if pondering some great mystery. Every so often, he would stretch, his muscles rippling under his shirt—a reminder of his status as a professional swimmer. His dark hair fell into place with a casual ease that somehow seemed to enhance his already perfect appearance. His blue eyes, though frustratingly handsome, were just another reminder of how undeserving he was of all the attention he got.

As I looked at him, I couldn't help but wonder how on earth anyone could fall for someone so self-assured and annoyingly attractive. Sure, he was tall, with dark hair and striking blue eyes, but in my opinion, his charm was more about confidence than actual substance.

The day had been a whirlwind of unpacking and organizing my belongings. I'd managed to get my things sorted out and had finally learned my class schedule, which was a small victory in itself. The sense of accomplishment was overshadowed by the frustration of having to share a space with someone I found insufferable.

Kylian, for his part, seemed to be perfectly content. Occasionally, I would hear the muffled sounds of him laughing at something on his phone or chatting with friends. It was clear he was used to being the center of attention and had no intention of letting the change in scenery affect him.

As I tried to focus on my own tasks, the dissonance between our worlds was glaring. I was here to focus on my studies and make a fresh start, while Kylian seemed to float through life with effortless charm. The more I observed him, the more I felt the weight of the four months ahead.

The silence in the room was a stark contrast to the chaos I had felt earlier, and as the evening wore on, I settled into a routine of trying to ignore Kylian's presence. It wasn't easy, but it was clear that if I wanted to survive this, I'd have to master the art of coexistence.

As we sat in the silence of the dorm room, the clatter of cereal against bowls was the only sound breaking the otherwise tense atmosphere. I was immersed in my breakfast, mentally reviewing the tasks I had to tackle for the day, while Kylian seemed absorbed in his phone, his face illuminated by the screen's glow.

Suddenly, the sound of the door opening cut through the silence. I looked up, bracing myself for whatever new development awaited us. My internal plea was simple: Please, let it not be a guy.

To my surprise, a cheerful blonde girl burst into the room, her excitement almost palpable. She was struggling with a couple of large suitcases but managed to greet us with an enthusiastic wave.

"Hi! I'm Regina!" she announced, her voice bright and friendly. "I hope I'm not interrupting. I'm moving in!"

Kylian barely looked up from his phone, offering only a brief nod in her direction. I, on the other hand, jumped up to help Regina with her bags, eager to make a good impression and escape the stifling atmosphere that had settled in the room.

"Hey, Regina! Welcome!" I said, grabbing one of her suitcases. "Let me help you with that."

"Oh, thank you so much!" Regina said with a beaming smile. "I wasn't sure where to start. I didn't expect to have so much help on the first day."

"No problem at all," I replied, helping her with her luggage. "We've been here a little while already, so I'm glad to lend a hand."

As we started to unpack her bags, Regina's gaze fell on Kylian, who was now half-heartedly glancing up from his phone.

"So, um, who's this?" Regina asked, her curiosity evident. "I thought I was moving in with another girl."

I hesitated for a moment, wondering how to explain the situation without sounding too bitter. "Oh, this is Kylian. He's, um, a temporary roommate."

Regina raised an eyebrow, looking between Kylian and me. "A temporary roommate? I didn't realize they allowed guys to stay in the dorms. Is everything okay?"

I forced a smile. "Yeah, it's just a bit of a mix-up. I'm sure it'll be sorted out soon. For now, we're just making the best of it."

Regina nodded slowly, still clearly puzzled. "Well, as long as it's okay with everyone, I'm sure we can make it work. I'm really excited to be here and meet everyone."

Kylian finally looked up from his phone, his expression neutral. "Nice to meet you, Regina. I'm sure we'll all get along just fine."

Regina, eager to settle in, continued to chat with me while we arranged her things. She seemed genuinely excited about starting this new chapter and her energy was a welcome distraction from the tension in the room. I couldn't help but feel a bit hopeful that having Regina around might make these next few months more bearable.

As we finished setting up her space, Regina's enthusiasm began to lift the mood, even if just a little. With any luck, her presence would bring some much-needed positivity to our makeshift trio.

As the clock ticked past midnight, the dorm was wrapped in a quiet stillness. The sounds of snoring from the various rooms were a comforting background to my own exhaustion. I had finally managed to get some sleep, but the peace was abruptly shattered by a strange noise coming from the common area.

Groaning inwardly, I dragged myself out of bed, the exhaustion from the day weighing heavily on my limbs. I stumbled towards the noise, my footsteps soft on the carpeted floor. As I reached the living room, I rubbed my eyes and squinted at the dim light.

There was Kylian, stretching his limbs with exaggerated grace. His movements were smooth, almost too smooth, as if he was performing a slow-motion ballet.

"What on earth are you doing?" I asked, my voice laced with sarcasm and fatigue. "Trying to wake up the entire building with your stretching routine?"

Kylian glanced over his shoulder, his face a picture of mock innocence. "It's well known that stretching before bed helps with relaxation. Didn't you know that?"

I rolled my eyes, crossing my arms. "Oh, of course. How could I not be aware of that essential pre-sleep ritual? Next time, maybe you could add some interpretive dance to really complete the effect."

He chuckled, his laughter low and slightly amused. "If you're lucky, maybe I will. Or maybe I'll just keep stretching in silence. Either way, I'm doing this for my own well-being."

As he continued his stretches, he suddenly paused and turned towards me with a curious expression. His gaze seemed to linger a bit longer than necessary, and I felt an involuntary shiver run down my spine.

"You know," he said, his voice softer now, "I never noticed before, but you have freckles. They're kind of...cute."

I stiffened, feeling my cheeks flush. "Well, thank you for the observation, but I'm trying to go back to sleep. Maybe save your commentary for a more appropriate time."

Kylian's eyes softened, but he didn't move. "Sure thing. Sorry if I woke you. I'll try to be quieter."

I gave him a curt nod, trying to ignore the unsettling way his gaze had made me feel. Turning on my heel, I headed back to my room, determined to get some rest despite the unexpected encounter.

As I climbed back into bed, I muttered to myself, "What an idiot." The day had been challenging enough without Kylian's antics. Despite my irritation, I was secretly relieved that he hadn't pushed it further.

I pulled the covers tightly around me, hoping for a few hours of uninterrupted sleep before the chaos of the next day.

The next morning, I woke to the sound of animated chatter coming from the kitchen. Groaning, I forced myself out of bed, the comfort of sleep now a distant memory. Today was the start of classes, and I needed to be sharp, despite feeling anything but.

As I shuffled into the kitchen, still half-asleep and disheveled, I was greeted by an unexpected sight: Regina and Kylian were seated at the breakfast table, engaged in cheerful conversation. Regina was laughing at something Kylian had said, her eyes sparkling with the kind of morning energy I wished I could summon.

I cleared my throat, ready to join in and make some semblance of social interaction. Just as I was about to speak, Kylian decided it was the perfect moment to start his blender. The loud whirring noise drowned out my attempt at greeting.

I tried again, but every time I opened my mouth, Kylian turned on the blender. It was like some twisted game of silent charades, with him playing the role of the obnoxious maestro.

Finally, after what felt like an eternity of blender noise, Kylian shut it off with an exaggerated flourish and flashed me that infuriatingly perfect smile of his. "Good morning! Hope you slept well."

I managed a tired smile that didn't quite reach my eyes. "Morning."

Kylian, oblivious to my frustration, grabbed his bag and gave Regina a quick hug before heading out. "See you at school, Regina. And, uh, see you around, Kathleen."

With that, he was gone, leaving me alone in the kitchen with Regina, who seemed genuinely sorry about the whole blender debacle.

"I'm really sorry about that," Regina said, looking slightly embarrassed. "Kylian can be a bit...persistent with his morning routines."

"It's fine," I said, trying to sound more gracious than I felt. "I just needed to get used to the whole living situation. I'm sure it'll be okay."

Regina nodded sympathetically. "If you need anything or want to chat later, just let me know. I'm here for you."

I appreciated the offer, but at that moment, I was too frazzled to take full advantage of it. I just needed to get ready for the day and face my new classes. I abandoned any further attempts at socializing and headed back to my room, where I could finally start preparing for the whirlwind of the day ahead.

As I got dressed and mentally braced myself for my first day of classes, I couldn't help but hope that things would settle into a more manageable routine. If Kylian and his blender became a regular part of my mornings, I might need a whole new strategy for survival.

As Regina and I made our way to campus, the excitement of the first day was palpable, at least for Regina, who buzzed with enthusiasm about everything from the architecture to the opportunities. I was more focused on surviving the day and figuring out how to manage my new living situation.

Classes began, and I quickly discovered that some were as thrilling as watching paint dry. There were moments, however, when certain subjects or professors had enough charm to make the time pass more pleasantly. Perhaps it was the undeniable fact that a few professors were rather easy on the eyes. Whatever it was, it was enough to make me hope for some more engaging lectures.

In my art class, which was marginally better due to the allure of the subject, I settled into my seat and began taking notes. As I was scribbling away, I felt a presence next to me. I looked up to see a guy settling into the seat beside me.

He leaned in and whispered, "Hey, do you happen to have an eraser?"

I glanced at my notes and shook my head. "Sorry, I'm writing in pen. No erasers here."

He grinned, clearly amused. "Pen, huh? So you're a risk-taker. I like that."

I chuckled softly, a bit thrown off by his casual attitude. "Yeah, I guess. I prefer to live on the edge."

His grin widened as he continued, still whispering. "So, are you going to the welcome party tonight? I hear it's going to be quite the event."

I hesitated, feeling a bit unsure. "I'm not sure. Parties aren't really my thing."

He tilted his head, giving me a curious look. "Not a fan of parties, huh? Well, if you change your mind, you might just miss out on something special."

The way he said it made me wonder if he was flirting. I felt my cheeks flush slightly. "Maybe I'll think about it."

I glanced over at him, trying to keep my composure. "I'm Kathleen, by the way."

"Aaron," he replied, his smile genuine. "Nice to meet you, Kathleen."

He was quite handsome—tall, with a friendly face and an easy charm. I turned my gaze away, feeling my face heat up even more. This was not how I expected my first day to go, but I had to admit, it was a pleasant distraction from the chaos of my living situation.

As the class continued, Aaron and I exchanged a few more whispers and laughs. His presence made the class more bearable and, for a moment, made me forget about the stress of starting over in a new place. I still wasn't sure if I would go to the party, but Aaron's company was certainly a welcome surprise.

The day had dragged on, and by the time classes ended, I found myself wandering through the labyrinthine halls of the university, searching for a quiet spot to study. I was feeling both lost and a little overwhelmed by the sheer size of the campus.

As I wandered, I stumbled upon the swimming pool area. Curious, I peered through the large glass windows. Inside, a group of swimmers glided through the water with effortless grace. I watched, trying to make sense of the appeal. The idea of strapping on a tight swim cap that pinched my head and goggles that dug into my eyes didn't exactly seem like a recipe for fun to me. And don't even get me started on the thought of water up my nose.

A few swimmers climbed out of the pool, and as they did, I couldn't help but notice the display of toned physiques. The guys emerging were a sight to behold—muscles rippling with each movement, their skin glistening slightly from the pool water. They were the kind of fit that seemed to belong on a magazine cover, with well-defined abs and broad shoulders that suggested both strength and discipline.

I felt my cheeks warm as I inadvertently studied their well-sculpted forms. Embarrassed by my own wandering gaze, I quickly averted my eyes and focused on finding my way out of this maze of confusion. My heart was racing a little faster now, and I couldn't help but feel a bit flustered by my accidental peep show.

Turning on my heel, I headed in the opposite direction, my thoughts a jumbled mess as I tried to focus on finding a study spot. My day had been full of new experiences and unexpected encounters, and this was just another twist in an already eventful start to my time at the university.

Chapter 3

Back in my room, I found myself twiddling my thumbs, staring blankly at the piles of books and random items scattered about. The question of whether I should go to the welcome party lingered in my mind. It could be a good way to meet people and perhaps take my mind off everything—plus, it would be a chance to get out of my room and socialize, even if the thought didn't thrill me.

As I debated with myself, there was a knock at the door. Regina's cheerful voice broke through my internal monologue. "Hey, Kathleen! Come on, it's time to get ready for the party. I've brought a dress for you to try!"

I opened the door to find Regina holding a light blue dress, a soft, flowy number that seemed both elegant and casual. I had to admit, it looked like it could be fun to wear.

With a mix of resignation and curiosity, I took the dress and headed to the bathroom to change. I slipped into the dress—it had a fitted bodice with a flared skirt that fell just above my knees. The fabric was a pleasant blend of comfort and style, and it was perfect for a casual party. The light blue color made my dark hair and eyes stand out, and the dress's subtle shimmer added a touch of sparkle.

After I'd dressed, I tackled my hair and makeup. I left my long, thick black hair loose, letting it cascade in gentle waves down my back. I opted for a simple yet polished look with a bit of makeup: a light foundation, a hint of blush, and a swipe of mascara. I wanted to look put-together but still like myself.

When I stepped out of my room, Regina was waiting for me, looking radiant in her own outfit. "Wow, you look great!" she exclaimed with genuine enthusiasm.

Kylian, who was lounging on the sofa with his phone, glanced up as I walked by. His eyes widened slightly before he smirked. "Well, well, look at you. Someone's all dressed up."

His comment, coupled with that infuriatingly smug smile, made me roll my eyes. "Thanks for the commentary, Kylian. I'm sure your opinion is exactly what I needed."

Regina, sensing the growing tension, quickly intervened. "Alright, let's not make this awkward. Kathleen, you look fantastic, and we're going to have a great time tonight. Come on!"

We headed out, and as we made our way to the party, I couldn't help but feel a mix of anticipation and dread. The evening promised to be an adventure, if nothing else. With any luck, it would be a chance to unwind and maybe even have a bit of fun. After all, I kept telling myself, I only had to survive four months with Kylian and his antics.

The party was in full swing, but to be honest, it was mostly a dull affair. The music was mediocre, and the crowd seemed more interested in their phones than actually mingling. Still, I made an effort to socialize and meet some of the other students.

As I scanned the room, I spotted Aaron from art class. He was standing by the snacks, and I decided to go say hi.

"Hey, Aaron! Fancy seeing you here," I said with a friendly smile.

He looked up and grinned, his eyes lighting up. "Kathleen! I was hoping you'd show up. You're looking great tonight."

"Thanks," I replied, feeling a bit flattered. "I'm just here trying to make the most of it."

Aaron leaned in slightly, his tone playful. "Well, you're certainly making the evening better. I have to say, I'm really glad we met earlier. I was thinking about how nice it would be to get to know you better."

I raised an eyebrow, a hint of amusement in my voice. "Oh really? Is that so? And how do you plan on doing that?"

He chuckled, looking genuinely interested. "Maybe we could grab coffee sometime? I'd love to hear more about what brought you here and what you think of Cambridge so far."

I was about to respond when I spotted Kylian nearby, talking with a group of swimmers. Seeing him reminded me of the less pleasant side of my living situation. I rolled my eyes and decided to get a drink to distract myself.

As I made my way to the drinks table, Regina appeared beside me, her energy infectious. "Come on, Kathleen! Let's go dance. We need to liven up this party!"

Before I could protest, she grabbed my hand and led me to the dance floor. I couldn't help but laugh as we joined the other students, moving to the beat of the music. Regina and I danced with abandon, enjoying the music and each other's company. It was a nice change from the earlier awkwardness, and for a while, I forgot about the less enjoyable aspects of the evening.

Despite the less-than-exciting atmosphere of the party, Regina's enthusiasm made it bearable. And who knew? Maybe the rest of the night would bring more surprises.

Regina and I stumbled back into the dorm, our laughter echoing through the halls as we tried to keep our balance. The party had left us both feeling quite tipsy, and we couldn't help but be a little rowdy as we navigated our way back to our rooms.

As we entered the dorm, the sound of muffled chatter and giggles came from the common area. I glanced over and, to my dismay, saw Kylian lounging on the couch with a girl draped over him. They seemed completely absorbed in each other, their heads close as they whispered and laughed.

Even in my tipsy state, I rolled my eyes. It was like something out of a bad soap opera. The last thing I needed was to be reminded of Kylian's charming yet obnoxious presence. Regina, blissfully unaware of my growing annoyance, started to chat animatedly about the evening's events.

Kylian looked up as we entered, his smirk widening when he saw us. "Well, well, if it isn't the dynamic duo, back from their big night out. Looks like someone had a little too much fun."

His voice was dripping with mockery, and I could feel the heat rising to my cheeks. "Yeah, well, not all of us have to stay up... um, late, with... people..." I tried to respond, but the words came out a jumbled mess as I stammered.

Kylian's laughter followed me as I made my way down the hall, desperately trying to escape the awkwardness. I muttered something incoherent under my breath as I pushed open the door to my room.

Once inside, I collapsed onto my bed, feeling both exhausted and relieved to be away from Kylian's annoying grin. My head was spinning slightly, and I could still hear the faint echoes of the party in the distance. I barely had the energy to change into pajamas before I sank into the softness of my mattress, letting out a sigh of relief.

I drifted off to sleep, grateful for the quiet and the comfort of my bed, hoping that tomorrow would be a better day—maybe even one without any more run-ins with Kylian.

The next morning, I woke up with a pounding headache, the aftermath of last night's festivities making itself known. I dragged myself out of bed, hoping a little food might help alleviate the throbbing pain in my temples.

As I shuffled into the kitchen, I saw the girl from last night emerging from our dormitory. Great, just what I needed—another reminder of Kylian's irritating presence. I tried to ignore the unpleasantness of the encounter and made my way to the cupboards in search of something to eat.

To my dismay, every single plate and bowl was stashed on the top shelves—just out of my reach. I stood on my tiptoes, stretching my arms as high as they would go, but it was no use. With Kylian being a towering 6 feet 2, I knew he'd made sure to put everything up there on purpose. Typical.

Frustrated and hungry, I sighed loudly. "Seriously?" I muttered, glaring at the shelves. "How is it fair that you get to make everything impossible just because you're taller?"

I considered trying to find a stool or something to stand on, but my headache and the sheer effort of it all made me rethink that plan. Defeated, I abandoned the idea of eating breakfast and slumped back into the common area.

The thought of Kylian and his selfish little tricks was almost enough to make me regret ever stepping into this dorm. The day had barely started, and I was already dreading the next interaction with him. I only hoped the rest of the day would be less exasperating.

A short while later, Kylian emerged from his room, still looking as smug and effortless as ever. He sauntered into the kitchen with a casual confidence that only seemed to aggravate my already pounding headache. Without even glancing in my direction, he reached up effortlessly and grabbed a bowl from the top shelf. Of course, he did it with the ease of someone who didn't have to struggle with his height.

He proceeded to pour himself a generous amount of cereal and milk, all while maintaining that insufferable air of nonchalance. The clinking of the spoon against the bowl was like nails on a chalkboard, and I couldn't help but sigh deeply.

"Must be nice," I muttered under my breath, though I knew he probably couldn't hear me over the crunch of his breakfast.

Kylian finally noticed me, catching my exasperated sigh. He raised an eyebrow, a smirk playing at the corners of his mouth. "Good morning, Kathleen. You look like you had quite a night."

"Good morning, Kylian," I said through gritted teeth. "Yeah, I did. And if you were wondering, I had a bit of trouble reaching the plates you so thoughtfully put on the top shelf."

He chuckled, not missing a beat. "I guess some things are just out of reach for some people."

I rolled my eyes and tried to ignore him as I slouched into a seat, still feeling the effects of my hangover. I wished I could escape this ridiculous dorm situation, but for now, I was stuck dealing with both Kylian and my persistent headache.

Kylian finished pouring his cereal and milk, then grabbed another bowl from the top shelf—of course, he could reach it effortlessly. To my surprise, he scooped up some cereal and milk, preparing a bowl specifically for me.

With an exaggerated flourish, he placed the bowl in front of me, his smirk wider than ever. "I thought you might be hungry," he said, his tone dripping with mock sweetness. "Figured I'd save you the trouble of stretching yourself."

I stared at the bowl, its contents staring back at me like a mocking reminder of how awkward and small I felt in this place. "I don't want it," I said firmly, pushing the bowl away. "I'm not a charity case."

Kylian's smirk didn't waver, but there was a glint of amusement in his eyes. "Oh, come on. I'm just trying to be nice," he said, leaning against the counter. "But if you'd rather starve..."

"Very funny," I replied, crossing my arms. "I'll find something else. Thanks, but no thanks."

He shrugged, apparently unbothered by my rejection. "Suit yourself. Just thought I'd make your morning a little easier."

I grabbed a glass of water and tried to ignore him as I sipped slowly, hoping the cool liquid would help with my headache. Kylian continued to eat his cereal with a casual ease, as if his small act of kindness was just another part of his daily routine.

The day at school seemed to drag on forever, each class blending into the next with a monotonous hum. The only highlight was a sudden announcement during one of my lectures: a new project assignment that required a practical study.

The project was to focus on learning swimming to better understand and analyze its effects on stress management and academic performance. Great. Just what I needed—an opportunity to dive into the sport I loathed more than anything. Not only did I have to observe swimmers, but I also had to learn how to swim myself. Perfect, right?

As the professor explained the details, I could feel a knot forming in my stomach. How could this be happening? I had never learned to swim, and now I was being forced into it by my dream school. The irony of the situation was almost too much to bear.

After class, I wandered through the hallways, trying to figure out how I was going to tackle this new requirement. My thoughts circled around the pool area I had glimpsed earlier. The idea of being in a swimsuit, floundering around in a pool, was beyond intimidating.

I considered asking for help, but there was no way I was turning to Kylian. He was already insufferable enough, and the thought of him knowing I needed swimming lessons was unbearable. Plus, knowing him, he'd probably find some way to make it a joke.

Instead, I decided to seek help from other sources. I started researching beginner swimming classes and tutors. I even scoured online forums and student groups for recommendations. The idea of facing Kylian, with his confident swagger and expert swimming skills, was the last thing I wanted to deal with.

By the end of the day, my head was spinning with information and the looming dread of my new swimming lessons. I tried to focus on the positives—at least I'd get to learn something new, right? But the thought of getting into a swimsuit and swimming in front of a crowd made me cringe.

As I walked back to the dorm, I couldn't help but feel that this project was shaping up to be the biggest challenge of my time at Cambridge.

That evening, I decided it was time to face my swimming fears. I pulled out the swimsuit I had bought two years ago—clearly destined to sit in my closet forever until now. It was a simple white one-piece, and as I looked at myself in the mirror, I couldn't help but think, "Seriously? This is what I have to wear?" I threw on a jacket to cover up and headed out, trying to muster some semblance of confidence.

When I arrived at the pool, I was greeted by the sight of a women's swim class in full swing. They moved through the water with grace and precision, making it look effortless. I stood at the edge, notebook in hand, scribbling down observations. Honestly, it was more amusing than anything else. Watching their synchronized strokes and the occasional splash of water was like observing a comedic performance.

As their class wrapped up, I took a deep breath and prepared to take my turn. The pool was intimidatingly empty except for me, which only added to the pressure. I climbed the ladder to enter the water, feeling the chill of the pool's temperature as it bit into my skin. It felt like I was stepping into a gigantic ice cube.

I counted to three—my personal countdown for brave attempts. On "three," I pushed off from the ladder and attempted to swim. The results were less than stellar. My strokes resembled a confused dog trying to navigate an alien landscape. At one point, I found myself on my back, flailing about like a fish out of water. My attempts to correct my position only led me to stare at the ceiling tiles, feeling like a stranded astronaut.

"Great start, Kathleen," I muttered to myself. "You've officially mastered the art of floating while looking utterly ridiculous."

As I continued to flounder about, I couldn't help but laugh at the absurdity of the situation. The pool was a minefield of misplaced strokes and splashes, and here I was, giving it my all and managing to create more waves than progress. I was definitely not the elegant swimmer I had hoped to be.

Chapter 4

As I lay there on my back, flailing in the water like a distressed starfish, I heard voices approaching. My immediate instinct was to scramble towards the ladder, but my attempts at swimming were more akin to a poorly executed flounder than anything graceful.

Then, I heard a familiar voice cut through the water's surface. "I'm going to grab my water bottle. The rest of you can leave," Kylian said, casually. Panic surged through me. I tried to find a spot to hide, but given the pool's limited options, my choice of concealment was less than stellar.

Kylian appeared at the edge of the pool, and as soon as his eyes fell on me, he burst into laughter. I attempted to keep my dignity intact, even though I was desperately trying not to splash around too much. "Shut up, Kylian!" I yelled, my voice echoing in the quiet pool area. His laughter continued, a reminder of my current predicament.

Kylian was decked out in a swim cap that made him look remarkably like Humpty Dumpty. He peeled it off, revealing his usual smirk. "Well, if it isn't the great swimmer of our time," he teased, taking in my less-than-stellar performance with amusement.

I finally managed to pull myself out of the pool, dripping wet and feeling the sting of embarrassment. As I tried to gather my things and escape, I slipped on the wet floor. Kylian was quick to grab my arm, his touch making my heart race for a completely different reason. I pulled away as soon as I could, clutching my bag tightly.

"Wait!" he called after me, but I was already making a beeline for the locker rooms. I dashed inside, the cool air of the changing area offering a brief respite from the humiliation. I knew I'd have to face him again soon enough, but for now, I was more than happy to hide away and mentally prepare for the next round of this swimming fiasco.

I was drying my hair in the locker room, feeling the sting of humiliation still fresh. What a disaster! I pulled on my jacket and sandals, trying to hide my face with the hoodie pulled low over my head. I barely managed to avoid eye contact with anyone as I trudged back to the dorm.

Entering the dorm, I was met with the sight of Kylian lounging casually, his trademark smirk plastered on his face. Regina was engrossed in her homework, seemingly unaffected by the drama that had just unfolded. I decided to ignore Kylian and headed straight to my room.

"Hey, what were you doing at the pool?" Kylian called out, his voice dripping with curiosity. I kept my back to him, pretending not to hear.

Regina, ever the one to play mediator, chimed in. "Oh, she was probably just working on the project. You know, the one that requires us to learn swimming."

Rolling my eyes, I tried to ignore the conversation, focusing instead on my frustration. Kylian didn't take the hint. "I can help you with the swimming project if you want. It's no big deal."

I turned to face him, exasperation clear in my voice. "I don't need your help."

He wasn't deterred. "Come on, it's really no trouble. I can show you the basics—"

"No, thanks!" I cut him off, the irritation evident in my tone. "I'll manage just fine on my own."

I didn't wait for his response, slamming the door to my room behind me. The sudden silence was a relief, giving me a moment to collect myself and escape the relentless teasing. As I leaned against the door, I couldn't help but wonder how I was ever going to survive the next few months with Kylian in my orbit.

In the days that followed, my attempts to observe the swimmers and absorb the intricacies of their strokes had been, to put it mildly, a spectacular failure. The only thing that really stuck with me was that the swimmers, in general, were incredibly attractive. Who knew that swimming pools could double as an ad for some kind of beachwear magazine? The way they moved through the water was, admittedly, mesmerizing. But, of course, that wasn't going to make me a fan of the sport.

Living with Kylian continued to be a nightmare of epic proportions. His presence was like a constant low-level hum of irritation in the background of my life. Here's a rundown of his daily shenanigans:

1. Morning Routine Mayhem: Kylian's morning routine was something out of a high-maintenance manual. He had this elaborate ritual involving an extensive selection of grooming products. The smell of his cologne filled the entire dorm room, making it feel like I was trapped in a cloud of his ego. Every morning, as I tried to get ready for the day, I had to endure his music blasting from his phone and the loud, animated conversations he had with his reflection in the mirror.

2. Messy Habits: His habit of leaving wet towels and swim gear strewn around was a daily annoyance. It was like living in a perpetual state of "youth hostel after swim meet." Finding his wet towel draped over my study desk or his swim cap lodged in the communal fridge was a new form of daily entertainment I didn't sign up for.

3. The Poolside Show: Whenever he had practice, which was often, he would leave for the pool in a cloud of arrogance, with a new set of teammates in tow. Their camaraderie and laughter seemed to follow him back to the dorm, with their locker room banter echoing through the walls. The constant chatter about swim times, competitions, and who had the best lap times was enough to make me yearn for some peace and quiet.

4. Food Wars: Kylian had a knack for raiding the kitchen, often leaving nothing but crumbs and empty containers in his wake. He would boast about his "athlete's appetite," which, quite frankly, only seemed to add to my list of grievances. I'd find my snack stash mysteriously depleted or discover that the fridge was empty except for his protein shakes and energy bars.

5. The Smug Athlete: His tendency to flaunt his swimming prowess, both in conversation and in his frequent gym sessions,

was just too much. He'd casually mention how he was getting ready for the next big meet or how many miles he'd swum that day. It was a continuous reminder of how effortlessly he excelled, making my own academic struggles feel all the more stark.

Despite all this, I had to admit that Kylian did have a certain charm, even if it was buried under layers of bravado and athleticism. But with every interaction, my patience was tested to its limits. I kept reminding myself that this was temporary, a mere phase before I could return to a less infuriating daily life. For now, though, it was a constant battle to keep my cool in the presence of my arrogant, wet-towel-wielding roommate.

As I watched the swimming practice from the sidelines, a slight boredom set in. The goal was to learn how to swim, but honestly, I was much more comfortable staying on solid ground. The tightness of my swimsuit beneath my clothes was a constant reminder of the commitment I had reluctantly made.

I glanced at the swimmers, focusing on one who stood out from the rest. He had a strong, fluid stroke and moved through the water with an effortless grace. His movements were powerful yet precise, and there was a certain elegance in how he cut through the waves. As he finished his lap, he pulled off his swim cap and goggles, revealing a mop of tousled hair and a face that seemed oddly familiar. It was Kylian.

"Ugh, really?" I thought, a mix of frustration and reluctant admiration bubbling inside me. How had I ever thought he was handsome? The realization made me cringe.

The practice came to an end, and Kylian approached me with a confident stride. "So, still thinking about learning to swim?" he asked, his tone annoyingly casual.

I sighed. "Yes, but definitely not with you."

Kylian raised an eyebrow. "Why not? You're going to get nowhere if you stay on the edge."

I shot him a withering look. "Because you're a smug, over-confident athlete who can't stop bragging about his swimming skills."

He grinned, completely unfazed. "And yet, I'm the one who can teach you. Unless you want to stay stuck on the edge."

Reluctantly, I acquiesced, feeling the weight of my decision. Kylian slipped off his jacket and draped it over a chair. "I'll be waiting for you at the poolside," he said, turning to head toward the water.

I steeled myself, stripping off my clothes to reveal the tight-fitting swimsuit beneath. Kylian's eyes flickered over me, and he couldn't resist a teasing smirk. "Nice suit," he called out, his voice dripping with sarcasm.

I shot him a glare, trying to ignore the flush creeping up my neck. "Just get on with it."

With a deep breath, I stepped into the water. It was cold and startling, making me shiver as I waded in. The water felt alien, and I clung to the edge of the pool, feeling a mix of nervousness and discomfort.

Kylian approached, and the smirk on his face grew wider. "This is going to be fun," he said, clearly enjoying the spectacle of my hesitation. "Come on, you've got to let go of the edge if you want to learn."

I tightened my grip on the side, determined to prove him wrong. "I can do this," I said, pushing off from the wall and attempting to swim.

But as soon as I was away from the safety of the poolside, panic set in. I flailed awkwardly, legs kicking in random directions, and quickly found myself struggling to stay afloat.

Kylian's laughter rang out as he saw my predicament. "See? It's not as easy as it looks!"

Before I could even think to react, he reached out, grabbing my hands and pulling me toward the edge. "Just breathe," he instructed, his touch surprisingly gentle despite his earlier teasing.

I pulled my hands away quickly, mortified and embarrassed. "I get it, okay? I need practice. But don't make me feel worse."

Kylian's grin softened, though he still looked amused. "Alright, alright. Just remember, it's all about persistence. And try not to flail like a fish out of water next time."

I clung to the edge, the sting of humiliation mixing with a newfound determination. Maybe this swimming thing wasn't so bad after all—if only Kylian could be a little less smug about it.

Kylian effortlessly joined me in the water without even needing the ladder—of course, he's a professional. He casually instructed me to put my head in the water and blow bubbles through my mouth.

"Why?" I asked, feeling utterly ridiculous.

"Stop asking questions and just do it," he replied, clearly annoyed.

I plunged my head into the water, blowing bubbles like a kid playing in a pool, and then surfaced three times in a row. Each time I came up, I noticed Kylian standing nonchalantly in the water, not even making an effort to stay afloat. I couldn't help but ask, "How are you standing there like that?"

He smirked. "We're in the shallow end. You can stand here without any trouble."

The realization made me feel incredibly foolish for gripping the pool's edge like a lifeline. I slowly let go, my feet touching the bottom. Kylian glanced at me expectantly. "So, what can you do?"

I puffed out my chest with a touch of pride. "I can float on my back."

He chuckled, an unmistakable glint of amusement in his eyes. "Alright then, let's start with that."

He guided me to lie on my back in the water. I hesitated, panic creeping in as I started to lower myself. Kylian placed his hands beneath my back, supporting me. "Just breathe and relax," he instructed.

I tried to focus on my breathing but couldn't help feeling self-conscious with his hands under me. He told me to kick my legs, and I kicked so vigorously that water splashed everywhere.

"Ease up on the kicking," he advised with a grin.

I adjusted my movements, trying to kick more gently. As I looked up at him, our eyes met, and my heart started to race for reasons I couldn't quite understand. Kylian's gaze lingered on me for a moment longer than necessary, and I couldn't help but feel a strange flutter in my chest.

He slowly removed his hands, letting me float on my own. I managed to move a few feet but quickly began to panic, my body tensing up. Kylian caught me effortlessly and couldn't resist a smirk.

"You're not exactly graceful," he teased.

I squirmed and pushed him away, feeling embarrassed and flustered. "Yeah, well, I'm a beginner, remember?"

Kylian chuckled, clearly enjoying my discomfort. "You're doing fine. Just try not to turn swimming into a splash zone next time."

I rolled my eyes but couldn't suppress a reluctant smile. "Thanks for the help, I guess. Just don't expect me to be an Olympic swimmer anytime soon."

He laughed, "I wouldn't dream of it."

As he continued to tease me, I tried to focus on my technique, hoping to improve while trying to ignore the awkward flutter of nerves whenever I looked his way.

Kylian adjusted his position in the water, his gaze steady as he explained, "To float on your back, you need to inflate your stomach and keep your body relaxed. It's all about buoyancy."

I barely heard him; my attention was fixated on his well-defined physique. For someone I was constantly annoyed with, he had an undeniably impressive body.

"Are you listening?" he asked, snapping me out of my reverie.

I blinked, my cheeks warming slightly. "Yeah, sure. I got it."

"Alright then, let's give it a shot." He helped me get into position, guiding me onto my back. "Remember, spread your arms and legs like a starfish and keep your stomach inflated."

I followed his instructions, stretching out and inflating my stomach. At first, the water lapped at my face, and Kylian's hands supported me.

"Hey, don't get too comfortable," he said, a mischievous grin on his face. "If you start sinking, it'll be a lot of fun trying to get you back up."

I tried to suppress a laugh. "Well, you're not exactly the best cheerleader."

"Hey, someone's gotta keep you on your toes," he teased. "Otherwise, you might just float away and leave me with all the glory."

As I continued to float, I managed to stabilize myself. "Look at that, I'm actually doing it!"

"Impressive," he said, sarcastically. "You're not just a beginner anymore. You're a floating starfish."

I rolled my eyes. "Yeah, well, don't get used to it. Next time, I'll be the one rescuing you from a sinking disaster."

He laughed, a low, easy sound that made me smile. "We'll see about that. I'm off to get some water. Don't go sinking without me."

He swam over to the edge of the pool, leaving me floating comfortably. As I adjusted to the sensation of gliding on my back, I couldn't help but think that this might not be as terrible as I'd originally thought.

Chapter 5

Once back in the dorm, I found Kylian already there, looking completely dry as if nothing had happened. Meanwhile, I was still dripping wet, my hair plastered to my face. He looked up from his phone and smirked.

"What happened to you? You look like someone who's just been through a traumatic experience."

"Gee, I wonder why," I shot back, rolling my eyes. "Maybe because some jerk decided to toss me into the deep end of the pool."

He laughed. "Oh come on, Humpty Dumpty, you needed a push. You can't learn to swim if you're scared of a little water."

"Humpty Dumpty?" I glared at him. "Really?"

"Hey, it suits you," he said with a grin.

Before I could retort, Regina popped her head in. "Hey guys, I'm ordering pizza. You want some?"

"Yes, please," I sighed, still feeling the sting of Kylian's teasing. "I need some comfort food."

I stomped off to my room, slamming the door behind me. How do people actually enjoy swimming? I wondered. How is flailing around in water supposed to help with stress? It's just a fast track to humiliation.

Changing into dry clothes, I flopped onto my bed, trying to push the memory of my awkward swimming attempts out of my mind. Maybe tomorrow would be better, but right now, I just wanted to forget.

Just as I was finally drifting off to sleep, I was awakened again by the sound of Kylian's stretching routine. Seriously, doesn't this guy ever sleep? Frustrated, I got out of bed and went to see what was going on.

When I found him, he was in the middle of his stretches, shirtless. Great. I could feel my face heating up despite myself. "What are you doing?" I demanded.

He glanced at me and rolled his eyes. "What does it look like I'm doing? Stretching. What do you want?"

I tried to maintain my composure. "Could you maybe do this some other time? Some of us are trying to sleep."

Ignoring me, he continued his stretches, flexing his muscles with each movement. "Whatever, Humpty Dumpty."

"Can you stop calling me that?" I snapped, feeling my irritation rise.

He walked over to me, getting uncomfortably close. "Why? It suits you." He reached out and gently removed my glasses, his face inches from mine. My heart pounded in my chest. "Could you go get me a bottle of water?" he said softly, his breath warm on my skin.

I pushed him away, feeling both flustered and angry. "Get it yourself."

He chuckled, seemingly amused by my reaction. "I thought you'd be like the other girls, but I guess you're different."

"For who do you think you are?" I shot back, crossing my arms.

He went to the fridge, grabbed a bottle of water, and handed me back my glasses. "You've got spirit, I'll give you that," he said, his tone surprisingly sincere.

I was about to storm off when he called after me, "Don't forget, I'll see you at the pool tomorrow night."

I sighed, feeling utterly exasperated. "Fine," I muttered, and retreated to my room, wondering how I was ever going to survive living with Kylian for the next few months.

My heart was a mess of emotions. Kylian had nearly drowned me earlier, and now he was acting like everything was normal. How could he be so infuriating and confusing at the same time?

As I lay in bed, I couldn't help but replay the events of the evening. His smug smile as he effortlessly moved through the water, the way he had looked at me when he took off my glasses, the unexpected compliment. It was maddening.

Why did my heart race when he got close? And why did I even care about what he thought? He was just some arrogant swimmer who enjoyed making my life difficult.

I rolled over, trying to push the thoughts out of my mind. But sleep wouldn't come easily. I kept thinking about his comment about seeing me at the pool tomorrow night. What did he really want from me?

Finally, I took a deep breath, telling myself to stay focused. This was just another hurdle, another challenge to overcome. I couldn't let Kylian get under my skin.

But as I drifted off to sleep, I couldn't help but wonder what it was about him that had me so unsettled. And why, despite everything, I felt a tiny flicker of excitement about seeing him again.

The next morning, I woke up and found a bowl of cereal already set on the counter. I blinked in disbelief, taking off my glasses and putting them back on to make sure I wasn't dreaming. Nope, it was real—someone had actually prepared breakfast for me.

I sat down and started eating, still puzzled by the unexpected gesture. Regina joined me a few minutes later, grabbing her own breakfast. We chatted about our plans for the day, but my mind kept drifting back to the cereal mystery.

After breakfast, I got dressed for the day, pulling on my usual jeans and a comfy top. With a sigh, I packed my swimsuit and a towel into my bag. The thought of another evening at the pool with Kylian was both annoying and...something else I couldn't quite identify.

"Ready for another exciting day?" Regina asked, giving me a playful nudge.

"Thrilled," I replied sarcastically, but with a smile.

We left the dorm together, heading to our classes. As the day went on, I couldn't shake the feeling of curiosity about Kylian's actions. Why had he made me breakfast? Was it some sort of peace offering after nearly drowning me? Or was he just messing with me again?

Classes were a blur of lectures and note-taking. During a break, I found myself zoning out, thinking about the evening ahead. I knew I needed to learn to swim, but the thought of spending more time with Kylian made my stomach twist.

When the last class ended, I headed back to the dorm to grab my bag. The pool awaited, and so did Kylian. I took a deep breath, steeling myself for whatever lay ahead. One way or another, I was going to learn to swim, and I wasn't going to let Kylian get the best of me.

"Here we go," I muttered to myself, leaving the dorm with my bag slung over my shoulder. A new day, a new challenge. And hopefully, a step closer to conquering my fear of the water.

I waited by the poolside, watching the swim class finish up. The guys moved through the water with effortless grace, Kylian included. I had to admit, he wasn't bad at all. As I scanned the pool, someone called my name.

"Kathleen!" Aaron's voice broke through my thoughts.

I turned and waved, "Hey, Aaron!"

He sauntered over, flashing a charming smile. "Fancy meeting you here. What brings you to the pool?"

I shrugged, trying to play it cool. "Just observing for a project."

Aaron raised an eyebrow, clearly intrigued. "A project, huh? Need any help? I'm pretty good at swimming, you know."

I laughed, shaking my head. "Thanks, but I think I've got it covered."

He leaned in a little closer, lowering his voice. "Well, if you ever need a private lesson, you know where to find me."

I felt my cheeks heat up. "I'll keep that in mind."

Aaron glanced over at the pool, noticing Kylian's slower pace and frequent glances our way. "Looks like someone's a bit distracted."

I rolled my eyes. "Yeah, he's... complicated."

Aaron chuckled. "Tell you what, why don't we grab a coffee sometime? You can tell me all about your project. And maybe about why Kylian keeps staring at you."

I blushed deeper, nodding. "Sure, that sounds nice."

"Great," Aaron said, giving me a wink. "I'll see you around, Kathleen."

With that, he headed off, leaving me flustered and a bit confused. I turned my attention back to the pool, where Kylian was still stealing glances in my direction. He was definitely slower than usual, and it was clear he wasn't as focused on his swimming.

I sighed, feeling a mix of amusement and frustration. What was with that guy? Trying to push the thoughts aside, I settled back into my seat and watched the rest of the training session, though my mind kept wandering back to Aaron's invitation and Kylian's bizarre behavior.

The practice finally ended, and Kylian made his way over to me, water dripping off his toned body. His muscles glistened under the pool lights, each movement showing off his athletic build. I quickly averted my eyes, trying not to stare.

"Who was that guy?" he asked, his tone slightly tense.

"Why do you want to know?" I shot back, trying to sound casual.

He ignored my question entirely, his eyes hardening. "I'll be waiting for you in the pool."

With a sigh, I made my way to the locker room. I found an empty stall and changed into my swimsuit, glancing at my reflection in the mirror. I couldn't help but feel self-conscious. There really wasn't anything special about me, I thought.

Stepping back out, I saw Kylian already in the water, waiting. Taking a deep breath, I carefully jumped into the pool, shivering as the cool water enveloped me.

He smirked, seeing my hesitation. "Careful there, don't want you drowning on your first lesson."

I rolled my eyes. "Very funny, Kylian."

"Alright, let's start with something simple. Do the windmill motion with your arms, like this." He demonstrated, his arms cutting through the water with ease.

I mimicked his movements, feeling awkward and clumsy. "I feel like a flailing chicken."

He laughed, his eyes sparkling with amusement. "More like a duck trying to take off."

"Hey, at least ducks can swim," I shot back, splashing him playfully.

"Touché," he said, grinning. "But I have to admit, you're doing better than I expected."

"Oh, so you had low expectations?" I teased, splashing him again.

He laughed, dodging the water. "Well, you did look pretty pathetic clinging to the edge yesterday."

"Thanks for the vote of confidence," I replied dryly.

"Just calling it like I see it," he said, still smiling. "Now, let's see if you can do this without looking like you're fighting for your life."

"Challenge accepted," I said, determined.

As we continued, the banter flowed easily between us. Every now and then, he would correct my form or give me a tip, but mostly, we just made fun of each other.

"Maybe if you keep this up, you'll be ready for the Olympics," he joked.

"Oh yeah, because I totally have Olympic aspirations," I retorted, rolling my eyes.

"Hey, you never know. Stranger things have happened," he said with a wink.

Kylian looked at me, his expression serious yet playful. "Alright, now you're going to float on your back, kick your legs, and do the arm windmill like I taught you."

I stared at him, bewildered. "Wait, what? You're asking me to do all that at once?"

He sighed, clearly exasperated. "Yes, all at once. It's not that complicated. Just trust me."

With that, he moved closer and gently guided me to lie on my back in the water. His hands were firm yet gentle on my shoulders as he positioned me. Our eyes met, and I couldn't help but notice how striking his gaze was. For a moment, I forgot I was in a pool and not having some intense staring contest.

"Okay, kick your legs now," he instructed, his voice soft but commanding.

I started kicking, but it was more like I was trying to stir up a whirlpool than swim. "Like this?"

"No, not so much like a jackhammer. Relax your legs," he said, his tone tinged with amusement.

I tried to calm my kicking, focusing on my legs. We kept staring at each other, and I could feel my heart racing—not just from the exercise. His eyes seemed to be saying something, but I couldn't quite put my finger on it.

"Now, do the windmill with your arms," he added, his voice low and encouraging.

I flailed my arms around, attempting to synchronize my movements. He smiled, and it was clear he was enjoying this more than he let on. Slowly, he moved forward, his hands gliding down my back, giving me that reassuring support.

"Look at that, you're actually doing it," he said, his smile widening.

Suddenly, I started to panic. My legs stopped working, and I flailed more than I floated. Kylian's smile turned into a look of concern, and before I knew it, he was beside me, scooping me up with effortless ease.

"Hey! What are you doing?" I yelped as he carried me to the edge of the pool.

"Just saving my favorite Humpty Dumpty from drowning," he teased, setting me down gently at the poolside.

I rolled my eyes, though a smile tugged at my lips. "Can you please stop calling me Humpty Dumpty? It's kind of embarrassing."

He chuckled, taking a sip from his water bottle. "You know, you're actually quite cute with that nickname."

I felt my cheeks flush. "You say that to all the girls, don't you?"

He shrugged nonchalantly, though his grin suggested he was enjoying my reaction. "Maybe, but it's true in your case."

As he walked away, leaving me there to process his comment, I couldn't help but wonder if there was more to his teasing than he let on. Maybe I wasn't the only one who found this swimming lesson a bit more interesting than expected.

Kylian returned to the poolside with a determined look. "Alright, let's do it again. I want you to focus, close your eyes, and just breathe."

I nodded, trying to ignore the fact that my heart was pounding at the prospect of another round. I shut my eyes and took a deep breath, trying to relax as Kylian guided me through the motions.

"Keep going, just like that," he said, his voice a soothing presence in the water.

Suddenly, I noticed that Kylian's hands were no longer supporting me. I was moving on my own! The sensation of gliding through the water without assistance was exhilarating. I pushed forward, feeling a surge of accomplishment—until, out of nowhere, my head collided with the pool's edge.

I gasped, quickly lifting my head out of the water and opening my eyes. To my surprise, I had made it to the end of the pool, completing my first length on my own.

Kylian was already by the poolside, towel in hand, drying off. He saw me and grinned, clearly pleased. "Nice job, Humpty Dumpty! You made it all the way."

I rolled my eyes but couldn't suppress a smile. "Yeah, well, don't get too used to it. I still don't like swimming."

He laughed, stepping closer and placing a hand gently on top of my head, ruffling my hair in an almost affectionate gesture. "You're a natural, you know. Just needed a little push."

I shivered slightly at the touch, not sure if it was from the cool air or something else entirely. "Thanks, I guess," I managed, trying to play it cool.

Kylian's smile widened, and he leaned in a bit closer, his voice dropping to a teasing whisper. "Just wait until next time. I'll be expecting even more from you."

With a final wink, he walked away, leaving me to stand there, still feeling the warmth of his touch and the thrill of my small victory in the pool.

I didn't understand what was happening inside me. After changing, I sat down to jot down my notes about the session. I had to admit, there was something undeniably calming about swimming, but that didn't mean I suddenly loved it.

I reflected on how Kylian's presence had affected me—his teasing, his encouragement, and that unexpected touch. It was confusing and, honestly, a bit overwhelming. My feelings were a tangled mess of irritation and something warmer, something I wasn't quite ready to label.

As I finished my notes, I noted the relaxing effect of the water but quickly reminded myself that it didn't change my fundamental dislike of the sport. I still preferred solid ground beneath my feet and a clear distance from any potential humiliation in the pool.

For now, I was left grappling with these mixed emotions and trying to figure out how to navigate this unexpected turn of events.

When I got back to the dorm, Regina was waiting for me, eager to hear how the swimming session had gone. I told her I'd managed to swim, and her excitement was palpable. She cheered and asked all sorts of questions about how I felt and whether Kylian had been a good coach.

As we chatted, Kylian walked out of his room with a towel draped over his shoulders. He headed to the kitchen and grabbed an apple. When he saw me, he couldn't resist teasing. "Look at you, swimming pro now," he said with that infuriatingly smug grin.

I rolled my eyes and shot back, "Oh, stop it. You're the one who practically had to drag me into the pool."

He just chuckled and waved his hand dismissively. "Yeah, yeah, whatever you say, Humpty Dumpty." He took a bite of his apple and headed back to his room, leaving me with a mix of frustration and...something else I couldn't quite put my finger on.

Regina, meanwhile, was still bubbling with excitement, but I couldn't shake the image of Kylian's grin from my mind.

Chapter 6

The next day, I met up with Kylian at the pool. He was already sitting in the bleachers, watching the girls' practice with an absorbed look. As I approached, I couldn't help but ask, "What's so fun about swimming, anyway?"

He glanced at me, his expression softening. "It's not just about the swimming itself. It's the feeling of gliding through the water, the sense of freedom, and how it clears your mind. It's almost like... escaping everything else for a while."

I was taken aback by his genuine response. It was different from the usual playful banter I was used to. He seemed to be a different Kylian than the one I'd known before. But of course, he couldn't stay serious for long.

With a smirk, he added, "Anyway, I'll be waiting down there. Don't keep me waiting too long, Humpty Dumpty."

I watched him leave, his teasing grin back in place, but there was something in his tone that made me pause. For a moment, I wondered if I was beginning to see a different side of him.

As I joined Kylian at the pool, slipping into the water became easier with each attempt. He instructed me to swim two lengths on my back. I agreed and started, finding it challenging at first. Each time his hands adjusted my position, I couldn't help but feel a strange sensation—a mix of confusion and something else that I couldn't quite place. Despite the difficulties, I managed to complete the task.

Kylian, with his usual teasing grin, commented, "Not bad, Humpty Dumpty. You're making progress."

I shot back, "Yeah, well, don't get used to it."

He then asked if I could do the same on my stomach. I blushed and replied, "No, not really."

"Of course, you can't!" Kylian laughed. "But don't worry, I'm here to teach you."

Before diving into the crawl technique, Kylian explained the principles: body position, breathing, and arm and leg movements. As he was about to demonstrate, he looked at me with a mischievous glint in his eye.

"Alright, let's see if you can float on your stomach. Get into position."

I sighed dramatically. "Great, floating on my stomach. Just what I always dreamed of."

Kylian chuckled. "Don't worry. Floating is like being a human noodle—just less flexible."

I rolled my eyes as I positioned myself on my stomach. "Is this how you see me? A noodle?"

He grinned. "Only the most graceful noodle in the pool."

With that, I tried to find my balance. Kylian watched, ready to step in if needed. I attempted to float, feeling like a clumsy, overcooked spaghetti. Kylian's hands were there to support me again, and I couldn't help but notice how his touch seemed to bring out both a sense of security and an odd flutter in my chest.

As I managed to stay afloat, I shot him a playful glare. "Is this the part where you tell me I'm a natural?"

Kylian smirked. "Not quite. But you're getting there. Just remember, if you start sinking, try not to look too surprised."

I laughed, trying to ignore the fluttering feeling and focus on mastering the crawl.

Kylian positioned himself by the edge of the pool, and I followed his instructions, trying to mimic the movements of my arms and legs. He demonstrated each technique with a practiced ease that made it seem effortless. As he showed me how to kick and stroke, I couldn't help but notice that he looked rather cute, even with the slight furrow of concentration on his face. It was about time I admitted it.

I glanced at him, my curiosity piqued. "So, how do you manage to breathe while you're in the water?"

He chuckled, his eyes twinkling with amusement. "It's all about timing. You turn your head to the side when you need to breathe. Think of it as a synchronized dance with the water."

I nodded, trying to imagine this dance. "And how does it feel for you when you're swimming? Does it ever get... weird?"

Kylian's expression softened as he answered genuinely, "When I'm in the water, it's like everything else fades away. It's just me and the water. It's peaceful, in a way."

I smiled, appreciating the sincerity in his voice. "That sounds kind of nice."

But just as I was about to enjoy this rare moment of connection, Kylian's playful side returned. "Just don't expect me to let you off easy. You still have a lot to learn."

I rolled my eyes with a grin. "Of course, I'm always the one who gets teased."

He smirked. "Well, if you weren't so adorable when you try to swim, maybe I'd be a bit nicer."

I laughed, shaking my head. "You're impossible."

Kylian's laughter was infectious, and for a moment, it felt like the teasing was just a part of our growing friendship.

Kylian slid into the pool with effortless grace, his movements a stark contrast to my own awkward flailing. He directed me to lie on my stomach, arms and legs splayed out like a starfish. I looked at him skeptically.

"Are you sure this is a good idea?" I asked, my apprehension clear.

"Stop asking questions and just do it," he replied, a hint of amusement in his voice.

Reluctantly, I complied. The water around me was oddly soothing, almost relaxing. Why was I feeling so calm? I popped up to the surface for a breath, and Kylian took the opportunity to tease me.

"Look at you, floating like a pro!" he said, his grin widening.

I rolled my eyes and took a deep breath before trying again. But this time, as I floated on my stomach, I could feel Kylian's hands on my hips. Every touch sent an unexpected jolt through me, making my heart race. What was going on?

Kylian was showing me how to align my body to reduce water resistance, but his explanations were drowned out by the sensation of his touch. "Keep your body straight, and raise your hips slightly," he said, positioning me.

I surfaced again, trying to focus on his words, but all I could think about was the way his hands felt on my hips. Why was I feeling this strange flutter every time he touched me?

"Just make sure to keep your body aligned," he continued, but his words seemed to fade into the background.

I gazed into his eyes, trying to ignore the heat rising in my cheeks. "Okay," I murmured, more absorbed in the weird feelings than the swimming lesson.

Kylian adjusted my position, his hands moving with a gentle precision that made my heart pound even faster. "You really need to focus on keeping your hips up," he explained, though his voice seemed to come from a distance.

I floated there, feeling more like I was floating in some strange, confusing sea of emotions rather than in the water. Why was this so distracting? Couldn't he just teach me how to swim without all these weird feelings?

Kylian climbed out of the pool, leaving me to wrestle with the wild beating of my heart. "It's just swimming, Kathleen," I muttered to myself, trying to regain some composure. He returned with a floating mat, laying it down beside the pool.

"We're going to practice lateral breathing," he announced, clearly not noticing—or perhaps ignoring—my internal turmoil.

"Can we take a break?" I pleaded, hoping for a moment to gather myself.

"Nope," he replied firmly.

"Seriously? You're such a slave driver," I complained.

"Are you calling me a slave driver because I want you to be a better swimmer?" he shot back, his tone light but with an edge of challenge.

"Maybe I don't want to be a better swimmer. Maybe I just want to survive this without feeling like I'm about to drown," I retorted, crossing my arms.

"Surviving isn't enough. You have to thrive," he said, mimicking a motivational coach.

"Thrive? In the water? Are you serious right now?" I asked, incredulous.

"Absolutely," he said with a grin. "Come on, give it a shot. It's not going to kill you. Besides, you don't want to be the only person here who can't swim, do you?"

I sighed in defeat. "Fine. Let's get this over with."

Climbing out of the pool, I reluctantly lay on my stomach on the mat. Kylian positioned himself beside me, demonstrating the technique with exaggerated motions. "Count to three before you breathe," he instructed. "Like this: one, two, three, breathe."

Feeling ridiculous, I mimicked his actions, pretending to swim on the mat. "This feels so stupid," I grumbled, moving my arms and legs as he showed me.

Kylian burst out laughing. "You look like you're trying to fly instead of swim!"

"Thanks for the encouragement," I said, rolling my eyes.

"Hey, you're the one who said you wanted a break. This is part of it," he teased, his laughter contagious despite my frustration.

"Part of the break or part of you just enjoying watching me struggle?" I shot back, unable to suppress a smile.

"A bit of both," he admitted with a mischievous grin. "But mostly the second part."

"You're such a jerk," I said, shaking my head but unable to stop the smile from spreading across my face.

"And yet, here you are, following my instructions," he pointed out, his tone playful.

"Only because I have no choice," I replied, continuing the mock swimming motions.

"Sure, keep telling yourself that," he teased.

Despite my frustration and embarrassment, there was something oddly comforting about our banter. It made the whole experience a little less daunting and a lot more bearable.

I slid back into the pool, water enveloping me like a cool blanket. Kylian stood at the edge, adjusting his goggles with a confident air. "I'm going to show you the final result," he announced, positioning himself for a perfect dive.

"Count to three," he instructed.

"Why do I have to—"

"Stop asking questions and just do it," he interrupted, his tone firm but teasing.

I rolled my eyes but complied. "One, two, three."

At three, he launched himself off the edge with a powerful push, slicing through the water with an effortless grace. His body stretched out, arms cutting forward in perfect rhythm, legs kicking with precise, controlled movements. He made it look so easy, each stroke propelling him forward with minimal splash. The water seemed to part willingly for him, allowing him to glide smoothly across the pool. His form was impeccable, streamlined and efficient, like he was born for this.

I watched, slightly mesmerized, my cheeks flushing a bit as I admired his skill. He was definitely good at this, and it was hard not to be impressed. His turns were sharp and quick, and before I knew it, he was back in front of me, barely out of breath.

"See? That's what you're aiming for," he said with a triumphant grin.

"Yeah, sure, just like that," I muttered, rolling my eyes again.

"What's the matter, Humpty Dumpty? Afraid you'll fall apart?" he teased.

"Can you stop with that nickname?" I retorted, but there was no heat in my voice. It was hard to stay mad at him, especially when he looked so genuinely happy.

"Not a chance," he replied, still smiling.

I climbed out of the pool and back onto the mat, resigning myself to more practice. Kylian knelt beside me again, ready to coach me through another round. Despite my reluctance, a small part of me was beginning to appreciate the challenge. And maybe, just maybe, the company wasn't so bad either.

Kylian motioned for me to stand, and I reluctantly obliged. As he positioned himself behind me, my heart began to race. His presence was palpable, making it hard to focus on anything else.

"I never realized you were this short," he remarked with a teasing tone.

"Yeah, well, I guess I never realized you were this annoying," I replied nonchalantly, though my voice wavered slightly. He laughed, the sound warm and genuine, and it made my heart skip a beat.

He gently lifted my arms, guiding them into the proper position. His touch was firm but careful, sending shivers down my spine. I could feel the heat of his body close behind me, making it difficult to concentrate on anything other than the pounding of my heart.

"I need a break," I blurted out, trying to catch my breath. He paused, clearly intrigued but willing to give me space.

"Sure, take a break," he said, stepping back.

I walked over to the bench and sat down, my eyes drifting to the pool as I tried to steady my breathing. Kylian, unfazed, returned to his swimming, gliding through the water with the same effortless grace he always had. I watched him, unable to tear my gaze away.

He moved like a fish in water, his body cutting through the pool with precision and strength. Each stroke was powerful and smooth, his legs kicking rhythmically as he propelled himself forward. The muscles in his back and arms flexed with each movement, glistening under the pool lights. It was hard not to be captivated by the sheer athleticism on display.

As I observed him, I couldn't help but feel a strange mix of admiration and frustration. Admiration for his skill and dedication, and frustration because of how he made my heart race with just a touch or a look. There was something different about him, something that was starting to get under my skin in ways I didn't quite understand.

Kylian finished his lap and looked up, catching me watching him. He smiled, that infuriatingly charming smile, and my heart fluttered despite myself. What was happening to me? Why did he have this effect on me? I shook my head, trying to clear my thoughts. This was just swimming practice, after all. Just swimming.

"Come on, get back in here," Kylian called out to me, a playful grin on his face.

I sighed, tying my hair up in a messy bun. I approached the pool's edge, intending to ease myself in gently, but Kylian's mocking chuckle stopped me.

"Just jump in already," he teased.

I shot him a look. "You know I don't like jumping in."

"The pool isn't even that deep," he countered. "I'll count to three, and if you don't jump, I'm coming to get you."

I closed my eyes, took a deep breath, and pinched my nose. "Fine," I muttered.

"One... Two... Three!"

I jumped in, water splashing everywhere. It wasn't as bad as I had imagined. Emerging from the water, I saw Kylian's triumphant smile.

"See? Not so bad, right?" he said.

"Whatever," I replied, brushing water from my face.

"Now, do a lap," he instructed.

"I'm not ready," I protested, rolling my eyes.

He sighed, moving closer. "Just get on your stomach. We'll break down the movements, like we did with the backstroke."

I reluctantly positioned myself on my stomach, feeling the cool water against my skin. Kylian's hands guided my arms and legs, showing me the proper technique. His touch sent shivers down my spine, making it hard to focus.

"Got it?" he asked, his face close to mine.

I nodded, feeling a mix of determination and nervousness. Giving myself a small push, I began to swim. Kylian's hands provided gentle support at first, but soon I was moving on my own. The rhythm came more naturally than I expected, and before I knew it, I had reached the end of the pool.

"I did it!" I exclaimed, my heart pounding with excitement.

Kylian chuckled, swimming up beside me. "Not bad for a beginner."

"Thanks, I think," I replied, grinning despite myself.

"Just keep practicing, and soon you'll be a pro," he said, ruffling my hair playfully.

"Yeah, yeah," I said, rolling my eyes but unable to hide my smile. "But seriously, why do you have to touch me every single time?"

"It's called coaching," he said with a wink. "Besides, I thought you liked it."

I felt my cheeks heat up and quickly splashed water at him. "You're impossible, you know that?"

He laughed, dodging the water. "And yet, here you are."

Shaking my head, I realized that maybe, just maybe, I was starting to enjoy this swimming thing—if only a little.

"The lesson's over for today," Kylian announced, swimming effortlessly to the edge of the pool.

"Do I have to come back tomorrow?" I asked, hoping for a break.

"Actually, I have a competition tomorrow," he said with a grin.

I sighed in relief. "Oh good, you're sparing me from drowning."

He climbed out of the pool with ease, water streaming off his toned body. I tried to follow suit but slipped slightly as I got out, earning a chuckle from Kylian.

"Nice exit," he teased, grabbing his towel.

"Shut up," I muttered, pushing him lightly as I went to get my own towel.

As he dried off, he turned to me. "You know, it would be nice if you came to my competition."

I scoffed, "Why would I want to watch you show off?"

He shrugged, a playful smile on his lips. "Maybe you'll learn something."

"Like what? How to annoy people?"

He laughed, shaking his head. "See you around, Humpty Dumpty."

I rolled my eyes, but couldn't help but smile as he walked away.

Chapter 7

The next morning, I finally woke up late. I stretched lazily and reached for my laptop on the nightstand. "Ten pages!" I groaned. My instructor wanted ten pages on my swimming project, and I had only written one.

Dragging myself out of bed, I greeted Regina as I stumbled into the kitchen.

"Morning," she said cheerily. "Are you going to the swim meet today?"

I frowned. "Why would I do that?"

She rolled her eyes. "Come on, it's a chance to see Kylian in action. And you might actually enjoy it."

"Enjoy watching people swim back and forth? Thrilling."

She grinned. "There'll be lots of cute guys in swim trunks. Think of it as research for your project."

I laughed. "Research, huh? Alright, alright. I'll go."

"Plus," she added with a wink, "it wouldn't hurt to see some abs up close."

I shook my head, laughing as she headed back to her room. With no sign of Kylian around, he was probably already at the competition. Finally, a peaceful morning to myself.

Sitting down with my laptop, I tried to get some work done. But my mind kept wandering to the meet. With a sigh, I closed my laptop. Maybe Regina was right. A bit of eye candy might be just the thing to kickstart my writing motivation.

After a few hours, Regina and I finally arrived at the swimming competition venue. The place was bustling with energy, filled with the sounds of cheering spectators and the rhythmic splashing of water. The pool was an Olympic-sized marvel, shimmering under the bright lights that lined the ceiling. Bleachers extended along the length of the pool, packed with enthusiastic fans and supporters waving banners for their favorite swimmers.

Regina and I found a spot in the middle of the bleachers, offering a perfect view of the pool. I sat down, trying to make sense of the appeal of swimming competitions. What exactly was so relaxing about them, and how on earth could they help "manage stress"? I scanned the pool area, watching the swimmers warm up with effortless strokes, cutting through the water like sleek, well-oiled machines.

"Check him out," Regina nudged me, pointing to a tall, muscular guy stretching by the pool. "And him," she added, gesturing to another swimmer adjusting his goggles. "Sexy, right?"

I rolled my eyes but couldn't help but chuckle. "Yeah, I guess. If you're into that sort of thing."

I continued to watch as the teams trained, their precise movements and sheer speed a testament to their dedication and skill.

Yet, despite the impressive display, I couldn't shake the feeling that this sport just wasn't my thing. The endless laps, the intense focus on shaving off fractions of a second – it all seemed more stressful than relaxing to me.

"Seriously," I muttered to myself, "what's so relaxing about all this?"

Regina was engrossed in pointing out more swimmers she found attractive, clearly enjoying herself. Meanwhile, I found myself pondering how anyone could find solace in such a high-pressure environment. But I had to admit, there was something mesmerizing about the fluidity and grace with which the swimmers moved. Maybe, just maybe, I'd find a way to appreciate it.

I spotted Aaron across the bleachers and waved hello. He noticed me and winked back. Okay, he was kind of cute, I had to admit.

Regina nudged me with a mischievous grin. "I'm gonna grab some drinks. Might take a bit longer if I decide to get a few numbers while I'm at it." She winked and disappeared into the crowd, leaving me alone to observe the swimmers.

I shifted my attention to our school's team. There he was, Kylian, with his black swim cap and green goggles, standing out among the other swimmers. I watched him as he stretched and prepared for his race. Despite my best efforts to roll my eyes and dismiss him, I found myself unable to look away.

He moved with a confidence that was hard to ignore, his muscles flexing and contracting with each warm-up motion. There was a certain intensity in his eyes, even from a distance, that hinted at his determination and focus. It was almost mesmerizing.

"What is it about you, Kylian?" I murmured to myself, shaking my head.

As much as I tried to convince myself that I was only here because of Regina, a part of me was genuinely curious to see how he performed in the competition. Maybe, just maybe, there was more to swimming – and to Kylian – than I had initially thought.

The competition started, and Regina returned, grinning from ear to ear.

"So, did you get any numbers?" I asked.

She winked. "Maybe a few."

I laughed, shaking my head at her antics. We both turned our attention to the pool, where Kylian was sitting, headphones on, looking completely in his zone. He seemed almost serene, a stark contrast to the usual teasing and taunting Kylian I knew.

His turn came, and I watched him as he got ready. He stepped onto the starting block, adjusting his goggles one last time, his focus unwavering. The countdown began, and at the signal, he launched himself into the water with a powerful dive.

He started with the butterfly stroke, which, honestly, looked pretty ridiculous. All that flailing and flapping, it was hard not to giggle. But Kylian made it look...well, slightly less ridiculous. His movements were strong and controlled, each stroke propelling him forward with impressive speed.

As he neared the end of the first length, it was clear he was neck and neck with another swimmer. The tension was palpable. I found myself leaning forward, fingers gripping the edge of my seat. They made the turn almost simultaneously, but Kylian's determination was visible in every muscle of his body.

In the final stretch, it was a close call. The two swimmers were nearly tied, but in the last few meters, Kylian gave an extra push, pulling ahead just enough to touch the wall first.

He won.

I surprised myself by clapping and cheering, feeling an unexpected rush of pride. Then I realized what I was doing and abruptly stopped, sitting back down and staring at my hands.

"Did I just...cheer for Kylian?" I muttered to myself, bewildered. Regina elbowed me playfully.

"Looks like someone's starting to care," she teased.

I rolled my eyes but couldn't help but smile a little. Maybe there was more to Kylian – and this whole swimming thing – than I had thought.

I took a sip of my soda, my eyes following Kylian as he remained calm and composed despite his victory. He really was an enigma. The team had secured first place, and I watched as the swimmers received their medals and posed for a team photo. Kylian's smile was surprisingly charming, and I quickly typed some notes on my phone, trying to capture the moment.

As I descended the bleachers, Aaron approached me with a shy grin.

"Hey," he said, rubbing the back of his neck nervously. "I saw you cheering for Kylian. Didn't know you were into swimming."

I shrugged, trying to play it cool. "I'm not, really. Just here supporting the team."

He smiled. "Well, it was great to see you here. Maybe we could hang out sometime? You know, outside of school or...the pool."

I raised an eyebrow, surprised by his sudden boldness. "Yeah, maybe. I'll think about it."

Just then, Aaron glanced behind me, his expression shifting from confidence to nervousness. He stammered something about having to go and quickly walked away. Confused, I turned around and saw Kylian standing there, a knowing smirk on his face.

Had he just scared Aaron off? Impossible. But the timing was too perfect to be a coincidence.

"You were pretty good out there," I said, trying to sound casual.

Kylian's smirk widened. "Thanks. Did you enjoy the show?"

I rolled my eyes. "Don't get too full of yourself."

He chuckled and placed his hand on my head, ruffling my hair. I swatted his hand away, glaring at him. "Stop that!"

"You're too easy to tease," he said, still laughing. "Catch you later, Humpty Dumpty."

I watched as he walked off to join his friends, feeling a strange mix of irritation and something else I couldn't quite place. Maybe Regina was right – there was something about Kylian that was starting to get under my skin.

Regina came up beside me, a mischievous grin on her face. "You two are so cute together."

I groaned. "Don't even think about it."

She laughed. "Why do you dislike him so much, anyway?"

I sighed. "Kylian has always been so arrogant, and he doesn't take academics seriously. He just coasts by on his swimming talent."

Regina shrugged. "Maybe he's changed."

I hesitated, not sure how to respond. Was it possible that he had changed? Kylian did seem different lately, more focused and, dare I say it, more genuine.

"I don't know," I finally said. "He's still the same Kylian to me."

Regina gave me a knowing look. "People can surprise you, you know. Maybe give him a chance?"

I rolled my eyes, but couldn't help but wonder if there was some truth to her words.

Just as I was about to shoot Regina a skeptical look, a group of rival swimmers approached us. They had that swagger that just screamed trouble.

"Do you owe them something?" I whispered to Regina, eyeing the group warily.

She shook her head. "Nope, never seen them before."

One of the guys, clearly the ringleader, started getting too close for comfort. "Hey there, ladies. Enjoying the competition?"

Regina and I exchanged uneasy glances. "Yeah, it's been great," Regina said, trying to keep things light.

"Maybe we can make it even better," another one of them chimed in, stepping closer and trying to touch my arm. I jerked away, feeling the tension rise.

"Don't touch her," I snapped, my voice wavering a bit despite my attempt to sound confident.

Before things could escalate further, Kylian appeared out of nowhere. "Back off, losers," he growled, shoving the guy away from me. "Or do you need a reminder of what happens when you mess with my friends?"

The rival swimmers exchanged looks, muttering insults under their breath, but eventually decided it wasn't worth the trouble. They slunk away, leaving us alone.

"Thanks," Regina said, relief evident in her voice.

Kylian turned to me, his usual smirk replaced with genuine concern. "You okay?"

I shrugged, trying to act nonchalant. "I'm fine. Thanks for stepping in."

He smiled, and before I could react, he placed his hand on my head. "You really need to stop getting into trouble, Humpty Dumpty," he murmured, his voice low and teasing.

My heart did that annoying flutter thing again. I quickly removed his hand from my head. "And you need to stop calling me that," I retorted, trying to ignore the way my cheeks were heating up.

Kylian laughed and headed back to his friends, leaving me standing there with Regina, who had a smug look on her face. "You like him," she teased.

I rolled my eyes, but my blush gave me away. "Shut up, Regina."

She just laughed. "You're blushing."

"Am not," I muttered, though we both knew it was a lie.

We head back to the dorm and settle in to do our homework together, laughing and joking around to keep things light. I manage to make some progress on my project—okay, it's only one page, but it's progress. Still, I can't stop thinking about Kylian's smile. Why can't I just get him out of my head?

Just as I'm trying to refocus on my work, Kylian bursts into the dorm with his sports bag slung over his shoulder. I immediately lose all concentration and find myself staring at him. Our eyes meet, and he looks at me with a curious expression. I quickly avert my gaze back to my laptop, feeling a blush creep up my cheeks.

Regina, of course, catches on immediately. She has this infuriatingly knowing smile on her face. Before I can tell her to shut up, Kylian strolls over and snatches a chip from the table.

"Is that all you've written?" he teases, glancing at my screen.

I roll my eyes. "Mind your own business."

"Oh, touchy," he says, a playful glint in his eyes. "Need some help? I could give you a few pointers."

"I'd rather fail," I shoot back, but my tone lacks its usual bite.

Regina steps in, sensing the growing tension. "Alright, you two, enough. Kylian, go take a shower or something."

He smirks at me one last time before heading to his room. "Just four months, Kathleen. Just four months," I mutter to myself, trying to regain my focus.

But as I stare at the screen, all I can think about is that stupid smirk and how much it's messing with my head.

Regina leans over and whispers with a mischievous grin, "You two are so cute together."

I deny it vehemently. "No, we're not! Stop it!"

She just keeps smiling, clearly not buying my denial. Feeling embarrassed and flustered, I decide I need to escape. "I'm going to continue my work in my room," I mumble, grabbing my laptop and heading for the door.

As I pass Kylian's room, I notice the door is slightly ajar. I can't help but glance inside. He's standing there with just a towel wrapped around his hips, clearly about to take a shower. Why does he have to be so annoyingly sexy?

I quickly dart into my room and shut the door behind me, leaning against it as if it can keep out all these confusing feelings. Why am I feeling all these things? It's just Kylian. He's arrogant, and annoying... and somehow incredibly attractive.

I sit down at my desk, opening my laptop and trying to focus on my project. But my mind keeps drifting back to the sight of him, the way his hair was still damp, the way his muscles moved as he walked. I groan in frustration, burying my face in my hands.

"Why does he have to mess with my head like this?" I mutter to myself, desperately trying to shake off the image of him from my thoughts.

Chapter 8

The next day, after my last class, I found myself waiting for Kylian at the pool. The atmosphere was buzzing with excitement as people dove off the platforms. I watched, fascinated, trying to figure out how they managed to make it look so effortless. Seriously, did they have some sort of secret gravity-defying power?

Suddenly, I felt a presence beside me. I glanced over and saw Kylian standing there, looking rather casual in his swimwear, as if he didn't have a care in the world. His presence was almost as surprising as a penguin at a beach party.

"Hey," I said, trying to sound nonchalant but failing miserably. "What's it like winning a competition? Does it come with a secret handshake or something?"

Kylian chuckled softly. "It's more about the satisfaction of a job well done. But yeah, there's no secret handshake, just a lot of hard work and a few bruised egos."

He seemed genuinely relaxed, a stark contrast to the Kylian I was used to. It was like meeting a new version of him who had swapped arrogance for, dare I say it, charm.

He continued with that soft tone, "I'll be waiting for you downstairs for the lesson. Don't keep me waiting too long."

I was taken aback. Was this really Kylian? The same guy who'd been a complete jerk just a few weeks ago now sounded almost... considerate? What kind of alternate universe had I stumbled into?

I watched him walk away, and couldn't help but notice how different he seemed. It was as if he had accidentally wandered out of a soap opera and into my life, bringing along a new script and a fresh attitude.

"Yeah, yeah, I'll be there," I called after him, shaking my head in disbelief. It seemed like I was in for another adventure with this new, improved version of Kylian.

As he disappeared down the hall, I couldn't help but wonder: was he still the same Kylian I knew, or had he just discovered a new way to confuse me?

In the locker room, I changed quickly, trying to ignore the chatter of the other girls as they arrived. They flashed me friendly smiles, and I returned the gesture, though my mind was preoccupied. I overheard snippets of their conversations about the competition, and I couldn't help but wonder how a sport could have such a profound positive effect on one's psyche.

I slipped into my swimsuit and tied my hair back, preparing myself mentally for the session ahead. It was time to face the pool again.

When I met up with Kylian, he was already in the water, looking effortlessly at ease. "To warm up, swim a length," he instructed. I nodded, and with a deep breath, I plunged into the pool, swimming on my stomach. I made it to the end and turned around to head back.

As I swam, I noticed a curious sensation of calm washing over me. It was strange but soothing, like the water was carrying away my stress and worries. Despite my initial resistance, I found myself enjoying the rhythm of my strokes and the tranquil embrace of the water.

I returned to the poolside and spotted Kylian chatting with a lifeguard. An odd feeling stirred inside me, a mix of curiosity and something else I couldn't quite pinpoint. As I watched them interact, I noticed the way he smiled and how natural their conversation seemed. The lifeguard, catching my gaze, gave Kylian a cheerful wish of good luck before walking away.

I couldn't help but feel a twinge of irritation. Who did she think she was? It wasn't jealousy, or was it?

Kylian came back over, a mischievous grin on his face. "Ready for some more training?" he teased. Before I could respond, I splashed him playfully, causing him to laugh.

"Alright, let me show you how to get a good push off the wall," he said, demonstrating how to align your body and propel yourself efficiently. As he guided me through the movements, I couldn't shake the unsettling emotion from earlier. I wondered why I had felt so unsettled seeing him with that girl. It seemed so out of place compared to the calm and focused Kylian I was used to.

The feeling lingered, like a ripple in the water that wouldn't settle. Maybe it was just me getting caught up in something that wasn't really there.

He asked if I understood, and I nodded. With a cheerful tone, he announced that we'd be practicing this in the deep end of the pool. I protested, suggesting it wasn't a great idea, but he teased me until I finally gave in.

As we walked to the deep end, my anxiety levels skyrocketed. Kylian demonstrated what he wanted to see—a smooth, effortless glide through the water. He showed how to push off the wall, stretching out, and slicing through the water like a torpedo. His demonstration was so fluid and graceful it almost made swimming look like a piece of cake.

I felt a strong urge to turn back, but he insisted I at least try. "Come on, don't be a chicken," he prodded. "If I'm going to drown you, I'll be right here."

I closed my eyes, took a deep breath, and counted to three. On "three," I pushed off, plunging into the water. When I surfaced, panic set in, and I flailed a bit.

Kylian swam over to me and pulled me into his arms. We locked eyes, and for a moment, I was struck by how incredibly blue his eyes were—like a calm sea on a sunny day. I could feel his arms tightening around me, providing a reassuring grip.

"Are you okay?" he asked, his voice laced with concern.

I stammered, "I-I think so."

He chuckled, clearly enjoying my flustered state. "You're not going to drown, you know."

I rolled my eyes, feeling a mix of embarrassment and relief. "Well, thanks for not letting me."

He grinned, still holding me close, and we floated together in the deep end for a moment longer, his teasing laughter echoing in the water.

He guided me back to the edge of the pool, and I clung to it as if my life depended on it. He couldn't help but tease me, "You look like you're holding on for dear life."

I shot back, "Well, maybe I am! Not everyone is as confident in the deep end."

When he got out of the pool, he asked, "Give me your hands."

I hesitated, "I don't want to touch you."

He smiled and said, "Remember how you clung to me a moment ago?"

I felt my cheeks flush and, reluctantly, I gave in.

He took my hands and pulled me up out of the water. As we walked towards the shallow end, he still had that teasing smile on his face. "See? Not so bad, right?"

As we walked, the lights went out, plunging the pool area into darkness. "Great, a power outage," I muttered, feeling a pang of panic. "We should probably head back."

Kylian, however, was undeterred. "We're not stopping the practice because of a little blackout."

I sighed, knowing I was fighting a losing battle. "Fine, let's keep going."

I entered the pool, and Kylian said we'd focus on aligning my body. He took my hand to guide me, his touch sending an unexpected shiver through me. He instructed me to lie on my stomach, and I obeyed, trying to ignore the strange sensation of his proximity.

The darkness seemed to amplify the closeness of our bodies. Was it just the lack of light, or was something more at play? I tried to focus on what he was saying, but his presence was incredibly distracting.

Kylian adjusted my position, aligning my body, his hands moving over my back, causing more frissons. The closeness was electric, and every touch seemed to linger longer than necessary.

When I surfaced, he told me I needed to improve the movement of my arms. He positioned himself behind me, and I could feel the warmth of his body radiating against mine. "Lift your arms," he instructed.

I raised my arms, and he placed his hands over mine to demonstrate the correct motion. His touch was firm yet gentle, guiding my movements. As he showed me how to move my arms properly, I found it nearly impossible to concentrate. The sensation of his hands on mine and the closeness of his body were too overwhelming.

Kylian continued his explanations, but I was barely listening. My focus was consumed by the heat and closeness of his body against mine.

Finally, he stopped and asked, "Did you get it?"

I turned to face him, our faces just inches apart in the darkness. Despite the lack of light, I could see the glint in his eyes. I tried to answer, but my voice came out in a stammer, "Y-yeah, I got it."

Kylian smirked, clearly amused by my reaction. "Good. Let's see if you can put it into practice."

As we continued the lesson, my heart raced, and I couldn't help but wonder if this blackout had turned into a rather strange, but somehow exciting, twist on our training.

I tried out the new technique Kylian had shown me, and to my surprise, I felt a significant improvement. It was as if I was swimming better than before.

I returned to Kylian, who looked impressed. "Hey, that was actually pretty good!" he said, giving me a thumbs up.

"Thanks," I replied, feeling a bit proud of myself.

But of course, Kylian couldn't resist his usual teasing. "Well, look at you, actually swimming like you know what you're doing. Who knew you had it in you?"

I rolled my eyes, but I couldn't help but smile. "Yeah, yeah, just let me get through this without any more jokes."

"Alright," he said, still grinning. "Next up, we need to practice your lateral breathing."

He gestured for me to get back into position. I lay on my stomach, and he placed his hands firmly on my hips to keep me steady. "Alright, I'm going to count to three. When I hit three, you need to take a breath, okay?"

I nodded, trying to steady my nerves. Kylian counted out loud, his voice echoing in the dark pool area, "One... two... three."

As I took a deep breath, I felt the cool water rush around me. Despite the darkness and the strange tension in the air, I managed to follow his instructions.

Kylian watched closely, still holding onto my hips to make sure I didn't lose my balance. His touch was reassuring, and I felt a mix of relief and awkwardness.

"Nice job," he said with a smirk. "You're getting the hang of this. Maybe I won't have to rescue you every time."

I shot him a playful glare. "Don't push your luck, Kylian."

With a final chuckle, he let go of my hips and gave me a mock salute. "Well done, Humpty Dumpty. Now, let's see if you can keep up this progress when the lights are back on."

A loud noise echoed through the pool area, making me jump. Without thinking, I grabbed Kylian's hand, holding on tight.

The lights flickered back on, illuminating the pool, and I quickly pulled my hand away, feeling embarrassed. "I... I think I should go," I stammered, trying to keep my voice steady.

Kylian looked intrigued but nodded. "Alright."

As I started to walk away, I felt his hand grab mine again, pulling me back effortlessly. He looked at me intently, his eyes searching mine. "Are you sure you're okay?" he asked, his voice soft and genuine.

I pulled away from him, trying to regain my composure. "Yes, I'm fine," I replied quickly.

Without waiting for his response, I turned and hurried to the locker rooms. My mind was racing. What is going on with you, Kathleen? I thought to myself as I slammed the locker door shut behind me.

I dressed quickly, yanking off the elastic from my hair and letting the wet strands drape over my sweatshirt. I slipped on my glasses, grabbed my bag, and left the locker room. As I walked past the pool, I saw Kylian swimming with effortless grace.

He cut through the water with powerful strokes, his muscles rippling under the surface. His rhythm was mesmerizing, each movement precise and controlled. I found myself stopping to watch, completely entranced by his skill.

Kylian finished his lap and noticed me standing there. He pulled off his goggles, a smirk spreading across his face. "Enjoying the view?" he teased, slightly breathless.

I tried to muster a cold reply, but my words came out weak. "Just... checking your form," I said, though even I wasn't convinced.

He climbed out of the pool, water streaming down his sculpted body. His shoulders were broad, his abs defined, and every movement seemed to highlight his athleticism. My heart started pounding, and I could feel my cheeks heating up as I took in the sight of him.

Kylian walked over to me, reaching into his bag and pulling out a black swim cap with "Rivera" written on it—the same one he wore. "I had an extra," he said, sounding a bit sheepish, "and I thought you might like it."

I took the cap, trying to ignore the butterflies in my stomach. "Thanks," I mumbled.

He grinned, back to his usual self. "Now you can look just like Humpty Dumpty."

I glared at him, calling him a name that probably wasn't very mature, and turned on my heel to leave. Behind me, I could hear him laughing, and despite myself, I couldn't help but smile a little.

Somehow, even when he was being an idiot, Kylian had a way of getting under my skin.

I looked down at the swim cap in my hand. Did he really just give me a swim cap with his last name on it? As if... No, don't even think about it.

I shook my head, trying to push the ridiculous thought away. But the more I tried not to think about it, the more it lingered in my mind. It was just a swim cap, right? No big deal. Just Kylian being Kylian.

I glanced back at the pool, catching one last look at him as he dove back into the water with perfect form. The cap felt strange in my hands, like it carried some sort of hidden meaning I couldn't quite grasp.

With a sigh, I shoved it into my bag and headed out of the pool area, determined to focus on anything but Kylian and his stupid swim cap.

Chapter 9

The next evening, I saw Regina all dressed up, looking ready for a night out. She asked, "What are you doing?"

"Reading," I replied, glancing up from my book.

"There's a student party tonight," she said, her eyes sparkling with excitement.

"I'm not really in the mood," I protested.

But Regina wouldn't hear any of it. "Come on, you have to come!" she insisted, practically dragging me to my room.

I sighed and went to my closet, pulling out a sleek black dress. It was simple yet elegant, with thin straps and a neckline that dipped just enough to be intriguing without being too revealing. The fabric hugged my figure in all the right places, falling just above my knees with a subtle flare.

Yeah, I had to admit, it was a sexy dress. I slipped it on and looked in the mirror, noticing how it accentuated my curves—or lack thereof. I felt a pang of insecurity but tried to push it aside. I took a deep breath, reminding myself to be confident. I removed my glasses and replaced them with my contact lenses, giving myself one last look in the mirror.

When I joined Regina, she gasped. "You look stunning!" she exclaimed.

"Thanks," I said, feeling a bit better. "You look amazing too."

We exchanged smiles and headed out together, ready for whatever the night had in store.

We arrived at the party, and the atmosphere was electric. People were drinking, dancing, and shouting over the loud music. The room was dimly lit with flashing neon lights, and the bass from the speakers made the floor vibrate. Students were packed together, laughing and swaying to the rhythm, some already a little too tipsy.

"I'm going to get us some drinks," I told Regina, who was already caught up in a conversation with some friends.

"Get me something strong!" she called after me with a laugh.

I chuckled and made my way through the throng of people, weaving between dancing bodies and avoiding the occasional drink spill. Just as I reached the makeshift bar, I collided with someone.

"Aaron!" I exclaimed, recognizing him.

"Hey, Kathleen. Want to dance?" he asked with a charming smile.

I glanced back at Regina, who was engrossed in her conversation, and decided why not. "Sure," I said.

As we started dancing, Aaron pulled me in closer, his grip a bit too tight, and our bodies pressed together uncomfortably. I tried to laugh it off, but I felt uneasy. "I need to go," I said, trying to pull away.

But Aaron didn't let go. "Stay a bit longer," he insisted, his hand squeezing my arm painfully.

"Aaron, stop, you're hurting me," I said, my voice rising in panic.

Suddenly, someone shoved Aaron away from me. It was Kylian. "Back off," he snarled at Aaron, his eyes flashing with anger. He grabbed my hand and led me away from the crowd.

Once we were in a quieter corner, Kylian turned to me, his eyes searching mine intensely. "Are you okay?" he asked, his voice filled with concern.

"I'm fine," I said, though my arm throbbed where Aaron had gripped it.

Kylian didn't seem convinced. He scanned me for any sign of injury. "Are you sure? You don't look hurt?"

"I'm fine, really," I insisted. "I didn't need your help, though."

He chuckled and, as if it was second nature, placed his hand on my head. "You know, you look really cute when you're flustered," he said, making me shiver slightly.

He turned to leave, heading back towards his friends. "I'm keeping an eye on you, Humpty Dumpty," he called over his shoulder with a grin.

I rolled my eyes but couldn't help feeling a little safer knowing he was watching out for me.

I grabbed a drink, then another, and another. The buzz of the alcohol started to take effect, making everything feel a bit lighter and more fun. It was time to enjoy this party, right?

I made my way to the dance floor, letting the music take over. The rhythm pulsed through me, and I felt a sense of freedom. I noticed Kylian standing with his friends. He was laughing, his usual confident smirk plastered on his face. His friends, a mix of guys and girls, were hanging on his every word. Kylian had that magnetic presence that drew people in effortlessly.

As I continued to dance, my moves became bolder, more daring. Was I trying to get his attention? No way. That couldn't be it. I just wanted to have fun. Right?

But I couldn't help glancing his way, noticing how he occasionally looked over in my direction, his eyes lingering a bit longer each time. I spun around, letting my hair fly, and swayed my hips to the beat. The alcohol gave me a confidence boost, and I danced with abandon, feeling the music in every part of my body.

It was impossible to ignore the way Kylian's gaze followed me. I told myself I didn't care, but a small part of me enjoyed the attention. After all, this was my night to let loose and enjoy myself.

I went to grab another drink, needing a moment to cool off from all the dancing. As I reached for the cup, I heard a familiar voice behind me.

"Having fun, Humpty Dumpty?" Kylian teased, his tone playful.

I turned to face him, responding coldly, "More fun than you'd ever know."

He stepped closer, his body now almost touching mine. The space between us felt charged with an inexplicable tension. Leaning in, he whispered a compliment, his voice low and sensual, "You look incredible tonight."

I glanced up at him, a mischievous smile playing on my lips. I decided to play along, feeling bolder than ever. Leaning in, I let my breath lightly brush against his ear, my lips just grazing his earlobe.

"Nice try, Kylian," I murmured, my voice dripping with mockery.

With that, I pulled back and walked away, leaving him standing there.

I continued to enjoy the evening, letting the music and drinks take me away. As I danced and mingled, I couldn't help but notice Kylian's gaze following me more intently than usual.

In the past, Kylian had always been the kind of guy who would effortlessly charm any girl in sight, leaving a trail of fluttering hearts and disappointed admirers. He had a knack for flirting with ease, bouncing from one girl to another, always surrounded by a small crowd of admirers. Tonight, however, his behavior seemed markedly different.

He was no longer the aloof, charming player who seemed more interested in collecting phone numbers than having an actual conversation. Instead, he appeared genuinely focused on me. It was almost as if he was studying me with a kind of intense curiosity, his eyes locked on me with an unsettling frequency. What was up with that?

As I observed, I noticed a curious pattern. Every time I engaged in conversation with another guy, they seemed to get nervous and eventually retreat. Was I really that unapproachable? Or was it something else entirely—like the fact that Kylian was lurking in the background?

It was a bizarre, frustrating situation. I wondered if I had suddenly developed some sort of repelling aura. Maybe my dancing was sending out invisible "stay away" signals. Or perhaps Kylian had some sort of weird, possessive problem. It made me wonder, what exactly was his issue?

Trying to shake off my confusion, I decided to focus on enjoying the night, even if Kylian's increasingly intense stares and the mysterious departure of every guy I talked to were starting to get under my skin.

The night had been a whirlwind, and as I stumbled into bed, I could barely keep my eyes open. I'd had a bit too much to drink, and my head was spinning slightly as I tried to drift off.

Then, there was a knock at the door. I groaned, half-asleep and grumbling as I threw on my glasses and dragged myself out of bed. I opened the door, expecting perhaps one of my friends or, at worst, some annoying party-goer. Instead, there stood Kylian.

Before I could even think about questioning his presence or demand an explanation, he placed a finger gently over my lips, shushing me. His closeness and the soft warmth of his breath on my ear sent an unexpected shiver down my spine.

Kylian leaned in and whispered a compliment so smooth and so unexpectedly sincere that it took me by surprise. "You've got a way of lighting up the room, even when you're not trying." His voice was low and warm, and it left me momentarily breathless.

He straightened up, his lips curling into that familiar, teasing smirk. "Good night, Humpty Dumpty," he said, his voice carrying a hint of playful affection. And then, just like that, he turned and walked away.

I closed the door, still in shock, and leaned against it for a moment, trying to calm my racing heart. What on earth had just happened? What was with Kylian's sudden change in behavior? His teasing nickname, his close proximity, and that oddly tender compliment—it was all too confusing. As I lay back down, I couldn't help but wonder if my head was spinning from the drinks or if Kylian was genuinely becoming something more than just an irritatingly charming guy.

As I sat through my last class of the day, my mind kept drifting back to the strange and confusing events of the previous night. Was it a dream? I could barely remember the details, but the lingering sense of Kylian's presence and his unexpected compliment kept making my heart flutter in a way I couldn't quite explain.

By the time the class ended, I had almost convinced myself to skip the swim practice. But something—maybe a stubbornness or a nagging curiosity—kept me moving toward the locker room. I walked at a slower pace than usual, each step feeling heavier than the last.

Once in the locker room, I changed in my usual stall, trying to ignore the voices around me. However, I couldn't help but catch snippets of conversation. One girl mentioned, quite casually, that she had spent the evening with Kylian Rivera. My stomach twisted into a knot. Was it jealousy I was feeling? No, surely not. I tried to dismiss the thought, but the uneasy feeling lingered.

I finished changing and pulled my hair into a ponytail, glancing at the mirror. The unmistakable black swim cap with "Rivera" emblazoned on it caught my eye. I hesitated, feeling a mix of reluctance and defiance. It was ridiculous, but maybe wearing it would be a way to deal with the lingering confusion from last night.

After a moment of struggling, I managed to put the cap on, feeling the snug fit around my head. I looked at my reflection and almost laughed out loud. With the cap on, I truly did resemble Humpty Dumpty. The image was absurd, yet it felt oddly fitting.

I sighed, trying to shake off the strange feeling. I needed to focus on swimming, not on whatever was going on with Kylian or how silly I looked in this ridiculous cap. As I walked toward the pool, I hoped that maybe, just maybe, the water would help clear my head and put things into perspective.

As I stepped into the water and watched the other girls train, I tried to focus on the rhythm of my strokes. But then, I felt a hand lightly rest on my head. I turned around to see Kylian standing there, his usual smirk on his face.

"You're really starting to annoy me," I said, trying to sound irritated as I pushed his hand away.

"Oh, come on, Humpty Dumpty," he teased, leaning in closer with that infuriating grin. "You look adorable in that cap."

I rolled my eyes, trying to ignore him. But as a girl swam past us, Kylian gave her a flirtatious wink. Great, he hadn't changed at all. Maybe I'd just imagined the more genuine side of him from last night.

"Here," he said, holding out a pair of bright pink goggles. "These will look great on you."

"I don't want them," I replied, hoping he'd get the hint. But before I could protest further, he had already put them on me.

He chuckled, apparently enjoying the sight of me in the ridiculous goggles. "I'm going to grab my water bottle. I'll be right back."

I watched him walk away, feeling a wave of frustration mixed with a hint of disappointment. How could I have thought he had changed? It seemed like the same old Kylian was still here—playful, flirtatious, and not taking anything seriously.

I sighed and adjusted the pink goggles, feeling the weight of their ridiculousness pressing down on me. Maybe I had overestimated him. Or maybe I was just making things more complicated than they needed to be. Either way, I was back to reality, and reality included Kylian's usual antics.

Chapter 10

Kylian returned with his water bottle, looking as casual as ever. "Alright, do two laps and we'll see how you're doing," he instructed.

I took a deep breath and dove into the water, completing the laps with relative ease. The rhythmic strokes and the coolness of the pool were soothing, calming my racing thoughts.

When I came back to the edge, Kylian was staring at me with a curious expression. "Is everything okay?" I asked, noticing his unusual gaze.

"Y-yeah, everything's fine," he stammered, looking away quickly. His cheeks were slightly flushed, which was odd.

He entered the water, shaking his head as he swam closer. "So, what's up? You need something?"

I hesitated for a moment before asking, "Could you teach me how to swim the butterfly stroke?"

He burst into laughter, shaking his head. "The butterfly stroke? You sure you're ready for that? It's not exactly beginner's level."

I rolled my eyes and decided to make him pay for his teasing. I splashed him with a generous amount of water, causing him to sputter and laugh even harder.

"Hey, no fair!" he exclaimed, wiping his face. "You're just trying to distract me from your lack of swimming skills!"

I smirked. "Maybe I just want to see you get all wet and flustered."

Kylian grinned, clearly enjoying our playful banter. "Alright, alright. I'll teach you. But be prepared; it's going to be a workout. And maybe next time, try not to splash your instructor!"

As he started to demonstrate the basic movements of the butterfly stroke, I couldn't help but feel a little excited. Despite his teasing, there was something about Kylian's presence that made the whole experience enjoyable.

I attempted to follow Kylian's instructions, but my movements were a chaotic mess. It seemed like I was flailing more than actually swimming. Kylian couldn't help but laugh, his smile widening as he watched me struggle.

"Oh, that's adorable," he teased, clearly enjoying my frustration. "You're not exactly a natural at this."

Determined to get a reaction out of him, I splashed him with water, sending him into a fit of laughter. He swam closer, and our faces were mere centimeters apart. He leaned in, his breath warm against my skin, and murmured, "You know, you might need a bit more practice before you master this."

I sighed in defeat. "Alright, alright, I'll wait before trying to learn the butterfly stroke."

Kylian's eyes sparkled with mischief. "Sure thing. Want to see how it's really done?"

I nodded, feeling a mix of irritation and curiosity. Kylian shrugged, his expression shifting to one of confidence. "Alright, let's see what you think."

He positioned himself at the edge of the pool, took a deep breath, and launched himself into the water. The way he moved was fluid and graceful, each stroke of the butterfly stroke seemingly effortless. I watched, captivated despite myself, as he glided through the water with precision.

When he returned, he was breathing heavily but grinning widely. "See? Not so hard once you get the hang of it."

I rolled my eyes at his cocky demeanor. "Yeah, yeah, you make it look easy."

Kylian's gaze softened as he looked at me, his smile slightly worn from the effort. "You know, you look pretty cute with those pink goggles on."

I felt my cheeks flush, and I stammered, "Uh, thanks. I guess they're not that bad."

He chuckled, clearly enjoying the effect his compliment had on me. "Just don't let it go to your head. We've got a lot more to work on if you want to keep up with me."

As he swam away, I couldn't help but smile. Despite the teasing and the difficulty, there was something undeniably enjoyable about our interactions.

Kylian asked if I wanted to go to the deep end now. I sighed but eventually nodded in agreement. We reached the deep end, and without a hint of hesitation, he dove into the water like it was the most natural thing in the world.

"Come on in!" he called out, his voice echoing through the water.

I took a deep breath and slowly entered the water, clinging to the edge as if my life depended on it. The moment my feet lost contact with the floor, a wave of panic washed over me. I felt like I was floating in the middle of nowhere, and the deep water seemed to mock my inability to swim freely.

Kylian swam over to me with a look of pure mischief. Before I could protest, he wrapped his arms around me, lifting me off the edge. My immediate reaction was to cling to him for dear life.

"Please, take me back to the edge!" I begged, my voice trembling with panic. But Kylian, in his typical fashion, seemed to ignore my pleas.

"Calm down," he said softly, his voice surprisingly soothing. "Just breathe. I'm here. Nothing's going to happen."

Despite my racing heart and the sudden urge to bolt back to the safety of the shallow end, I closed my eyes and focused on his reassuring voice. I tightened my grip on him, trying to steady my breathing.

"Just breathe," he repeated, his words a gentle anchor in my sea of anxiety. "I've got you."

Slowly, I opened my eyes to find his gaze locked onto mine. His eyes were a deep, reassuring blue, and for a moment, my panic subsided as I stared into them.

"You know," I said, trying to lighten the mood despite my nerves, "you're really not making this any easier by being so calm."

Kylian chuckled softly. "Well, I figured you'd appreciate a bit of support, even if it's just me floating with you."

I managed a weak smile, still holding onto him tightly. "Yeah, support. Right. More like making me feel like I'm on a precarious tightrope in the middle of an ocean."

He laughed, his warmth and humor making me feel a little better. "Well, at least you're not sinking. That's a start."

With his reassurance and steady presence, I began to relax a bit, though I still clung to him. Kylian's calm demeanor was oddly comforting, even if his method of support was a bit unconventional.

Kylian looked at me with an intense gaze, his eyes searching mine as if trying to uncover some deep secret. "Why don't you like swimming?" he asked, genuinely curious.

I took a deep breath, feeling a bit vulnerable under his scrutiny. "Well, it's not that I don't like it. It's just... I've always felt out of my depth, you know? Like, I never really got the hang of it. It's kind of like trying to dance on ice—slippery and unpredictable."

Kylian burst out laughing, the sound echoing around us. "That's ridiculous," he said with a grin. "You're not dancing on ice. It's just water."

I rolled my eyes, trying to mask my embarrassment. "Thanks for that enlightening perspective."

As I tried to wriggle free from his embrace, he tightened his grip, holding me close. He wrapped my legs around his waist, making it clear that he wasn't about to let me go. My heart skipped a beat as I realized how close we were.

"Seriously?" I exclaimed, feeling my cheeks heat up. "Can you please not—"

Ignoring my protests, Kylian swam us back toward the edge of the pool. As we reached the side, he gently helped me climb out. I scrambled out of the water, my heart racing from both the exertion and the proximity.

I collapsed onto the floor, staring up at the ceiling, feeling the cool air on my wet skin. Safe and sound! The relief was palpable as I lay there, trying to regain my composure.

Kylian leaned over the edge, looking down at me with a mischievous smile. "See? That wasn't so bad, was it?"

I shot him a tired but grateful smile. "Let's just say I'm glad to be on solid ground."

He laughed softly, his eyes twinkling with amusement. "Well, if you ever need a personal lifeguard, you know where to find me."

I shook my head, trying to suppress a smile. "I'll keep that in mind. Thanks, I guess."

As Kylian offered me a hand to help me up, I couldn't help but feel a strange mixture of gratitude and exasperation. Despite the chaos, there was something undeniably comforting about his presence.

Kylian turned around and casually mentioned, "In a few hours, I have a competition."

I raised an eyebrow, not quite catching the significance. "And?"

He looked back at me with a seriousness I hadn't seen before. "It's really important to me. I'd really like it if you came."

I squinted at him, trying to read his expression. Was he... blushing? It was subtle, but there was something in his cheeks that made me think I might be imagining it.

I sighed, trying to sound casual despite the flutter in my chest. "Alright, I'll come."

His face lit up with a wide, genuine smile. "Great! Well, the class is over now, and I need to go train with the team."

As he turned to leave, I watched him walk away, feeling a strange mix of curiosity and anticipation. There was something undeniably appealing about seeing him so invested in something that mattered so much to him.

I stood there for a moment, the reality of my decision sinking in. I was actually going to his competition. Why was I feeling so nervous about it? I shrugged it off, figuring it was just another one of those inexplicable feelings I seemed to be having around Kylian lately.

A few hours later, I was already at the competition, still with damp hair from the pool. The arena was bustling with teams from all over the country, and the air was charged with excitement and nervous energy.

Suddenly, I spotted Kylian. He made a beeline for me, his eyes lighting up when he saw me. He enveloped me in a hug that caught me completely off guard. I stood there, frozen, as he whispered in my ear, "I'm really glad you came."

When he finally pulled away, I felt a flush of embarrassment creeping up my cheeks. "Good luck," I managed to say, trying to sound casual but failing miserably.

Kylian flashed that mischievous grin of his and teased, "Don't worry, I'll try not to embarrass myself too much."

I rolled my eyes at him, but couldn't help but smile. My gaze lingered on him as he adjusted his swim cap, which had his name emblazoned on it—clearly a sign of his dedication and pride.

He placed his hand on my head, ruffling my hair lightly. "Your support means more than anything here."

Before I could respond, he was off, joining his team with that same confident stride. I watched him with a mix of amusement and bewilderment. What had happened to the Kylian I knew? The one who was always so flippant and carefree? This new, earnest version was almost too endearing.

I took my seat in the stands, feeling slightly out of place but also strangely content. I glanced back down at Kylian every now and then. Each time, our eyes met, and he would shoot me a quick, reassuring smile.

I settled into my spot, trying to absorb the atmosphere. My thoughts kept drifting back to Kylian. What a peculiar guy. From the teasing to the unexpected tenderness, he had managed to flip my world upside down in more ways than one. I shook my head, chuckling to myself. "What have they done with the old Kylian?" I wondered aloud, amused by the way he'd managed to get under my skin.

As the competition began, I found myself more invested than I'd expected. It wasn't just about watching the races—it was about rooting for someone who had somehow become important to me.

A woman plops down beside me, and I immediately recognize her as one of the girls from the pool earlier. She casts a curious glance at me and asks, "Is Kylian your boyfriend?"

I turn to her, caught off guard by the question. My cheeks heat up, and I stammer, "Uh, why do you ask?"

She looks a bit flustered and explains, "I was just wondering because I'm interested in him. I wanted to know if I had a chance."

Without thinking, I blurt out, "Yes, he's my boyfriend."

Her eyes widen in surprise, and she quickly mumbles an apology before making a hasty exit. I'm left sitting there, my mouth hanging open in disbelief at my own words.

What on earth is happening to me, Kathleen? Kylian isn't my boyfriend—not by a long shot. My heart races, and I try to process what just happened. Was I seriously feeling jealous?

I watch as the woman disappears into the crowd, my mind spinning. The idea of Kylian being with someone else suddenly feels like a jab to my gut, and I can't help but question why I reacted that way.

I shake my head, trying to dismiss the strange feeling. Kylian and I are just friends—right? But then why did it bother me so much when she showed interest in him? My heart thumps loudly as I try to refocus on the competition, but my thoughts keep drifting back to the unsettling mix of jealousy and confusion I'm feeling.

As the competition kicks off, I find myself getting completely swept up in the excitement. I'm shouting and cheering like a madwoman every time Kylian dives into the pool. My throat gets sore from all the yelling, but I don't care—each victory he secures makes me more elated.

The energy in the arena is electric, and I can't help but feel this bubbling excitement every time Kylian touches the wall first. I'm practically on my feet, clapping and hollering, and my enthusiasm seems to catch on with those around me.

I catch myself in the midst of all this cheering, and I have to wonder: do I still hate him? The truth is, I'm not so sure anymore. Watching him compete with such intensity, seeing him focus and push himself, it's hard to maintain the same feelings I had before.

In fact, as I cheer him on, I realize that I'm genuinely rooting for him. I might have been annoyed with him before, but right now, I'm just incredibly proud and thrilled for his success. Maybe my feelings towards Kylian aren't so straightforward after all.

Chapter 11

The competition was over, and I watched as Kylian and his team received their medals. Their faces were alight with triumph, and I couldn't help but feel a surge of pride for him. I was scribbling notes for my project, but my throat felt like sandpaper. I decided to search for a water fountain, hoping to quench my thirst.

As I wandered through the building, I accidentally bumped into him. He looked exhausted but exhilarated, his damp hair sticking to his forehead. We stood there for a moment, just staring at each other, a strange silence settling between us. Despite myself, I found my arms wrapping around him in a hug. "You're not so bad for a pain in the ass," I said, my voice muffled against his shoulder.

Kylian chuckled and pulled away slightly, his eyes twinkling with amusement. "I'm glad you think so," he replied, trying to feign seriousness. "Though I'm pretty sure you were still supposed to hate me."

I tried to keep my tone cool, offering him my congratulations. He smirked, clearly enjoying the playful banter. "You did great," I said, though I couldn't quite mask the warmth in my voice.

"Thanks," he grinned, leaning closer. "I'd say you were pretty great yourself."

He then took off his medal and draped it around my neck. I protested, "This is yours!"

He waved off my concern. "I had plenty more," he said with a wink. "Besides, I thought it looked better on you."

As my heart raced, I was about to reply when his teammates called out to him. He gave me one last, lingering look. "See you later, Humpty Dumpty," he said, and before I could respond, he turned and walked away.

I watched him leave, feeling a mix of confusion and something else. Glancing down at the medal around my neck, I wondered what was happening with me. Why did it feel like everything was shifting? What was going on with us?

A group of girls from school passed by, their eyes fixed on the medal around my neck with obvious envy. I felt my cheeks heat up and smiled awkwardly, trying to shrug off the attention. Great, now everyone probably thought Kylian and I were together.

Despite the slight discomfort of the situation, I found that I didn't mind it as much as I'd expected. The idea lingered, a confusing mix of annoyance and something oddly pleasant.

"Focus, Kathleen!" I told myself, shaking off the stray thoughts. I quickly tucked the medal inside my sweatshirt, hoping to hide it from view and divert any further speculation.

I walked into the dormitory, still feeling a bit dazed from the day. Regina was lounging on her bed when she spotted the medal around my neck and instantly sprang up.

"What's that around your neck?" she asked, her eyes sparkling with curiosity.

I shrugged, trying to downplay it. "It's just a medal."

Her eyes widened, and she practically bounced with excitement. "Just a medal? Are you kidding me? That's Kylian Rivera's medal! He must have a thing for you."

I rolled my eyes, feeling my face heat up. "It's really nothing. Just a small gesture."

Regina wasn't convinced. "Oh, come on. He definitely has a thing for you."

I shook my head. "No way. Kylian? Never."

Just as I finished, Kylian walked in with his bag. Our conversation stopped abruptly. He came over, pretending to grab an apple from the kitchen, but as he leaned in close, he whispered in a soft, teasing voice, "You know, you look even more amazing with that medal on."

I tried to maintain my composure, but my heart raced. Kylian gave me a playful wink and left.

Regina stared at me with a mischievous grin. "See? I told you."

I couldn't deny the fluttering in my chest, but I brushed it off. "Oh, come on, Regina. It's just a little joke." Even as I said it, I wasn't entirely sure myself.

I walked into my room, my mind buzzing with conflicting emotions. I carefully removed the medal from around my neck and tucked it away in a drawer. Regina followed me in, her eyes bright with curiosity.

"Why are you putting it away?" she asked, almost pleadingly.

I shook my head. "It's not a good idea. It's just a medal."

Regina's expression turned serious. "But it means something to him. It's important."

Her words made me pause. Why was I feeling these strange emotions? I thought about it and, despite my attempts to deny it, I realized I might have feelings for him.

I turned to Regina, looked her in the eye, and placed my hands on her shoulders. "Okay, fine. I admit it. I'm a bit... well, I might have feelings for him. It's just... complicated."

Regina's face lit up with pure joy. She started bouncing on her heels, practically vibrating with excitement. "I knew it! I knew it!"

I watched her, a mix of embarrassment and relief flooding through me. Even though I was a bit flustered, admitting my feelings felt like a weight had been lifted.

Regina's phone rang, and she scrambled to answer it, her eyes widening in panic as Kylian's name flashed on the screen. "Oh no, where's my charger?" he asked through the phone.

Without missing a beat, Regina snatched the medal from the drawer and fastened it around my neck, giving me a quick, mischievous grin. I tried to protest, but she was already shoving me towards the door.

"Go on, it'll be fine!" she said, practically shoving me out of the way as Kylian walked in.

I froze in place as Kylian entered the room. His eyes widened slightly when he saw me with the medal. He gave me a shy, almost hesitant smile that made my heart skip a beat. I stood there, frozen and awkward, caught in a moment that felt both incredibly cliché and ridiculously embarrassing. Regina, playing the ultimate third wheel, waved cheerily before slipping out the door with Kylian.

And there I was, left alone with my rapidly deteriorating composure. I flopped onto my bed, face first, and groaned into the pillow.

"Seriously, Kathleen?" I muttered into the fabric, feeling the weight of my feelings press down on me like an overly dramatic soap opera. "Of all the people in the world, why did it have to be him? Why did I have to go and catch feelings?"

The pillow provided no answers, but it did cushion my face as I buried it, wondering why life had decided to throw me into this ridiculously tangled mess of emotions.

Regina burst back into the room, practically glowing with excitement. "Kathleen, that was amazing! Did you see how he looked at you? He totally has a thing for you!"

I barely lifted my head from the pillow, my voice muffled but tinged with frustration. "Yeah, sure. He looked at me like I was a giant walking, talking embarrassment."

Regina chuckled, sitting down beside me and gently rubbing my back. "Oh, come on. You saw how happy he was to see you with the medal. He won it for you, you know."

I shot her a skeptical glance, raising an eyebrow. "Really? He won it for me? I doubt it. He probably just tossed it at me because he's nice or something."

Regina shook her head, a knowing smile playing on her lips. "No way. He was totally excited when he saw you wearing it. Trust me, Kathleen, this medal means something special. He was practically glowing when he handed it to you."

I sighed, staring at the medal hanging around my neck. "Do you really think so? I mean, it's just a medal."

Regina grinned, patting my back comfortingly. "Oh, it's not just a medal. It's a symbol of how much he cares. He wanted you to have it. It's like a little piece of his win that he's sharing with you. It's really sweet, don't you think?"

I bit my lip, feeling a confusing mix of hope and doubt. "Maybe you're right. Maybe he did mean it like that."

Regina's eyes sparkled with excitement as she hugged me. "See? I told you! Now go on, wear that medal with pride. You've got a fan in Kylian Rivera."

I managed a small smile, though my heart was still racing with the uncertainty of it all. Could it be that Kylian really did have something special in mind?

I was hunched over my laptop, typing furiously and fighting off the desire to throw my notes out the window. I had four pages left to finish for my project, and honestly, I was tempted to skip my swimming lessons just to get it done. But I had to admit, I liked being around Kylian, even if he could be a bit of a pain.

Groaning in frustration, I closed my laptop with a decisive click and decided I needed a break. Maybe some food would help clear my mind. I shuffled out of my room and headed to the kitchen, my mind still preoccupied with the project.

As I entered the kitchen, I almost walked straight into Kylian, who was in the middle of his usual stretching routine. I tried to play it cool, but my heart did a little somersault. I focused on the cereal cabinet, determined to ignore him.

"Are you sure you're not trying out for a gymnastics competition?" I quipped, reaching for a box of cereal.

Kylian chuckled, his eyes glinting with amusement. "Not a bad idea. Might be more fun than dealing with you."

I shot him a look. "Well, don't let me interrupt your Olympic-level stretches."

He raised an eyebrow and waggled his fingers at me. "You know, you're not very subtle with the whole 'trying to ignore me' thing."

I tried to maintain my cool, but he was getting under my skin. "Oh, am I supposed to be flattered that you noticed?"

His laughter was infectious, and I couldn't help but crack a smile. "Definitely. It means you're paying attention."

Kylian sauntered over to the cabinet and pulled out a bowl. As he handed it to me, our hands brushed lightly. A jolt of electricity—or maybe it was just the cereal bowl—shot up my arm.

"Why aren't you asleep?" I asked, trying to sound nonchalant.

"Insomnia," he said, grabbing a spoon. "And you? Why are you avoiding my eyes?"

I felt my face flush. "I'm not avoiding your eyes. I just—"

He cut me off with a playful smirk. "It's okay. I get it. My charm is overwhelming."

My cheeks turned an embarrassing shade of red. "Sure, let's go with that."

Kylian's smile softened as he leaned closer. "If it helps, you're the best part of my insomnia."

I grabbed my cereal bowl with a hasty, awkward movement, trying to hide my flustered expression. "Thanks for the bowl. I'm going to... um... go back to my room now."

"See you around, Humpty Dumpty," he called after me.

I scurried back to my room, my heart pounding and my mind a jumbled mess. Ugh, why did he have to be so insufferably charming?

The next morning, I woke up slumped over my desk, my head resting next to an almost empty bowl of soggy cereal. My laptop screen had gone dark, and my neck ached from the awkward sleeping position. Groaning, I stretched and rubbed my eyes before dragging myself out of my room.

As luck would have it, I bumped into Kylian in the hallway. He was already up, looking annoyingly fresh and alert. He had on his usual athletic gear, his hair still slightly damp from a morning shower, and that infuriatingly confident smirk was plastered across his face.

"Oh look, it's Sleeping Beauty," he teased, his eyes glinting with mischief.

I rolled my eyes at him, trying to ignore the flutter in my stomach. "Yeah, yeah. Don't you have a pool to jump into or something?"

He laughed, a sound that somehow managed to be both irritating and endearing. "Sure, but first, I have to deal with you."

I shoved him lightly, but he quickly responded by slinging an arm around my shoulders, pulling me close. My heart skipped a beat, and I felt my cheeks heat up. "Kylian, get off me," I snapped, trying to sound annoyed but failing miserably as my voice wavered.

"Why should I?" he asked, his grin widening as he leaned closer.

"Because... because..." I stammered, my frustration growing. "Just because!"

He chuckled and finally let go, but not before ruffling my hair. "Fine, fine. Calm down, Humpty Dumpty."

I glared at him, trying to ignore the way my heart was racing. He leaned in, his voice dropping to a low, sleepy murmur. "You know, you're kinda cute when you're mad."

With that, he sauntered off, leaving me standing there with a pounding heart and a flustered expression. His voice, low and rough from fatigue, had an unexpectedly sexy quality that sent shivers down my spine.

As I watched him walk away, I couldn't help but think about how infuriatingly attractive he was. Ugh, why did he have to be so insufferable?

Regina stepped out of her room and joined Kylian in the hallway. I could hear their voices carrying over, laughing and chatting like old friends. I tried not to listen, but their conversation echoed in my mind, a stark contrast to the way he was with me.

Why did he have to be like that with me and not with others? It was as if he had a special reserve of teasing and mockery just for me.

I lingered in the doorway, half-hidden, watching them. Regina was animated, her gestures wide and expressive, and Kylian looked relaxed, genuinely enjoying her company. The way he laughed with her, so easy and natural, made my chest tighten with an inexplicable pang.

It was infuriating. Why couldn't he be that way with me? Why did he always have to push my buttons and get under my skin?

Regina spotted me lurking and waved. "Hey, Kathleen! Come join us!"

I hesitated, but Kylian turned and flashed me a grin, the same infuriatingly charming smile that always managed to fluster me. "Yeah, Humpty Dumpty, come over here. We were just talking about how you nearly drowned yesterday."

I scowled at him, crossing my arms over my chest. "Very funny, Kylian."

Regina laughed, unaware of the tension I felt. "Come on, Kathleen. Don't be shy."

I reluctantly walked over, feeling like I was stepping into the lion's den. Regina looped her arm through mine, pulling me closer to Kylian. "So, are you two ready for another swimming lesson today?"

I shot Kylian a glare. "As long as he doesn't try to drown me again."

Kylian put on an exaggeratedly innocent face. "Hey, I was just trying to help. You're the one who clung to me like a lifeline."

Regina giggled, and I felt my cheeks flush. "Only because you wouldn't let go!"

He smirked, leaning in closer. "Maybe I just like having you around, Humpty Dumpty."

I rolled my eyes, trying to ignore the way my heart was racing again. Why did he have to be so maddening?

Regina, still holding onto me, whispered, "You know, he might actually like you."

I stared at her, bewildered. "Yeah, right."

But she just winked at me and said, "You never know, Kathleen."

As they continued chatting and laughing, I couldn't help but wonder if there was a grain of truth in Regina's words. Why did he have to be so different with me? And more importantly, why did I care so much?

Chapter 12

That evening, I decided to skip the swimming lesson. I just didn't have the energy for it. As I walked towards the school's exit, I heard Kylian's voice calling out to me. A few students looked our way, and I felt my cheeks heat up with embarrassment.

"Hey, were you about to stand me up?" he asked, catching up to me with that infuriatingly charming grin.

I quickly scrambled for an excuse. "I... I forgot."

He raised an eyebrow, clearly not buying it. "Sure you did. But today, we're doing something different."

I sighed, knowing I wasn't getting out of this one. "Fine."

I headed to the locker room to change, trying to ignore the butterflies in my stomach. Once I was ready, I joined him at the pool. He simply told me to lie on my back and focus on relaxing. I slipped into the water and did as he said, letting the cool water support me.

I started to understand how this could be calming. Kylian floated beside me, and we stayed in companionable silence for a while. Eventually, he broke the silence.

"Do you ever wonder why I started swimming?"

I turned my head slightly to look at him. "Yeah, actually. Why did you?"

He let out a long breath, his eyes fixed on the ceiling. "When I was a kid, my mom got really sick. Cancer. She loved swimming, and it was something we did together. After she passed, I just... kept doing it. It made me feel close to her, I guess."

My heart ached for him. "I'm so sorry, Kylian. I had no idea."

He gave a small, sad smile. "It's okay. It's been a long time."

The silence fell again, but it was a comfortable one. We floated there, side by side, sharing a moment of vulnerability.

"So, what about you?" he asked after a while. "Why did you choose this school?"

I shrugged, feeling the water ripple around me. "It was mostly my parents' choice. They thought it would be good for me to be in a structured environment. Plus, it's got a good reputation."

He nodded thoughtfully. "Makes sense. Do you like it here?"

I hesitated. "I guess. It's just... a lot sometimes. But there are good things too."

He chuckled softly. "Like me?"

I rolled my eyes, even though he couldn't see it. "You wish."

We both laughed, the tension easing a bit more.

"You know," he said, "I've never really opened up to anyone about my mom before."

I looked over at him, surprised. "Really? Why tell me?"

He shrugged, still gazing up at the ceiling. "I don't know. You just... seemed like you'd understand."

I felt a warmth in my chest at his words. "Thanks for trusting me with that, Kylian."

He turned his head to look at me, his eyes soft and sincere. "Thanks for listening, Kathleen."

We floated there in silence for a bit longer, the water cradling us in its gentle embrace. For the first time, I felt a connection to Kylian that went beyond the teasing and the banter. It was a strange, comforting feeling, and I wasn't sure what to make of it. But for now, I was content to just be there, floating beside him, sharing the quiet.

We both straightened up and climbed out of the pool, sitting on the edge with our feet dangling in the water. Our shoulders touched, sending a small shiver through me. I took a deep breath, trying to gather the courage to ask what had been on my mind for a while.

"Why did you insist so much on teaching me how to swim?" I asked, my voice barely above a whisper.

He turned his head slightly to look at me, a small smile playing on his lips. "Because I knew you could do it. And maybe I wanted to spend more time with you."

His answer was simple, yet it made my heart skip a beat. I looked down at the water, trying to hide the smile that was threatening to break across my face.

"You really think I can do it?" I asked, feeling a bit vulnerable.

"Absolutely," he replied, his voice filled with a sincerity that made me believe him. "You just need to trust yourself a little more."

I felt his hand brush against mine, and my heart rate sped up. I glanced over at him, but he was looking straight ahead, acting as if nothing had happened. I was sure he had no idea how much he was driving me crazy in that moment.

Suddenly, a burst of boldness surged through me. "You know what? I have this crazy urge to swim right now."

He turned to me, intrigued. "Really? Now that's the spirit. Let's do it."

Without waiting for a response, he stood up and pulled me gently back into the pool. The water felt different this time, almost welcoming. We swam side by side, and for once, I didn't feel the overwhelming fear that usually accompanied me in the water.

As we floated there, I turned to him. "You know, Kylian, you're not as bad as I thought."

He laughed, a genuine, warm sound that echoed in the empty pool area. "I'll take that as a compliment."

We continued to swim, and with each stroke, I felt more comfortable and more confident. It was as if a barrier had been broken, and I wasn't just learning to swim. I was learning to trust, to open up, and to let someone in.

After a while, we stopped to catch our breath. He turned to me, his eyes shining with a mixture of pride and something else I couldn't quite place. "You did great, Kathleen. I'm proud of you."

For a moment, we just stood there, water dripping off us, breathing heavily. I felt a connection to him that I hadn't felt with anyone in a long time. It was terrifying and exhilarating all at once.

"Thanks, Kylian," I said, my voice soft. "For everything."

He reached out and gently squeezed my hand. "Anytime."

We climbed out of the pool again, this time feeling a sense of accomplishment and closeness that hadn't been there before.

As we sat back down with our feet in the water, our shoulders touching once more, I knew that things had changed between us. And for the first time, I was excited to see where it would lead.

He pointed to the diving board, and I immediately shook my head. "No way am I doing that," I said firmly.

"Please," he begged, his eyes wide and imploring.

"I'll never make it," I replied, shaking my head more vigorously.

He gently placed his hand on my cheek, and my heart pounded furiously. "You'll be fine," he said, laughing at my exaggerated fear. I rolled my eyes and pushed his hand away.

"Fine, I'll do it," I muttered, mostly to prove him wrong.

We walked over to the diving board, and as we climbed up the steps, I could feel my anxiety rising. I glanced at him and said, "I don't think I can do this."

"You've got this," he reassured me, his voice calm and steady. "Just breathe."

I shot him a challenging look. "If I do this, you owe me," I said, trying to sound braver than I felt.

He chuckled, "Deal."

Standing at the edge of the board, I felt the panic set in. "Count to three," I demanded, squeezing my eyes shut.

"One, two, three!" he called out.

On three, I jumped. The fall seemed to last forever, but when I hit the water, a sense of triumph washed over me. I swam to the edge, and before I could catch my breath, Kylian splashed into the water next to me.

"See? You did it!" he said, a grin spreading across his face.

I pushed him gently, playfully. "You're so annoying," I said, but I couldn't help the smile tugging at my lips.

He looked at me deeply, his eyes softening. He reached out and brushed a strand of hair away from my face. My heart pounded even faster.

"I, uh, need some water," I stammered, looking for an excuse to break the tension.

He nodded, his gaze never leaving mine. "Sure," he said softly.

I scrambled out of the pool, my mind racing. Why did he have to be so... intense? As I grabbed a bottle of water and took a long drink, I tried to steady my breathing. Being around Kylian was starting to feel like a different kind of plunge—one that had nothing to do with water and everything to do with my heart.

As I slipped back into the water, Kylian swam over and asked, "Are you okay?"

I tried to muster up the old attitude, the one where I was annoyed by him, but it felt forced and hollow. "Yeah, I'm fine," I said, but my voice lacked its usual bite. He looked at me with curiosity, as if he could tell I was struggling to keep up the façade.

Just then, a group of girls arrived for their training session. We both froze, realizing we weren't supposed to be there. Without missing a beat, Kylian and I dove underwater, our breaths held tightly.

I found myself wedged between the edge of the pool and him, and I could feel his body pressing against mine. My heart raced not just from the lack of air, but from the proximity. It was a tight squeeze, and I couldn't deny the odd comfort in being so close.

When the coast was clear, we surfaced, gasping for air. We looked at each other, and a wave of laughter bubbled up between us.

"That was close," he said, still close enough that I could feel the warmth of his breath on my skin. His voice was lighter, almost playful.

"Yeah, definitely," I replied, my laughter mingling with his. I couldn't help but notice how his gaze lingered on me, how his closeness felt strangely comforting.

We both laughed more freely now, the tension from earlier melting away. He was still pressed up against me, his arms lightly brushing mine. It felt like a bubble of intimacy, and even though I tried to ignore it, it was hard not to feel the electric charge between us.

"You know," he said, his eyes twinkling with mischief, "I never thought I'd be hiding in a pool with you."

"Neither did I," I admitted, trying to hide my smile.

He shrugged, his closeness becoming more noticeable. "Guess we're making memories," he said, his voice softening.

As we continued to laugh and joke, the space between us seemed to shrink. Even though we were just two people caught in an unexpected moment, there was something undeniably electric about it. And as much as I tried to keep my feelings in check, I couldn't ignore the way my heart skipped a beat every time he looked at me with that easy smile.

Out of breath, I finally managed to ask Kylian, "Can you let me go?"

He looked at me with a grin and said, "I don't really want to."

I blinked, thinking I must have misheard him. "Could you repeat that?"

He chuckled, "Yeah, I can let you pass."

I raised an eyebrow, intrigued by his playful demeanor. Reluctantly, I slipped out of the pool and began to dry off. Just as I was about to leave, Kylian's teammates arrived, greeting him with cheers. They dove into the pool and started doing laps, their chatter filling the air.

Kylian, however, decided to join me outside the pool. "So, you're leaving already?" he teased, his eyes twinkling.

"I'm heading out," I said, turning away.

As he put his hand gently on my head, he said with a mischievous grin, "You know, you look pretty cute when you're all flustered."

I swatted his hand away, feeling a mix of annoyance and affection. "Cut it out," I said, rolling my eyes.

He smirked and teased, "Or what? You'll throw me in the pool?"

Before I could respond, one of his teammates shouted from the pool, "Hey Kylian! Stop chatting with your 'girlfriend' and get back to practice!"

Kylian's face turned beet red, and I could feel my own cheeks warming up in response. "Sorry about that," he said, looking sheepish. "I didn't mean to—"

"It's fine," I interrupted, trying to brush off the embarrassment. "See you later."

He gave me a small, apologetic smile and said, "Catch you later, Humpty Dumpty."

As I headed towards the locker rooms, I couldn't help but reflect on how things had shifted between us. The playful banter, the unexpected moments of closeness—things had definitely changed. And though I tried to ignore the flutter in my chest, I knew that this was just the beginning of something new.

I quickly dressed, tying my hair up and putting on my glasses. As I made my way towards the exit, I noticed Kylian's teammates eyeing me with curiosity. They began to bombard me with questions, making me feel increasingly awkward and flustered.

Kylian, noticing my discomfort, stepped in and said, "Hey, guys, give her some space, will you?"

The teammates fell silent, but not before Kylian added with a laugh, "Come on, let her go. You're making her blush!"

He glanced at me with a smirk, his eyes full of mischief. I could feel my cheeks burning even more under his gaze. Trying to avoid drawing any more attention, I picked up my pace and headed toward the exit, my heart racing with both embarrassment and a flutter of excitement.

As I walked away, I could feel Kylian's eyes on me, and I couldn't help but glance back. He gave me a wink, and I quickly turned back around, my face flushed. The moment felt both thrilling and confusing, and I was left with the lingering question of what exactly was happening between us.

I walked into the dormitory, still feeling the buzz of the afternoon. Regina was already there, sprawled on her bed with a book. As soon as she saw me, she bounced up, her eyes wide with curiosity.

"So, how did it go?" she asked, practically bouncing with excitement.

I sighed, recounting the entire afternoon from beginning to end. I told her about Kylian's teasing, the close encounters, and the way his teammates had stared at me. I even mentioned how Kylian had defended me from his friends' prying questions. It felt good to get it all off my chest, even if it was a bit embarrassing.

Regina's eyes twinkled mischievously as she listened. When I finished, she raised an eyebrow and said, "You know, it sounds like he was really into you. He probably wanted to kiss you."

I rolled my eyes, shaking my head with a smirk. "Oh, come on, Regina. Don't be ridiculous. He's just messing around, as usual."

Regina gave me a knowing look but didn't press the issue. Instead, she flopped back onto her bed with a contented sigh. "Well, whatever you say. Just don't be surprised if something more happens."

I tried to ignore the flutter of nerves in my stomach as I changed the subject, but Regina's words lingered in my mind.

As I lay in bed that night, I couldn't shake the memory of that moment underwater with Kylian. The way he had held me so close, the warmth of his body against mine, and the way our faces had been just inches apart—it was all replaying in my mind.

I remembered the rush of adrenaline when we had dived in to avoid being seen, the tight squeeze of his arms around me, and the way his presence had made me feel safe despite my fear. There was something incredibly intimate about being so close, the soft brush of his skin against mine, and the way he had whispered reassurances into my ear.

Even now, lying in bed with the room dimly lit, I couldn't help but wish I could experience that moment again. It had been so different from how I usually felt around him—less about irritation and more about something softer, more vulnerable. I found myself replaying his gentle touch, the way he had looked at me, and the way he seemed to melt away my fears with just his presence.

Maybe Regina wasn't completely off the mark. Maybe there was something more to those moments than I'd been willing to admit. I sighed, turning over and trying to push the thoughts away, but they lingered, making it hard to fall asleep.

I stepped out of my room, still lost in my thoughts about the earlier swim. Kylian was sitting on the couch, engrossed in his phone. He looked up as I approached, and with a sheepish smile, said, "Hey, sorry about my friends earlier. They can be a bit overwhelming."

I tried to wave off his apology, forcing a smile. "It's okay. Honestly, I'd prefer to forget that part."

Kylian chuckled softly, his eyes crinkling at the corners. "Alright, if you say so. But I've got to say, I'm kind of glad you were there."

I raised an eyebrow, intrigued. "Oh really? Why's that?"

He leaned forward, a playful grin on his face. "Because now I have an excuse to spend more time with you. You know, in and out of the water."

I rolled my eyes, trying to keep a straight face. "You're incorrigible."

Just as I was about to respond further, a girl emerged from the bathroom, her eyes flickering between us. I felt a sudden wave of embarrassment and muttered, "Sorry," before quickly retreating to my room.

Once inside, I sat on my bed, feeling tears prick at the corners of my eyes. I wasn't sure why I was so upset. Maybe it was the sudden realization that no matter how close I felt to Kylian, he was still surrounded by a world that felt so different from mine. Maybe it was the fear that he might always be the charming, elusive player, never really changing.

Why had I let myself believe that he could be different? That he could be someone who might understand and care for me in a way that was more than just a fleeting moment? It felt like my heart was betraying me, investing in a possibility that seemed so far out of reach.

I wiped away the tears, shaking my head in frustration. "Why did I even think he could change?" I whispered to myself. It was a painful reminder that some things—people, habits, the way they see the world—might never truly change, no matter how much we hope or wish.

Chapter 13

The days that followed, I made a conscious effort to completely ignore Kylian. I wasn't about to let him play with my heart. I stopped going to the swimming lessons and threw myself into my studies instead, trying to drown out any thoughts of him with equations, essays, and endless reading.

In the mornings, I avoided the common areas where I might run into him, choosing instead to head straight to the library. I buried myself in textbooks, my fingers furiously typing away on my laptop, determined to keep my mind off the charming swimmer who had managed to get under my skin.

During lunch breaks, I found quiet corners of the campus where I could eat alone, away from prying eyes and any chance of bumping into Kylian. My friends noticed my sudden change in routine, but I brushed off their concerns with excuses about upcoming exams and assignments.

Regina, of course, was not so easily fooled. One evening, as I sat hunched over my desk, highlighting passages in my textbook, she walked in and plopped down on my bed.

"You've been avoiding him," she stated, rather than asked.

I didn't look up from my book. "I have no idea what you're talking about."

"Oh please," she scoffed. "You've been hiding out like a hermit. What happened to the girl who couldn't stop talking about swimming?"

I sighed, finally setting my highlighter down. "I'm just... focusing on my studies. That's all."

Regina gave me a knowing look. "You can't hide forever, you know. Especially from your own feelings."

I rolled my eyes. "Feelings are overrated."

She didn't press further, but her words lingered in my mind. I knew she was right, but I wasn't ready to face Kylian or the confusing emotions he stirred in me. So, I continued my self-imposed isolation, hoping that the distance would help me regain my balance.

But even as I tried to convince myself that I was better off without the distraction, I couldn't completely shake off the memories of his smile, the sound of his laugh, and the way he made me feel. It was frustrating, to say the least, and every day was a struggle to push those thoughts aside.

One afternoon, while I was studying in the library, I overheard a couple of students talking about the upcoming swimming competition. I felt a pang of longing but quickly squashed it, reminding myself that my priorities had shifted. I was determined to succeed academically, and that meant staying focused, no matter how much a part of me missed the water—and him.

So, I stayed the course, pushing through the days with a single-minded dedication to my studies, hoping that, eventually, the ache in my chest would fade and I could move on without looking back.

One morning, determined to avoid Kylian at all costs, I woke up even earlier than usual. The sun was barely up, casting a soft glow through the windows of our dormitory. I tiptoed out of my room, hoping to make a quick escape. But as soon as I stepped into the hallway, there he was, leaning against the wall, clearly waiting for me.

My heart skipped a beat, but I took a deep breath and tried to ignore him. I kept my eyes forward, walking with purpose.

"Kathleen, wait," he called out.

I quickened my pace, pretending not to hear him.

"Why have you been ignoring me?" His voice was closer now, and I could hear the frustration in it.

"I'm not ignoring you," I replied, my tone flat, still not looking at him.

He stepped in front of me, forcing me to stop. "Don't lie to me. You've been avoiding me for days."

I shook my head, trying to sidestep him. "I have a lot of work to do. I'm just busy."

He didn't move. "That's not it, and you know it. What happened? Did I do something wrong?"

"No," I said quickly, too quickly. "You didn't do anything."

"Kathleen," he said softly, his eyes searching mine, "I know you better than that. Just tell me what's going on."

I bit my lip, trying to hold back the emotions threatening to spill over. "I just... I need to focus on my studies, okay?"

He looked hurt but didn't press further. "If that's what you want."

I nodded, pushing past him. "It is."

I made it out of the dormitory, my heart pounding in my chest. As I walked away, I couldn't help but feel a pang of guilt. But I convinced myself that this was for the best. I needed to stay focused, and Kylian was too much of a distraction.

Yet, as I headed to the library, a part of me couldn't shake the image of his disappointed face. I forced myself to push it aside, reminding myself of my priorities. But deep down, I knew I wasn't just running from him—I was running from my own feelings.

Throughout the day, whispers and excited chatter about the upcoming swim competition filled the hallways. I overheard students discussing their plans to attend, the anticipation palpable. But I had made up my mind—I wasn't going to go. I needed to forget these confusing feelings I had for Kylian. To him, this was probably all just a game.

As I sat in the library, my laptop open in front of me, I stared at the document for my swimming project. The cursor blinked tauntingly at me, a reminder of my lack of progress. I hadn't written a single word since I started avoiding Kylian.

I sighed, leaning back in my chair. The truth was, I missed it. I missed the water, the challenge, and even Kylian's infuriating yet somehow endearing presence. I never thought I'd admit it, but the swimming lessons had become a highlight of my day. Without them, and without him, something felt incomplete.

I shook my head, trying to refocus. This was ridiculous. I had to stay strong, had to keep my priorities straight. My project was important, and I needed to finish it.

But no matter how hard I tried to concentrate, my thoughts kept drifting back to Kylian. The way he looked at me, the moments we shared in the pool, the unspoken connection I felt when we were together—it was all too much to ignore.

I closed my laptop with a frustrated sigh and packed up my things. Maybe a walk would clear my head. As I made my way out of the library, I couldn't help but wonder if avoiding Kylian was really the right choice. I needed to find a way to balance my emotions and my responsibilities. But how?

The evening wore on, and despite my resolve, I found myself drawn toward the pool area. As I walked, I argued with myself internally. I needed to forget about Kylian, about swimming, about everything. But the pull was too strong.

Before I knew it, I was standing outside the doors to the pool. I could hear the sounds of splashing and cheers from inside. My heart ached with a mix of longing and uncertainty.

Taking a deep breath, I turned away, forcing myself to walk in the opposite direction. I needed to stick to my decision. I couldn't let my feelings for Kylian derail everything I had worked so hard for.

But as I walked away, a small voice in the back of my mind whispered that maybe, just maybe, I was making a mistake.

Instead of going to the competition, I buried myself in my homework. The minutes dragged on, each page I turned feeling like an eternity. I was bored out of my mind, but I tried to convince myself it was better than facing my feelings for Kylian.

When the competition finally ended, I noticed a sense of disappointment hanging in the air as people returned from the pool area. Curious, I spotted Regina and approached her.

"Why does everyone look so disappointed?" I asked, unable to hide my curiosity.

Regina sighed, her expression mirroring the general mood. "Our school came in fifth place."

"Fifth?" I repeated, surprised. That was unusually low for our team. "What happened?"

She hesitated for a moment, studying my face. "You want to know about Kylian, don't you?"

I didn't even have to ask. She knew me too well. "What about him?" I asked, trying to sound casual.

Regina shook her head, looking genuinely baffled. "Kylian lost all his races. He didn't even make it to the podium."

I was stunned. "What? That's... that's unheard of. He hasn't lost a race in ages."

"I know," she said, her voice low. "It was like he wasn't even trying. Something was off."

I stood there, processing the news. Kylian, the star swimmer, losing every race? It was hard to believe. "Well, that's... surprising," I said, struggling to find the right words.

Regina patted my shoulder. "I know it's weird. Anyway, I'll see you later."

I nodded absently, watching her walk away. My mind was racing. Kylian losing? What could have happened to him? The thought of him struggling made my heart ache. Even if I was trying to distance myself from him, I couldn't deny that I still cared.

As I made my way back to my room, I couldn't shake the image of Kylian at the competition, not performing like his usual self. What had changed? Had my absence affected him that much?

I tried to push the thoughts aside, telling myself it wasn't my problem. But deep down, I knew I couldn't ignore it. Not when it came to Kylian.

I entered my room and immediately closed the door, not wanting to risk running into Kylian. The shock of his losses still lingered in my mind. But hey, it happens, right? Everyone has an off day.

I heard him come in, his voice low as he talked to Regina. He sounded disgusted, frustrated. Moments later, I heard the door to his room slam shut.

I glanced over at my desk and saw the medal he'd given me. I picked it up, turning it over in my hands. Was all of this really just a game to him? I couldn't help but wonder. After all, it seemed to be his style, didn't it? What could be so special about me anyway? He could have any girl he wanted.

I sighed, sitting down on the edge of my bed, still holding the medal. The more I thought about it, the more confused I became. Kylian had always been surrounded by girls, always the center of attention. So why me? Why go through all the trouble to teach me how to swim, to give me this medal?

I tried to brush it off, telling myself it didn't matter. But deep down, I couldn't shake the feeling that maybe, just maybe, there was more to Kylian than I had given him credit for.

I finished my last class and walked past the pool, peeking through the large windows at the athletes swimming inside. I couldn't help but smile faintly. God, how I missed it.

As I continued walking, I looked up and saw Kylian standing there. My heart raced despite my best efforts to stay composed. I muttered to myself that this wasn't the time and tried to sidestep him, but he planted himself firmly in my path.

"Hey, you didn't show up yesterday," he said, his eyes locked on mine.

"Yeah, so what?" I shot back, trying to sound nonchalant.

He scrutinized me with that intense gaze of his. "Why are you avoiding me?"

"I'm not avoiding you," I insisted, though I could feel my cheeks warming.

He raised an eyebrow, clearly unconvinced. "Sure you're not."

I tried to ignore the way his gaze made me feel, and I maneuvered around him.

"Come on, Kathleen. Just talk to me," he called after me.

I ignored him and kept walking, leaving him standing there, looking frustrated. For once, I managed to put some distance between us.

That evening, I was struggling to make any headway on my assignment when I heard a knock at my door. I opened it to find Regina standing there. She slipped past me into the room, closed the door, and fixed me with a serious look.

"Okay, what's going on?" she demanded.

"Nothing's going on," I replied, trying to sound as casual as possible.

"Stop denying it, Kathleen," she said firmly. "You've been ignoring Kylian for days. Why?"

I shrugged, pretending not to be bothered. "It's nothing. I just needed some space."

Regina wasn't buying it. She reached into her bag and pulled out my swimsuit, holding it out to me. "Here. You're going. No arguments."

I stared at the swimsuit in disbelief. "I don't know, Regina..."

"Just go. You need to talk to him. It's not just about swimming, you know." With that, she turned and walked out, leaving me alone in my room.

I sat down on my bed, feeling a wave of frustration and confusion. Why was it so hard to just sort things out? Regina's words echoed in my mind, and I couldn't shake the feeling that I was about to dive into something more complicated than just a swim.

The next morning, I found myself standing outside the pool, staring at the water through the large windows. My heart raced, torn between my stubborn pride and the pull of something I couldn't quite ignore. Regina's insistence was still fresh in my mind. I knew I had to go in, if only to satisfy her.

I took a deep breath and walked toward the locker rooms, hoping against hope that Kylian wouldn't be there. The idea of running into him was enough to make my stomach churn. I was just going to do this for Regina, nothing more.

I changed quickly, the familiar feeling of the swimsuit bringing a mix of nostalgia and anxiety. The sound of splashing water grew louder as I approached the pool area. I peeked out cautiously, scanning for any sign of Kylian. To my relief, he wasn't in sight.

With a deep breath, I stepped out of the locker room and onto the pool deck. The water looked inviting, a stark contrast to the chaos in my head. I walked to the edge of the pool and dipped a toe in, trying to steady myself.

Maybe this wouldn't be so bad after all.

CHAPTER 14

I stepped carefully into the water, feeling the coolness embrace my feet. With each step, I felt a sense of calm settling over me. Just as I started to relax, I heard a familiar voice. It was Kylian.

I glanced over, trying to keep my tone casual. "I'm not here for you," I said, though my heart wasn't entirely convinced.

Kylian chuckled softly and took a seat beside me. "Then why are you here? Since when did you like swimming?"

I looked out at the water, the ripples reflecting the light. "Since you taught me to appreciate it," I replied, my voice softer than intended.

A comfortable silence stretched between us, broken only by the sound of splashing water. Kylian finally spoke up. "So, why didn't you come to the competition?"

I shrugged, trying to sound nonchalant. "I had to study."

He looked at me, his gaze distant as he watched the swimmers practice. "I really needed you there," he admitted, his voice carrying a hint of vulnerability.

I turned to him, taken aback. "Why?"

He smiled, a genuine, warm smile that made my heart skip a beat. "Because it wouldn't have been the same without you cheering me on."

I felt a faint blush creep onto my cheeks. I opened my mouth to apologize, but he shook his head. "Don't worry about it," he said gently. "It's okay."

We sat there together, the silence between us now filled with a shared understanding, the water gently lapping at our feet.

He looked at me with those intense eyes and asked, "Why have you been avoiding me?"

I shook my head, trying to sound convincing. "I haven't been avoiding you."

He raised an eyebrow, clearly not buying it, but he let it go. Without another word, he stepped into the water and turned to face me. With a shy smile, he extended his hand towards me. "How about we make peace?"

I hesitated, weighing the idea of giving him another chance. Finally, I sighed and reached out to shake his hand. Without warning, he pulled me into the water.

"Hey! That's not fair!" I spluttered, water streaming down my face.

Kylian laughed, his eyes twinkling with mischief. "I missed you," he said, grinning.

I retaliated by splashing him with water. He put his hand on my head, playfully ruffling my hair. "Oh, really?" I said, trying to sound annoyed but unable to hide my smile.

I couldn't stop splashing him, my laughter mingling with the water droplets. Kylian, still laughing, reached out and grabbed my hands, pulling me closer. We ended up face to face, our eyes locked. For a moment, the playful splashing stopped as we just stared at each other. Then he awkwardly let go of my hands, a blush creeping onto his cheeks.

"Okay, okay," he said, trying to change the subject. "So, what's your favorite part of swimming?"

Before I could answer, Jared and Scott, two of Kylian's teammates, came into view. They greeted me with enthusiastic waves and cheeky winks.

"Hey, Kylian! Who's this?" Jared asked, his grin widening.

Scott joined in, "Yeah, you two look pretty cozy. Are you guys, like, a thing now?"

Kylian's face turned a deep shade of red. He elbowed both Jared and Scott in a futile attempt to quiet them. "Shut up, guys! She's just a friend."

Jared smirked. "Sure, just a friend. You two seem pretty close to me."

Scott, noticing Kylian's discomfort, decided to switch gears. "I'm going to grab the stopwatch for our drills. Catch you in a bit."

As Scott headed off, Kylian looked at me, his expression softening. "Do you want to stay and watch? We're going to start training soon."

I nodded, and he placed his hand on top of my head in a reassuring gesture. The warmth of his hand felt oddly comforting, though it also made my heart race. Ugh, why did he have to be so... well, him? I tried to ignore the fluttering feelings and gently removed his hand.

He noticed and smirked. "What's wrong? Can't handle a little touch?"

I rolled my eyes at his teasing and climbed out of the pool, taking a seat on the edge. The cool air on my wet skin felt refreshing. As I watched Kylian interact with his teammates, I couldn't help but feel a mix of emotions. Sure, his hand on my head was infuriatingly sweet, but it didn't change the fact that I was trying my best to keep my heart in check.

Despite my resolve, the playful banter and Kylian's easy charm made it hard to stick to my plan. It was like trying to ignore a delicious dessert right in front of you—impossible, but oh-so tempting.

I watched as Jared and Scott began their stretching routine. Jared, tall and broad-shouldered, had a serious expression as he bent forward, trying to touch his toes. His muscles strained visibly under the effort. Scott, on the other hand, was more relaxed, casually stretching his arms and chatting with Kylian about their upcoming drills. He was lean and agile, his movements smooth and practiced.

Scott approached me with a stopwatch in hand, a friendly smile on his face. "Here you go. Just press this button to start the timer, and press it again to stop. Pretty simple."

I took the stopwatch, feeling a bit uncertain. "I'm not sure I'll get this right."

Scott chuckled softly. "Don't worry, it's easy. Just follow along, and if you mess up, we'll deal with it."

Kylian glanced over, catching my eye. He gave me a quick nod, a silent check-in to see if everything was okay. I nodded back, feeling a small smile tug at the corners of my lips. He was unexpectedly considerate, and it was hard not to find him endearing.

As I started the timer, Kylian and his teammates dove into the pool. Their strokes were powerful and efficient, cutting through the water with practiced ease. Kylian's movements were particularly fluid; he seemed to glide effortlessly, his form perfect. His strong, rhythmic strokes made it clear why he was such a skilled swimmer.

Jared swam with a determined focus, his strokes slightly more forceful, each push against the water a testament to his competitive spirit. Scott, meanwhile, had a more relaxed style, but still moved with impressive speed.

I watched intently, my eyes moving between the stopwatch and the swimmers. The stopwatch felt heavier in my hand than I expected, but I managed to keep track of their times, glancing up occasionally to watch their technique.

Kylian's performance was captivating. His focus and grace in the water were mesmerizing, and I found myself lost in the rhythm of his strokes. Every so often, he would glance towards me, a flicker of amusement in his eyes as if he knew the effect he was having.

As the session continued, I found it surprisingly enjoyable, despite the fact that I was supposed to be just a spectator. The combination of their skill and the peaceful rhythm of the water was oddly soothing, making me wish I could be in the pool with them.

When the practice finally concluded, Kylian swam over to me, his expression a mix of satisfaction and curiosity. "How'd I do?" he asked, leaning on the edge of the pool.

I glanced at the stopwatch, then at him, trying to hide my smile. "Not too bad. You were pretty impressive."

He grinned, water dripping from his hair. "Thanks. It's good to know someone's keeping track of our times."

As he climbed out of the pool, dripping and breathing heavily, I couldn't help but admire how effortlessly he transitioned from fierce competitor to laid-back teammate. It made me wonder how I had ever managed to stay so indifferent to him.

Kylian plopped down next to me, his damp hair sticking to his forehead. He glanced at me and noticed I was shivering slightly. Without a word, he grabbed his towel from the bench and wrapped it around my shoulders.

"You don't have to," I protested, trying to shrug it off.

"It's freezing out here," he said with a grin. "Just keep it."

Before I could argue further, Jared and Scott approached, their curiosity piqued. Jared, still catching his breath, gave me a playful smile. "Looks like Kylian's taking good care of you."

Scott, who was drying off with his own towel, raised an eyebrow. "Yeah, seems like you two have a pretty close thing going on. Did we miss something?"

I felt my face turn beet red. I stammered, "It's not like that. He just—"

Kylian interrupted with a casual shrug. "Oh, come on. Don't make it weird. I'm just being nice."

Jared smirked. "Nice, huh? Because that looks like more than just a friendly gesture to me."

Scott chuckled and added, "Yeah, I've seen how you two act around each other. You're practically inseparable."

Kylian laughed and looked at me, his eyes twinkling with amusement. "Looks like they've figured us out. What do you think? Should we just go along with it?"

I tried to focus on the conversation, but the heat from my cheeks made it hard to think straight. "We're not—"

"Sure, sure," Jared interrupted, laughing. "Whatever you say."

Kylian gave me a reassuring pat on the back. "Ignore them. They're just trying to get a rise out of us."

Despite his casual demeanor, I couldn't help but feel a mix of embarrassment and warmth. His easygoing attitude made it hard to stay annoyed, even if I was blushing like mad.

Scott threw his arm around Jared's shoulders, clearly enjoying the banter. "We're just messing with you. But seriously, you two make a good team."

Kylian shrugged and smiled at me. "I guess we do."

As Jared and Scott wandered off to get changed, Kylian stayed by my side. "You okay?" he asked, his voice softening.

"Yeah," I replied, still feeling a bit flustered. "Thanks for the towel."

"No problem," he said, giving me a warm smile. "Anytime."

Curiosity got the better of me as I watched Kylian's casual demeanor, his laughter still lingering from the earlier teasing. I hesitated for a moment before asking, "So, who was that girl the other night?"

Kylian raised an eyebrow and grinned. "Oh, you're interested? Is that why you've been ignoring me?"

I tried to maintain a cool front, crossing my arms defensively. "No, I just thought it was worth asking."

He chuckled, clearly amused by my reaction. "She was just a classmate who came over to help me with some homework. Nothing serious."

I forced myself to look uninterested, though my mind was buzzing. "Oh, right. Well, good for you."

A comfortable silence fell between us as we sat there. I tried to ignore the way his presence seemed to make the air crackle with tension. Suddenly, I felt his hand gently rest on top of mine. The warmth of his touch was surprisingly comforting.

He looked at me with a soft smile and said, "You know, sometimes the best things in life are the simplest. Like this moment right here."

I felt my cheeks flush as I glanced at him, my heart skipping a beat. Before I could respond, he pulled his hand away, his playful side returning.

"Come on, Kathleen," he said with a mischievous grin. "You're turning into a puddle over here. I'm going to hit the showers. Try not to miss me too much."

I rolled my eyes, trying to hide my embarrassment. "Yeah, yeah. Go get changed, Kylian."

He laughed and jogged off towards the locker room, leaving me alone with my racing thoughts. I stared at my hand where his had been, trying to steady my breathing.

Kathleen, it's probably just a game for him. Why should you let it get to you? I reminded myself, but it was hard to ignore the fluttering in my chest.

I stood up, feeling the need to clear my head, and made my way to the locker room. The warm shower was a welcome respite, washing away some of the tension from the morning. After drying off, I dressed quickly, opting for a simple outfit, and tied my hair into a neat braid. My glasses went on last, helping me see the world with clearer eyes.

As I exited the locker room, I noticed Kylian chatting with Jared and Scott. The moment he saw me, he broke away from their conversation and approached with a playful grin.

"Hey, Kathleen," he teased, blocking my path. "Leaving without saying goodbye?"

I tried to sidestep him, but he grabbed my hand gently. "You know," he said, looking into my eyes, "you make my day better just by being around."

My heart pounded at his words, and I felt a blush creeping up my neck. I pulled my hand away, stammering, "Uh, thanks, Kylian. I, uh, should get going."

He chuckled, clearly enjoying my flustered state. "See you later, Humpty Dumpty."

As he walked back to his friends, I could hear their whistles and teasing. My face turned bright red as Kylian gave them playful elbow jabs to get them to stop.

I hurried away, feeling both annoyed and inexplicably drawn to him. Why does he have to be so infuriating yet so charming at the same time?

He said she was just helping him with his homework. So why did that make me feel so relieved all of a sudden? Shouldn't he have told me earlier? Did he actually manage to make me... jealous?

I shook my head, trying to clear the conflicting thoughts. It was ridiculous. He shouldn't have this kind of power over my emotions. Yet, here I was, feeling like an emotional yo-yo because of him.

I replayed his words in my mind. "Just helping with homework." It seemed so innocent, so straightforward. But then why did I feel a strange flutter of happiness when he explained? And why was there a pang of disappointment that he hadn't clarified sooner?

Was I actually jealous?

The realization hit me harder than I expected. Yes, I was. I was jealous of the idea that someone else could be close to him, even if it was just for something as mundane as homework. And that jealousy had driven me to ignore him, to avoid the pool, and to let my mind wander into places it shouldn't have gone.

This was getting too complicated. I needed to sort out my feelings, but every time I thought I had a grip on them, Kylian would do or say something that sent my heart racing all over again.

Maybe it was time for a change. Maybe it was time to confront these feelings head-on instead of running away from them.

But first, I needed to breathe and take it one step at a time.

Chapter 15

The next morning, as I was rummaging through my bag in the locker room, I was horrified to find a bikini instead of my usual swimsuit. Regina! I groaned inwardly. I had no time to go back to the dorm and retrieve my actual swimwear. It was either wear the bikini or skip swimming altogether.

So, with a resigned sigh, I put on the bikini. It was a cute, floral number that seemed more appropriate for lounging on a beach rather than swimming laps in a pool. I felt exposed and slightly awkward, but there was no turning back now. I just hoped Kylian wouldn't notice.

I ducked into one of the changing stalls, trying to adjust the bikini to a more comfortable fit. As I did, I overheard a group of girls talking excitedly outside my stall. Their conversation drifted through the thin walls, and it was impossible to ignore.

"Did you see Kylian's new swim cap?" one of them asked. "He looks so hot in it. I swear, the way he swims—"

"I know, right?" another girl chimed in. "I heard he's training harder than ever. He's always so focused. And did you see him the other day with that girl? They looked pretty cozy."

"Oh, you mean Kathleen Davis?" the third girl said, her tone dripping with jealousy. "Yeah, I saw them too. They were practically inseparable."

My heart skipped a beat. Were they talking about me? It sounded like they were speculating about my connection with Kylian, and the way they spoke made me feel a strange mix of embarrassment and irritation.

I held my breath, trying to stay as quiet as possible. I had to wait for them to leave before I could make my grand exit.

The girls finally left, their chatter fading into the distance. I peeked out of my stall, relieved to find the locker room empty. My mind was racing. The conversation had made my cheeks flush with heat. Not only was I dealing with the discomfort of wearing an ill-fitting bikini, but I was also faced with the reality that I was jealous.

It was absurd. I was standing here in a bikini that made me feel like I should be sipping a piña colada instead of swimming, all while stewing in my own jealousy. This wasn't how I had planned my day at all.

I took a deep breath and tried to regain my composure. I was determined to get through this swim practice without making a bigger fool of myself than I already felt. If Kylian noticed, well, I'd just have to explain why I was in a bikini instead of my usual swimwear.

And if he did happen to tease me about it, I'd just have to remind myself that I wasn't about to let him get under my skin—or let his presence dictate my emotions any more than it already had.

I stepped out of the locker room, ready to face whatever the day had in store for me.

I wrapped my towel tightly around myself, trying to keep the awkwardness at bay as I saw Kylian waiting by the pool. He greeted me with a curious look, clearly puzzled by my choice of attire.

"Hey," he said, eyeing the bikini with a mix of confusion and amusement. "Aren't you going to swim today?"

I tried to sound casual. "Actually, I thought I'd just watch today. I'm not really feeling up for it."

He wasn't buying it. "Why not? You're usually the first one in the water."

I hesitated, scrambling for an excuse. "Oh, I just thought I'd take a break today. You know, relax a bit."

Kylian wasn't convinced and, before I could react, he playfully grabbed my towel and yanked it away.

I could feel my face turn beet red as he took in the sight of me in the bikini. His eyes widened slightly, and he quickly averted his gaze, mumbling, "Uh, I'll be waiting in the pool."

I snatched the towel back from him, wrapping it around myself again. My cheeks burned with embarrassment, but also with a pang of irritation as I noticed the girls around the pool eyeing Kylian with obvious interest.

Why did that bother me so much?

Trying to shake off the discomfort, I made my way to the water and slipped in, hoping to find some relief from the awkward situation. As soon as I entered, Kylian swam over, his eyes gleaming with mischief.

"So, you've decided to join the party after all?" he teased.

I rolled my eyes. "I'm just here to get some exercise. Don't get too excited."

He smirked and started to swim alongside me. "Oh, really? Well, I'm glad you're here. Now you can show me what you've got."

I raised an eyebrow. "Is that a challenge?"

"Definitely," he grinned, splashing water at me. "Let's see if you can keep up."

We swam back and forth, engaging in a playful back-and-forth. Kylian's teasing only spurred me on, and I found myself getting caught up in the game. His laughter and the challenge made it hard to stay annoyed.

Out of breath, I turned to Kylian with a grin. "How about a race?" I challenged, knowing full well that I had little chance of winning.

He laughed, shaking his head. "You know you can't beat me, right?"

"Don't be so sure," I shot back, provoking him. "Let's see what you've got."

"Alright," he said with a smirk, clearly indulging me. "But don't cry when you lose."

We set ourselves up at the starting line, and with a quick countdown, we were off. I swam with all my might, and to my surprise, I reached the end first. Panting, I turned to see Kylian arrive a moment later, a knowing smile on his face.

"You totally let me win," I accused, splashing water at him playfully.

He laughed, dodging the splash. "Maybe I did, maybe I didn't. But you should enjoy your victory while it lasts."

Just then, a group of girls approached the pool and entered the water. They looked at Kylian with obvious admiration, and their expressions turned cold as they noticed me. One of them swam up to us, introducing herself as Shauna.

"Hey, Kylian!" she greeted him with a bright smile. "Long time no see."

"Shauna," he replied, sounding genuinely pleased. "It's been a while. How have you been?"

They started chatting, and I suddenly felt like the fifth wheel, awkwardly standing by as they caught up. Shauna was clearly enjoying the attention, and the other girls circled around, giggling and giving me frosty looks.

I forced a smile, trying not to let it bother me. Kylian noticed my discomfort and leaned in. "Don't mind them," he whispered.

Before I could respond, I felt his hand under the water, slipping into mine. My heart raced, but Kylian continued talking to Shauna as if nothing had happened.

Shauna was all smiles and flirty gestures, clearly trying to impress Kylian. "We should hang out more often," she suggested, twirling a strand of her hair.

"Yeah, maybe," Kylian replied noncommittally, his thumb gently stroking my hand under the water. It was a small, secret gesture, but it sent a thrill through me.

The other girls tried to join the conversation, but Kylian's attention kept drifting back to me. "So, are you up for another race?" he asked, looking directly at me with a playful challenge in his eyes.

"Sure," I replied, squeezing his hand back before letting go. "But this time, no holding back."

Shauna and her friends watched with a mix of curiosity and annoyance as Kylian and I swam off to the starting line again. My heart was still pounding, but not just from the anticipation of the race. Kylian's touch, his subtle way of showing he cared, was making it hard to think straight.

As we raced again, I couldn't help but smile, knowing that despite the competition, the teasing, and the presence of other girls, Kylian's attention was firmly on me.

As I swam, my heart raced, not just from the exertion but from the confusion swirling in my mind. He's just a friend, right? There's nothing more to it. We took a break, and Kylian turned to me with a teasing grin.

"Nice bikini," he said, a playful glint in his eyes. "Didn't know you had it in you."

I felt my cheeks burn and shot back, "It's just a swimsuit, Kylian. Don't make a big deal out of it."

"Oh, come on," he continued, clearly enjoying my discomfort. "You look good. No need to be so defensive."

"I'm not being defensive," I snapped, crossing my arms. "Why do you always have to tease me?"

"Because it's fun seeing you all flustered," he admitted with a chuckle. "You make it too easy."

I scowled at him. "Well, maybe you should find a new hobby."

He pretended to ponder that for a moment, then suddenly reached out as if to push me into the water. I reacted instinctively, shoving him back, harder than I intended.

"Whoa!" he laughed, regaining his balance. "Feisty today, aren't we?"

Before I could respond, he grabbed me and lifted me into his arms. "Kylian, put me down!" I protested, squirming in his grip.

"Not a chance," he said, grinning mischievously. "We're going for a swim."

Without warning, he jumped into the pool, taking me with him. The cold water enveloped us as we plunged beneath the surface, and I let out a startled yelp. When we resurfaced, I was still in his arms, my hair plastered to my face, and my annoyance mixed with reluctant amusement.

"You're impossible," I muttered, trying to sound angry but failing miserably.

"And you love it," he teased back, finally letting me go.

I splashed water at him, still trying to maintain my composure. "You're such a jerk."

"Yeah, but I'm your jerk," he said with a wink, dodging my splash. "Admit it, you missed me."

I rolled my eyes, but a small smile tugged at my lips. "Maybe a little."

"That's all I needed to hear," he said, splashing me back playfully.

I couldn't help but laugh, the tension easing as we returned to our usual banter. Despite the chaos and confusion, there was something undeniably comforting about being with Kylian, even if he drove me crazy.

Kylian wrapped his arms around me again, pulling me close. Our noses touched, and I could feel his breath warm against my face. For a moment, we just stayed like that, the world around us fading away.

"It feels like something's changed between us," he said softly, his voice barely more than a whisper.

I swallowed hard, my heart pounding in my chest. "I—I have to go," I stammered, pushing him away. "I have a... a date."

Kylian's eyes narrowed slightly, curiosity and something else flickering in his gaze. "A date? With who?"

"Just a guy from my class," I lied, trying to sound nonchalant.

He seemed to tense at my words, a hint of jealousy creeping into his voice. "Oh, I see. Well, have fun."

I hurriedly climbed out of the pool, my heart still racing. "Thanks," I muttered, grabbing my towel and heading towards the changing rooms.

As I walked away, I could feel Kylian's eyes on me, a mixture of confusion and hurt in his expression. I slipped into the locker room, my mind a whirlwind of emotions. Why did he have to make things so complicated?

Inside the changing room, I leaned against the wall, trying to catch my breath. My heart was still racing, and my mind was a jumble of thoughts. I quickly changed back into my clothes, my hands trembling slightly. As I finished, I glanced at my reflection in the mirror. My cheeks were flushed, and I could still feel the ghost of Kylian's touch on my skin.

Why does he have to be so confusing? Why does he have to be so... everything?

As I stepped out of the changing room, there he was, leaning against the wall with a towel draped over his shoulders. His eyes locked onto mine, an intensity in them that made my heart skip a beat.

"So, who's the guy?" Kylian asked, trying to sound casual but failing miserably.

I shrugged, trying to act indifferent. "Just a guy from my math class. Nothing serious."

His jaw tightened, and I could see the flash of jealousy in his eyes. "Math class, huh? What's his name?"

I hesitated for a moment, scrambling for a name. "Um, Ethan."

Kylian scoffed. "Ethan, right. And what makes him so special?"

"Why do you care, Kylian?" I shot back, feeling defensive. "It's not like it matters to you."

He stepped closer, his eyes searching mine. "It does matter. I don't like the idea of you with someone else."

I felt my cheeks flush with a mix of anger and something else. "Well, that's not really your decision, is it?"

He looked like he wanted to say more, but I couldn't handle it. I needed to get out of there before my emotions got the better of me.

"I have to go," I muttered, sidestepping him.

As I walked away, I could feel his gaze burning into my back. I didn't look back, even though every part of me wanted to. I needed space, and right now, Kylian was making everything too complicated.

With each step, I tried to steady my racing heart. Why did he have to act so jealous? And why did it bother me so much that he did?

I couldn't go back to the dormitory—Kylian would realize I had lied about my so-called date. Instead, I made my way to a small café in town. My hair was still damp from the pool, and I could feel the cool breeze against my skin as I walked.

Inside the café, the warmth was a welcome contrast to the chilly air outside. I walked up to the counter and ordered a coffee, hoping the caffeine would help clear my head.

As I waited for my drink, I replayed the events at the pool over and over in my mind. Kylian's intense gaze, his jealousy, the way he held me in the water. It was all so confusing.

"Just friends, Kathleen," I muttered to myself. "He's never going to see you as more than that."

The barista called my name, and I took my coffee, finding a quiet corner to sit and think. I wrapped my hands around the warm cup, letting the steam rise and warm my face. Despite my best efforts to convince myself otherwise, I couldn't shake the feeling that there was something more between Kylian and me. Something that scared me as much as it excited me.

I took a sip of my coffee, trying to focus on anything but Kylian. The familiar taste and the hum of conversation around me provided a small distraction, but it wasn't enough to drown out my thoughts. I was torn between the undeniable chemistry we had and the fear of getting hurt.

"He's just a friend," I repeated, trying to make myself believe it. "Nothing more."

But deep down, I knew that was a lie. The way my heart raced when he was near, the way his touch sent shivers down my spine—it was all too real to ignore. And the worst part was, I didn't know what to do about it.

Chapter 16

I walked into the dormitory, the late hour adding a tired edge to my steps. As I made my way to the kitchen, I saw Kylian sitting at the counter. He glanced up, his face momentarily showing a flicker of stress before smoothing into his usual confident expression.

"Hey," he said casually. "How was your evening?"

I hesitated, not sure how to respond. "It was fine," I said, trying to sound indifferent. "Just had a coffee."

He raised an eyebrow, clearly not buying it. "That's it? I thought you had a... 'date' or something."

I sighed, feeling the familiar tension creep in. "Yeah, well, it wasn't anything special."

Kylian leaned back, crossing his arms. "Oh, really? You seemed pretty worked up about it earlier."

Before I could respond, Regina, who was engrossed in her phone, looked up. "Guys, chill. Kylian, are you still stressing about this?"

Kylian shrugged, but I noticed a hint of discomfort in his eyes. "I'm not stressing. Just curious."

Regina, always the peacemaker, tried to diffuse the situation. "Kathleen, why don't you tell us what happened? We're all friends here."

I glanced at Kylian, who was now shifting uncomfortably. "Actually, we did kiss," I blurted out, half surprised by my own confession.

Kylian's face went through a rapid series of emotions—surprise, confusion, and something that looked suspiciously like jealousy. "Oh. Well, that's... interesting."

Regina's face lit up with a smile. "Wow, Kathleen! That's awesome! I'm happy for you."

Kylian's expression tightened slightly as he tried to mask his feelings. "Yeah, great. Well, I guess I'll... see you around."

His tone was strangely distant, and I couldn't help but wonder if I had read too much into his reaction. I shot him a curious look but chose to keep my thoughts to myself. "Sure, Kylian."

Without another word, I turned on my heel and walked to my room, feeling a mix of confusion and frustration. The way Kylian acted—like he was trying to play it cool but clearly wasn't—left me more puzzled than ever. And as I closed my door behind me, I couldn't shake the feeling that this was far from over.

The next day, after finishing my classes, I was determined to skip the pool. As I headed out of the building, I felt a tap on my shoulder and turned to see Kylian catching up with me.

"So, are you planning on going out with your boyfriend today?" he asked, his tone casual but laced with an edge of curiosity.

I raised an eyebrow, already feeling the annoyance bubbling up. "What's it to you?" I shot back.

Kylian's eyes softened slightly, and he flashed me a teasing smile. "Just trying to make sure you don't get too attached to him. You know, I'd hate to see you settle for anything less than amazing."

I rolled my eyes, trying to ignore the flutter in my chest. "I was actually planning to head back to the dorm."

"Really?" Kylian's grin widened, and he leaned in slightly. "How about we go somewhere a bit more... interesting instead?"

"Interesting?" I echoed, raising an eyebrow. "Like where?"

"Somewhere that's definitely more fun than your date last night," he replied with a smirk.

I couldn't help but laugh, despite myself. "And what makes you think I want to hang out with you?"

"Because, Kathleen," he said, his voice dropping to a softer, more sincere tone, "sometimes a little adventure is exactly what you need."

I was caught off guard by the genuine look in his eyes, but I tried to play it cool. "Alright, fine. Where do you want to go?"

Kylian's eyes sparkled with a mix of mischief and something softer. "There's this cool place I've been wanting to check out. I promise, it'll be way better than your usual routine."

I sighed dramatically, though a smile was tugging at my lips. "Alright, Kylian. Lead the way."

We walked side by side, the air between us charged with a mix of tension and something else I couldn't quite place. Kylian's attempts to act nonchalant were at odds with the way his eyes kept darting toward me, and I could tell he was trying not to let on how much he actually wanted this outing to go well.

As we made our way, I couldn't help but wonder why he was so keen on spending time with me outside of school. Was it really just a friendly gesture, or was there something more?

Despite my best efforts to stay aloof, I found myself looking forward to whatever Kylian had planned. After all, he had a way of turning the ordinary into something unexpectedly memorable. And as we walked, I felt a flicker of excitement, mingled with the usual skepticism I had for his charm.

As Kylian led me to a picturesque spot by the lake, I was struck by how beautiful the scene was. The lake's surface was calm, mirroring the colorful hues of autumn—reds, oranges, and golds—that framed the landscape. It was the kind of view that made you forget about everything else.

We settled on a cozy patch of grass, a comfortable distance apart. The crisp autumn air made me shiver slightly, so I slipped my hands into my pockets to warm them.

Kylian glanced over at me with a smirk. "So, I hope your boyfriend isn't too jealous of this beautiful view," he said, his tone teasing but with an undercurrent of genuine curiosity.

I looked at him with a mix of amusement and mild annoyance. "He's not my boyfriend, Kylian."

He raised an eyebrow, clearly surprised. "Oh really? I thought you two were getting pretty close."

I rolled my eyes and nudged him gently with my elbow. "I wouldn't say that. Besides, why do you care?"

Kylian chuckled and rubbed his hands together to warm them up. "Just making sure you're not letting him steal all your attention. It's not every day I get to spend time with someone as intriguing as you."

I couldn't help but laugh at his over-the-top flattery. "Intriguing, huh? Is that your way of saying you're still trying to figure me out?"

He grinned, clearly enjoying the playful banter. "Maybe. Or maybe I just like knowing that you're not completely off-limits. It keeps things interesting."

I pushed him lightly, still laughing. "You're impossible, you know that?"

Kylian leaned back on his elbows, looking out at the lake with a thoughtful expression. "And you're surprisingly easy to talk to. I guess I'm just trying to make the most of our time together."

As we sat there, the silence between us felt comfortable, not awkward. The autumn breeze rustled the leaves, and for a moment, it seemed like nothing else mattered but this simple, shared experience.

As we continued to enjoy the view by the lake, the temperature began to drop, and I noticed myself shivering slightly. Kylian, ever observant, glanced at me and then at his jacket, which was draped over his shoulders.

"You're shivering," he said, his voice soft but concerned. "Here, take my jacket."

I shook my head, trying to be polite. "I'm fine, really. It's not that cold."

Kylian gave me a look that clearly said he wasn't buying it. "Come on, it's chilly out here. I'm not going to let you freeze just because you're too stubborn to admit you're cold."

I rolled my eyes but couldn't help smiling at his persistence. "Okay, okay. If it'll make you feel better, I'll take it."

He grinned triumphantly and slipped out of his jacket, handing it to me with a playful flourish. "See, that wasn't so hard, was it?"

I took the jacket and slid it on, finding it surprisingly warm and comfortable. It smelled faintly of his cologne, which was oddly comforting. "Thanks," I said, adjusting the jacket around me.

Kylian looked at me with a satisfied smile. "You look better now. It suits you."

I laughed lightly, feeling a little self-conscious. "Well, I guess I do appreciate the extra warmth."

He shifted closer, his arm brushing against mine as he settled back down. "I'm glad. I wouldn't want you to catch a cold just because I dragged you out here."

I glanced at him, noticing how close we were now. The warmth of his jacket mixed with the warmth of his presence, making it hard to ignore the subtle shift in our dynamic. "You really are something, you know that?"

Kylian's smile softened, and he met my gaze. "Just trying to be a decent human being. And maybe a little more if you'll let me."

The air between us felt charged, and for a moment, I found myself leaning in a bit, the warmth of his jacket making me feel more at ease. "Well, I guess it's nice to have someone looking out for me."

Kylian's gaze held mine, and he seemed to hesitate for a moment before he spoke again. "It's more than just looking out for you. I actually enjoy spending time with you."

I could feel my cheeks warming up as I smiled. "I've noticed. And I'm starting to enjoy it too."

We stayed like that for a while, the conversation drifting off as we both simply enjoyed each other's company. The crisp air, the beautiful lake, and the warmth of Kylian's jacket made it feel like the world had narrowed down to just the two of us.

As we walked back to campus, the crisp autumn air seemed to have gotten colder. Kylian made a show of yawning, as if he were starring in a movie. He casually draped his arm around my shoulders, pulling me closer. I felt a slight blush creep up my cheeks.

"You know," he said with a playful grin, "you really are quite small compared to me."

I nudged him gently. "Shut up, Kylian. You're not exactly a giant yourself."

He chuckled, the sound warm and comforting. "I'll keep that in mind."

We continued walking, and Kylian looked at me with a faint, genuine concern. "Are you still cold? I don't want you to freeze."

I shook my head, but he still looked a bit cold himself, shivering slightly. "I'm okay. Really, you should take your jacket back."

He waved me off with a smile. "No way. I'd rather be freezing than have you shiver. Besides, it's kind of nice having you so close."

I looked up at him, touched by his words. "You're impossible, you know that?"

Kylian's smile softened, and he glanced down at me. "Maybe. But if being impossible means making sure you're warm and happy, I think I can live with that."

He tightened his grip on my shoulders just a little, and I found myself leaning into the warmth of his presence. The walk back felt shorter, the cold less biting, and I couldn't help but feel that this evening had brought us a little closer.

As we arrived at the dormitory, Regina looked at us with a curious expression. I pulled away from Kylian, feeling a flush of embarrassment. He leaned in close, his breath tickling my ear.

"Oh, I forgot to mention," he whispered with a teasing grin, "today was supposed to be a date. I guess I got so caught up in it that I forgot to tell you."

I felt my cheeks warm even more, and I tried to hide my blush. "Seriously, Kylian?"

He gave me a playful wink. "Well, now you know. I think it went pretty well for a surprise date, don't you?"

With a final chuckle, he headed towards his room, leaving me standing there with his jacket draped over my shoulders. I watched him walk away, feeling a mix of frustration and amusement.

I turned and headed to my own room, the jacket still warm from his body. Kylian was driving me crazy, but in the most confusingly charming way possible.

Chapter 17

The next day, I went to Kylian's practice, telling myself it wasn't to watch him. At least, I hoped it wasn't. As I walked in, I spotted him immediately. He waved at me with a warm smile, and I nodded back, trying to keep my expression neutral and distant. I took a seat and tried to focus on something else, but my eyes kept drifting back to him.

Kylian and his teammates were practicing intensely. Jared and Scott were there, pushing each other to do better, laughing and joking in between laps. Their camaraderie was evident, a mix of friendly competition and genuine support. Kylian moved with a fluid grace in the water, his strokes powerful and precise. It was hard not to admire his dedication and skill.

A group of girls arrived at the pool, giggling and chatting amongst themselves. They gathered near the edge, clearly excited to be there. Some of them shyly approached Kylian, and he greeted them with his usual charm. One girl, in particular, seemed especially interested. She handed him a towel, and he helped her adjust her goggles, his hand lingering just a bit longer than necessary.

I felt a twinge of jealousy. It was ridiculous, I thought, trying to shake it off. But as I watched him interact with them, I couldn't help but feel a pang of something unpleasant. He seemed so comfortable, so at ease with them. They laughed together, and he flashed that charming smile, making it hard for me to focus on anything else.

I reminded myself that I was just there to watch the practice, not to get caught up in my feelings. But as I sat there, trying to keep my emotions in check, it was impossible not to feel a little possessive. After all, he did call yesterday a date, didn't he?

I started typing my swimming project on my laptop, glancing up every now and then to observe the practice. They took a break, and I watched as Kylian and that girl sat together on a bench. They were deep in conversation, laughing and sipping water from their bottles. She leaned in closer, clearly enjoying his company, and he seemed relaxed, his eyes sparkling as he spoke.

"Kathleen, you're here for your assignment, not for him," I reminded myself. But my gaze kept drifting back to them. Kylian's athletic frame contrasted with his gentle demeanor, and the way he interacted with her made me feel a strange mix of admiration and irritation. She had long, wavy hair that shimmered under the lights of the pool, and her laughter was light and melodic.

As I watched, she playfully nudged his shoulder, and he responded with a grin, showing those perfect teeth of his. My fingers hovered over the keyboard, but my attention was firmly fixed on the scene unfolding before me. He said something that made her laugh even harder, and she lightly touched his arm, sending another pang of jealousy through me.

"Focus, Kathleen," I muttered under my breath. But it was easier said than done. My eyes kept darting back to them, and each time, I felt that nagging jealousy grow stronger. I tried to push the feeling away, reminding myself that I was here for my project. But every time I looked up, there he was, making it impossible to concentrate.

I let out a sigh, forcing myself to look at my screen. The words blurred together as my mind wandered back to Kylian and the girl. "Just friends," I tried to convince myself, but it wasn't helping. It was hard not to feel something when the person you were trying to ignore was the one person you couldn't stop thinking about.

Practice resumed, and I refocused on my project, trying to block out everything else. The rhythmic sound of the swimmers cutting through the water was almost soothing as I typed. Just as I was getting back into the flow, someone sat down beside me. I turned and found a guy from my class, someone I vaguely recognized.

"Hey, Kathleen, right?" he asked with a friendly smile.

"Yeah, that's me," I replied, a little surprised but not unwelcome to the company.

"I'm Caleb. Are you here for the project too?" he asked, setting down his bag and opening his laptop.

"Yep," I nodded, smiling. "Trying to get some work done between all the distractions."

"Distractions?" Caleb raised an eyebrow playfully. "Like what?"

"Oh, you know, just... the general chaos of the pool," I said, trying to sound casual.

He chuckled. "Yeah, it's hard to focus with all the splashing and... well, everything else going on around here."

I couldn't help but notice the way Caleb's eyes lingered on mine, and I felt a little flutter in my stomach. He was cute, with messy dark hair and an easygoing smile that put me at ease.

"Do you come here often?" he asked, his tone light and conversational.

"Not really," I replied. "Just today, for the project. What about you?"

"Same. But I might come more often if it means running into people like you," he said with a wink.

I laughed softly, a little flattered by his attention. "Well, I guess we'll see each other around then."

"Sounds like a plan," Caleb grinned, opening his laptop and getting ready to work. "Maybe we could compare notes sometime, you know, to make sure we're both on the right track."

"I'd like that," I said, still smiling.

Just as he was setting up, I glanced back at the pool, out of habit more than anything else. That's when I noticed Kylian looking straight at me. His expression was hard to read, but there was something intense in his gaze. It caught me off guard, and I quickly looked away, feeling a sudden rush of confusion.

What was that about? I wondered. But before I could dwell on it, Caleb leaned in a little closer, drawing my attention back to him.

"So, what part of the project are you working on?" he asked, clearly eager to keep our conversation going.

I tried to push thoughts of Kylian out of my mind and focus on Caleb instead. "I'm just working on the data analysis. It's the most time-consuming part, but I think I'm getting the hang of it."

"Maybe you could show me what you've got so far," Caleb suggested, his tone flirtatious but still warm. "I could use all the help I can get."

"Sure," I agreed, feeling a little more at ease. But even as I spoke, I couldn't shake the feeling of Kylian's eyes on me.

Caleb and I chatted and laughed, making surprisingly good progress on our project. His British accent was charming, and he had a way of making even the most mundane parts of the assignment seem interesting. I was starting to feel more at ease, enjoying his company far more than I had expected.

As the practice wound down, Caleb glanced at his watch. "I've got to head out, but this was fun. We should definitely work together again tomorrow in class."

"Yeah, sounds good," I replied with a smile, nodding in agreement.

He grinned back, gathering his things. "See you then, Kathleen."

"See you, Caleb," I said, watching him leave. He really was cute.

Once he was gone, I put on my coat and started packing up my own things, my mind still replaying parts of our conversation. As I headed down the stairs, lost in thought, I looked up and saw Kylian waiting for me at the bottom, leaning casually against the wall. His expression was hard to read, but there was a certain tension in his stance.

"Hey," I greeted him, trying to keep my tone cool and distant.

"Hey," he replied, pushing off the wall and walking towards me. "So, you and Caleb, huh? Looked like you two were having a pretty good time."

I shrugged, trying to act nonchalant. "We were just working on our project. What's it to you?"

Kylian narrowed his eyes slightly, his lips twitching into a smirk. "Just working on the project? Seemed like more than that from where I was standing."

I rolled my eyes, refusing to give in to whatever game he was trying to play. "You know, not everything is about you, Kylian. Some of us actually have other things going on."

"Oh, is that so?" he shot back, his tone teasing but with an edge to it. "I just didn't realize you had such a thing for British accents. Maybe I should start practicing mine."

I couldn't help but laugh, despite myself. "Please, you'd sound ridiculous."

He pretended to be offended, clutching his chest dramatically. "Ridiculous? I'll have you know, I'd make a fantastic Brit."

"Sure you would," I said, shaking my head, still trying to maintain my cool demeanor. "But seriously, what's your problem?"

"My problem?" Kylian repeated, his tone suddenly more serious. He took a step closer, his gaze locking onto mine. "I just don't like seeing you with someone else, that's all."

I blinked, caught off guard by his bluntness. "Kylian, we're not... It's not like that."

"Isn't it?" he challenged, his voice dropping a little. "Because it sure feels like something."

I hesitated, unsure of how to respond. "I don't know what you're talking about. Caleb's just a friend."

"Uh-huh," Kylian said, clearly unconvinced. "You seemed pretty cozy for 'just friends.'"

"And what if we are?" I shot back, feeling defensive now. "Why do you care?"

He looked at me for a long moment, then sighed, his expression softening. "I just... I don't want to lose whatever this is between us. Even if it's nothing."

His words hung in the air between us, and I felt my heart skip a beat. Was he being serious?

"Kylian, you're impossible," I muttered, feeling flustered and more than a little confused.

"That's part of my charm," he said with a grin, though there was something vulnerable in his eyes that made me pause.

"Yeah, sure," I said, trying to brush off the tension. "Anyway, I need to go."

"Fine, fine," he said, holding up his hands in surrender. But as I turned to leave, he called after me, "But if Caleb doesn't appreciate your taste in swimwear, just let me know. I'll take care of it."

I couldn't help but smile, despite the frustration bubbling up inside me. "Goodbye, Kylian."

"See you later, Humpty Dumpty," he replied with a wink, making me blush as I walked away. Why did he have to be so infuriatingly charming?

I stepped outside, and the cold wind hit me like a wall, cutting through the thin fabric of my coat. I shoved my hands into my pockets, trying to fight off the chill. But it wasn't just the wind that had me feeling uneasy.

Why does he have to be so... him?

The way Kylian acted, the way he looked at me, the way he couldn't help but throw in those little jabs—was he actually jealous? The thought made my heart race in a way I wasn't ready to admit. Was it really possible that someone like him could be jealous over me?

And why did that thought make me feel so strange inside? It was a mix of confusion, a little bit of thrill, and a whole lot of something I couldn't quite name. The more I tried to brush it off, the more it lingered in my mind.

As I walked, I felt my phone buzz in my pocket. I pulled it out and saw a message from Caleb.

"Hey Kathleen, it was great working with you today. Looking forward to seeing you in class tomorrow. Maybe we can grab a coffee afterward? :)"

I couldn't help but smile as I read his message. Caleb was sweet, charming even, with that British accent that made everything sound just a bit more interesting. The idea of getting coffee with him after class made me feel a little flutter in my chest.

But then, as if on cue, Kylian's face popped into my mind. His smirk, the way he always found a way to tease me, the way he'd seemed almost... jealous earlier. The smile on my face faltered slightly as I thought about it.

Why did Kylian have to creep into my thoughts just when I was feeling good about someone else? It was as if he had this unshakable presence, always lingering in the back of my mind, making it impossible to just enjoy the moment.

As I walked back to the dorm, I took in the crisp autumn air, the kind that carried a slight bite but was still refreshing. The leaves crunched beneath my feet, their vibrant reds, oranges, and yellows creating a colorful path that made the campus look like something out of a postcard.

I took a deep breath, letting the coolness of the air fill my lungs. There was something about autumn that I loved—maybe it was the way everything seemed to slow down just a little, or how the world felt a bit more peaceful as it prepared for the coming winter.

As I neared the dorm, I couldn't help but think about how much had happened lately. Between Kylian's unexpected jealousy and Caleb's flirty message, my mind was spinning. But here, in the quiet of the late afternoon, with the golden light filtering through the trees, I let myself just be in the moment.

The wind picked up slightly, tugging at the edges of my coat, reminding me that I still had Kylian's jacket at home. I pulled it tighter around me, a small smile tugging at my lips as I thought about how he'd insisted I keep it. It was a nice gesture, really, even if it did complicate things.

Finally, I reached the dorm, feeling both more relaxed and more confused than ever. Autumn had always been my favorite season, but this one was shaping up to be far more complicated than I'd anticipated.

Chapter 18

As Halloween approached, I found myself buried under a mountain of textbooks, not-so-discreetly procrastinating my way through my study sessions with a plethora of distractions. My desk was strewn with notes and textbooks, the occasional crumpled piece of paper making a bid for freedom.

My project on swimming was taking over my life. I was knee-deep in diagrams of stroke techniques and graphs plotting swim times. If anyone had peered into my room, they might have thought I was preparing for the Olympics, rather than just working on a project. I'd even gone so far as to draw a rudimentary pool on my whiteboard, complete with stick figures engaging in various swimming styles. Art, it seemed, was not my calling.

The Halloween decorations in the dorm didn't help my concentration. Fake cobwebs hung from every corner, and plastic spiders seemed to be plotting an uprising on my textbooks. I tried to ignore the eerie glow of the jack-o'-lanterns that seemed to stare right through me, their carved faces forever locked in mischievous grins.

In an effort to remain focused, I decided to embrace the spirit of Halloween and incorporate it into my study routine. I wore a pumpkin-themed sweater that had "I'm here for the boos" emblazoned across the front. Every time I felt my concentration waning, I'd remind myself that if I didn't finish this project, the only thing I'd be getting this Halloween was a well-deserved trick from my grades.

To make matters worse, my study playlist had morphed into an array of Halloween-themed songs. Instead of relaxing instrumental music, I was now subjected to a looping medley of spooky sound effects and "Monster Mash." There was nothing like trying to concentrate on swim techniques while ghostly wails and creaking doors provided an unsettling background soundtrack.

Every time I glanced at the calendar, I was reminded of the looming Halloween festivities, but I stayed focused, determined not to let a few ghostly distractions get in the way of my academic ambitions.

Still, with Halloween just around the corner, I couldn't help but wonder if my dedication to my studies was worth missing out on the costume parties and pumpkin carving. For now, though, it was back to the grind, with the occasional chuckle at my own absurdity—after all, there was always time to be spooked by my own overzealous academic spirit.

One evening, as I was sitting at the dinner table with my two roommates, Regina and Kylian, the topic of Halloween costumes inevitably came up. I was enjoying my meal, trying to ignore the fact that Kylian was once again being his usual teasing self, when he leaned in with a nonchalant air and asked, "So, what are you dressing up as for Halloween?"

I tried to play it cool, shrugging as if it were no big deal. "Oh, I'm not really dressing up."

Regina's eyes widened with disbelief. "What do you mean you're not dressing up? Halloween is the perfect excuse to be someone else for a night!"

I was about to insist that it wasn't necessary, but Regina's enthusiasm was relentless. She poked and prodded, insisting that I must come up with a costume. Her excitement was contagious, though slightly overwhelming.

I glanced around the kitchen, trying to buy some time. My eyes landed on a book on the shelf with the name "Alice" written in elegant script on the cover. Inspiration struck me like a bolt of lightning. I sighed dramatically and said, "Fine, fine. I'll dress up as Alice from Alice in Wonderland."

Regina's face lit up like a jack-o'-lantern. "Oh, that's going to be adorable! I can't wait to see it!"

Kylian, ever the opportunist, smirked and couldn't resist chiming in. "Alice, huh? So, what's next? Are you going to start talking to rabbits and having tea parties with Mad Hatters?"

I rolled my eyes, feigning annoyance but secretly amused. "Very funny, Kylian. Maybe I'll even invite you to join my tea party. I'm sure the Mad Hatter would love to have you."

Kylian leaned back in his chair, still smirking. "Well, if you're going to be Alice, I guess I'll have to find a Cheshire Cat costume to match. Wouldn't want to be left out of your fantasy world."

I shook my head, chuckling despite myself. "You'd make an excellent Cheshire Cat, Kylian. With that grin of yours, it's practically your signature look."

As dinner continued, Regina and I planned out the details of my costume, much to Kylian's amusement. He continued to tease me about my choice, but there was something oddly satisfying about getting under his skin. In the end, despite the ribbing, I was actually looking forward to putting together my Alice costume. After all, Halloween was supposed to be fun, and if Kylian's playful mockery was part of the deal, then so be it.

The big day had finally arrived. I woke up slowly, my enthusiasm for the Halloween party somewhat lacking. Regina, dressed as Little Red Riding Hood, was already bustling around with excitement. She helped me with my makeup and costume, and we chatted and laughed as we got ready.

Regina adjusted my Alice costume one last time, adding a touch of extra sparkle to my makeup. "There we go! You look absolutely adorable. I bet you'll steal the show tonight."

I grinned at her in the mirror. "Thanks, Regina. I'm just hoping I don't trip over my costume or accidentally eat a magical mushroom."

"Don't worry, Alice. I'm sure you'll find Wonderland a bit less chaotic than the real world," she teased.

Once I was finally ready, I stepped out of my room, eager to see how everyone else was dressed. And there, standing in the hallway, was Kylian in a rather peculiar costume. He was dressed as a Mad Hatter, complete with a colorful, oversized hat and a wild, mismatched outfit.

I couldn't help but laugh when I saw him. "Kylian, seriously? A Mad Hatter? You look like you're about to host a tea party for a bunch of very confused rabbits."

He struck a dramatic pose, tipping his hat with a flourish. "Why, thank you, Alice! I've been waiting for you to come join my tea party. Although, it seems you've forgotten your tea cup. How do you plan to join in the festivities without one?"

I playfully rolled my eyes. "Well, if anyone's going to need a cup of tea tonight, it's definitely going to be you. I'm just here to see if your hat is as magical as it looks."

Kylian chuckled, his eyes twinkling mischievously. "Oh, it's quite magical. It's been known to transport people to all sorts of adventures. Though I must say, you make quite a lovely Alice. I didn't realize Wonderland was going to be so stylish this year."

I smirked. "Well, you know what they say: even in Wonderland, you've got to dress to impress. But judging by your costume, it looks like you're ready to steal the show yourself."

He laughed, and for a moment, the playful banter made me forget how reluctant I was to attend the party. Kylian's Mad Hatter costume was both ridiculous and charming, and his genuine smile was enough to lift my spirits.

"You know," I said as we made our way to the party, "maybe Wonderland isn't such a bad place after all."

"Not with you around, Alice," he replied, grinning from ear to ear.

As we walked together, I couldn't help but feel a bit of excitement. Maybe this Halloween party was going to be more fun than I'd anticipated.

We entered the party, and the atmosphere was electric. The room was decked out in Halloween decorations—spooky cobwebs, flickering orange lights, and an assortment of carved pumpkins. The music was loud, pulsing with an energetic beat that made it impossible to stand still. Laughter and chatter filled the air as everyone mingled, their costumes ranging from eerie to extravagant.

Regina and I joined our friends, and we danced in a lively group, our Alice and Little Red Riding Hood costumes twirling with every spin. The dance floor was a swirl of colors and movement, with people losing themselves in the rhythm of the music.

In the middle of the chaos, I felt a tap on my shoulder and turned to find Caleb standing there, looking a bit nervous but determined. He flashed a charming smile and asked, "Hey, Kathleen. Would you like to dance with me?"

I raised an eyebrow, feigning skepticism. "Oh? And why should I accept your offer? What's in it for me?"

Caleb chuckled, his eyes twinkling. "Well, I've heard Alice has some pretty impressive dance moves. I'd love to see if the rumors are true."

I laughed, shaking my head playfully. "Alright, fine. Let's see if you can keep up."

Caleb took my hand, leading me to a spot on the dance floor. We began to dance together, our movements syncing with the rhythm of the music. He was a surprisingly good dancer, and we quickly fell into an easy, enjoyable groove. We moved together effortlessly, laughing and sharing glances as we followed the beat.

As we danced, I couldn't help but glance over Caleb's shoulder, only to spot Kylian standing a little ways off, leaning against a wall with his arms crossed. His Mad Hatter hat seemed slightly out of place amid the sea of other costumes. He was watching us with a thoughtful expression, and the sight made me feel a bit self-conscious.

I quickly turned my gaze back to Caleb, trying to focus on the dance and not on the fact that Kylian's eyes were on us. Caleb's presence was comforting, and his smile was genuine, which helped me push aside any lingering feelings of awkwardness.

The music continued to play, and I let myself enjoy the dance, feeling the beat of the music and the warmth of the room. Despite the occasional glance at Kylian, the evening was turning out to be more enjoyable than I'd initially thought.

As "You Don't Own Me" started playing, I felt the beat through the floor and the energy of the room pick up. Caleb's gaze was warm, but there was a hint of something more intense in his eyes. I could sense he was thinking about leaning in closer, maybe even kissing me. It was flattering, but I found myself strangely preoccupied with thoughts of Kylian.

Caleb leaned in, his breath warm against my ear as he murmured, "You know, you're an incredible dancer, Alice. I'm glad I asked you to dance."

His words made me smile, but the sight of Kylian's intense gaze from across the room pulled me back to reality. His eyes were fixed on us, and the weight of his attention was almost palpable. I felt my cheeks flush, and the smile I had been wearing faltered.

"Sorry, Caleb," I said, feeling a sudden wave of awkwardness. "I need to... use the restroom."

I quickly excused myself and made my way through the crowd, trying to ignore the curious glances and the sinking feeling in my stomach. I headed towards the bathroom, taking a deep breath as I tried to steady my nerves. Why was I so affected by Kylian's gaze?

As I stepped out of the bathroom, I noticed a group of people gathered around a game of Truth or Dare. It looked like a lot of fun, so I decided to join in. I settled onto the couch, trying not to glance too much in Kylian's direction. He was there, surrounded by friends, but I could feel his presence even without looking directly at him.

The game was in full swing. There were plenty of interesting truths and spicy dares being exchanged, and everyone seemed to be having a great time. Regina, ever the instigator, took her turn and spun the bottle. It came to a halt, pointing directly at me.

"Alright, Kathleen," Regina said with a mischievous glint in her eye. "Truth or dare?"

"I'll take truth," I replied, trying to sound confident.

Regina leaned in, a sly grin on her face. "If you could kiss any one person in this room, who would it be?"

I felt my face heat up immediately. My eyes darted around the room, catching glimpses of Caleb and Kylian's curious stares. My mind raced, but I needed an answer. "Um, I-I guess I'd, uh, kiss someone who's, uh, a good friend," I stammered, trying to sound nonchalant. My heart was pounding, and I could feel the blush spreading across my cheeks.

I took my turn spinning the bottle, and of course, it landed on Kylian. Great. The room buzzed with anticipation. I shot him a quick glance before asking, "Kylian, truth or dare?"

"Truth," he said, his usual confident smile in place.

I tried to keep my voice steady as I asked, "Why do you keep staring at me tonight?"

His smile widened into that familiar smirk, and he leaned forward slightly. "Well, if you really want to know, I was just curious about why you seem so flustered around me."

I felt my cheeks turn a deeper shade of red. "Oh, well... I, uh, guess I didn't realize I was making it so obvious," I mumbled, trying to hide my embarrassment. Was he serious, or had he had too much to drink?

The game continued, but my mind kept drifting back to Kylian's words. I tried to focus on the fun of the game, but the heat of his gaze and the implication of his answer lingered in my thoughts.

As Regina spun the bottle, it stopped on Kylian. The room fell silent, everyone eagerly waiting to see what he would choose. With a confident grin, he announced, "Action."

Regina's eyes sparkled mischievously as she set the challenge. "Alright, Kylian, your action is to get locked in the closet with the girl you think is the most beautiful tonight for ten minutes."

My heart skipped a beat. Did she really just say that? I shot Regina a look that could've melted ice, but she just smirked back at me. Kylian stood up, and I immediately looked away, trying to avoid his gaze. Surely, he would pick someone else. Why would he choose me?

But then, I felt him stop in front of me. I reluctantly lifted my eyes and saw Kylian extending his hand towards me. A sigh escaped my lips as I took his hand, feeling the warmth of his touch.

"Guess we're off to the closet," I said, trying to sound indifferent but failing miserably.

He chuckled softly. "Looks like it. Ready for a bit of adventure?"

I rolled my eyes. "Oh, absolutely. This is exactly how I imagined spending my Halloween evening."

Kylian guided me towards the closet, and as we squeezed ourselves into the tight space, I couldn't help but feel a bit self-conscious. The closet was dark and cramped, and we were pressed close together. I could feel the heat from his body and hear his steady breathing.

"So," I began, trying to break the awkward silence. "Is this your way of spending quality time with me?"

He laughed quietly, the sound vibrating against my skin. "I suppose it is. But if it's any consolation, you're not the worst person I could be stuck with."

I shifted slightly, feeling his hand still holding mine. "And who would be the worst?"

Kylian paused for a moment before replying, "Hmm, I guess anyone who doesn't enjoy a good adventure. But you seem to handle these situations quite well."

"Flattery will get you nowhere," I said, though I could feel myself softening a bit.

He squeezed my hand gently. "Just being honest. Besides, you're not exactly making this easy for me to stay distant."

I tried to suppress a smile. "Oh, so you're admitting you're struggling to keep your distance?"

He leaned in slightly, his breath warm against my ear. "Just a little. It's hard when you're so close."

We were silent for a moment, the darkness of the closet amplifying the closeness between us. I could feel his thumb brushing lightly against my hand.

"So, how's your Halloween so far?" I asked, trying to keep the conversation light.

"Not too bad," he replied. "It's definitely more interesting than I expected."

I laughed softly. "Well, it's certainly an experience."

Kylian's fingers traced small circles on my hand, and I felt my heart race. "Yeah, I guess it is. But I'm glad I'm spending it with you."

I looked up at him, but the darkness made it hard to see his expression. "That's... nice to hear."

We stayed like that, our hands entwined, the closeness and the conversation making the time pass quickly. Despite the situation, I felt a strange sense of comfort, mixed with a flutter of something more.

As we huddled together in the dark, Kylian broke the silence with a teasing tone. "So, how was your evening with Caleb? Did he sweep you off your feet?"

I pushed him lightly, trying to hide my growing embarrassment. "Oh, you know, just a dance and some small talk. Nothing earth-shattering."

Kylian laughed, his voice a soft rumble in the darkness. "Nothing earth-shattering, huh? That's not the impression you gave me. You seemed pretty engrossed."

I shifted uncomfortably, trying to ignore the way his laugh made my heart flutter. "Well, he's a nice guy. But he's not the one who managed to corner me in a closet tonight."

Kylian chuckled, and I felt his hand leave mine. I watched as he placed it gently on my head, but I quickly batted it away. "Hey, don't get too comfy now," I said, trying to sound assertive.

Kylian's voice took on a more playful tone. "Oh, come on. I'm just trying to make the best of our little predicament."

Before I could react, he wrapped his arm around my shoulders, pulling me closer to him. I stiffened slightly, but I could feel the warmth of his body and the gentle pressure of his arm.

"You know," he said softly, "you look pretty cute in that costume. Even if you're acting all cool and distant."

I tried to stay composed, but his closeness was making it hard. "Yeah, well, you're not exactly dressed for the occasion either."

He laughed, his breath warm against my ear. "Ah, but that's the charm, isn't it? A little unpredictability keeps things interesting."

I felt my resolve melting away as he tightened his hold slightly. "You're incorrigible."

"I know," he whispered, his voice low and teasing. "But you're the one who's letting me be this close."

I bit my lip, trying to maintain my composure. "Maybe I'm just a glutton for punishment."

Kylian's arm stayed around me, his touch gentle but firm. "Or maybe you're just enjoying it more than you'd like to admit."

I could feel myself slowly relaxing into his embrace, despite my efforts to remain distant. "You're impossible."

He grinned, his face still hidden in the darkness. "And you're just as bad, letting me get away with all this."

We stayed like that, the closeness between us growing more comfortable by the minute. Despite my attempts to stay cool, I found myself sinking into the warmth of his presence, the playful banter slowly giving way to a more tender feeling.

I told him, trying to sound nonchalant, "You can back off, you know."

He chuckled softly, his breath warm against my skin. "But I don't want to. I'm enjoying this too much."

I moved to face him, though it was still difficult to make out his features in the darkness. "Why? What's the point of staying so close?"

Kylian leaned in, his face just inches from mine. "Maybe I'm just curious to see how you'll react."

I could feel his breath mingling with mine, the tension between us palpable. "Curious, huh?"

"Yeah," he said, his voice a low whisper. "Curious to see if you'll give in."

I felt his lips brush against mine, the contact so light it sent a shiver down my spine. I wanted to respond, to close the gap between us, but I couldn't bring myself to move.

Kylian pulled back slightly, his lips curling into a playful smirk. "Still playing hard to get?"

I rolled my eyes, trying to mask the fluttering in my chest. "You're such a tease."

He laughed softly, his hand gently resting on my head. "And you're not too bad yourself. I guess I'll just have to keep trying."

I let him keep his hand there, the warmth of his touch soothing despite the teasing. "You're impossible."

"And you," he said, his voice tender now, "are impossible to resist."

Despite the darkness, I could sense his smile, and it made me feel a little more at ease. We stayed like that for a moment, the playful banter giving way to a more comfortable silence, both of us savoring the closeness in our own way.

Chapter 19

Kylian slowly removed his hand from my head, the warmth of his touch lingering even after he pulled away. "You know," he said, his voice low and smooth, "you're quite the enigma. I can't quite figure you out."

I shot him a look. "Can you just stop? We're just friends."

He leaned in a little closer, his voice barely above a whisper. "Friends, huh? Then why does it feel like there's something more between us?"

My heart skipped a beat, and I stayed silent, unsure how to respond. His words hung in the air, making the space between us feel charged.

The darkness of the closet seemed to stretch on as we both waited. Finally, the timer buzzed, signaling the end of our time in the small, enclosed space. We stepped out, and as we emerged, Kylian leaned in again, his voice soft but firm. "Caleb better not get too close to you."

I blinked, taken aback by his sudden shift. "And who do you think you are, to say that?"

He gave me a half-smile, a hint of mischief in his eyes. "Just someone who's looking out for you. Maybe I don't like sharing."

Despite my irritation at his possessiveness, I couldn't deny the thrill it gave me. The way he looked at me, the intensity in his voice—he made me feel a whirlwind of emotions. It was confusing, yet exciting.

I returned to the game, trying to ignore the way Kylian's eyes were fixed on me from across the room. Regina caught my eye, her expression one of barely concealed amusement. I shot her a few sharp looks, trying to convey my frustration and embarrassment.

Regina, ever the troublemaker, only grinned wider. It was as if she enjoyed watching me squirm. I could feel the heat rising to my cheeks, and I did my best to focus on the game, determined to avoid Kylian's gaze as much as possible.

But as I glanced around, I could feel his eyes on me, making it impossible to ignore the knot of excitement and confusion that had settled in my stomach.

The bottle spun slowly on the floor, coming to a stop with Caleb's name pointed directly at me. The room erupted in anticipation as someone called out, "Caleb, you have to kiss the girl you're most interested in."

Caleb's eyes locked onto mine, and he began walking toward me with a confident stride. The air seemed to grow thicker with every step he took. I felt a mix of nerves and excitement swirl in my stomach. When he reached me, he leaned in and pressed his lips against mine.

The kiss was brief, but it was enough to make my cheeks flush a deep shade of red. I pulled back, trying to steady my breathing, and my gaze instinctively shifted toward Kylian. His face was a mask of frustration, his jaw clenched and his eyes narrowed as he watched the exchange.

Regina, noticing the tension, leaned in and whispered, "Looks like someone's a little jealous."

I shot her a withering glance, my eyes flashing with annoyance. "Oh, please. Just keep it to yourself."

Regina merely grinned, clearly enjoying the drama unfolding. The frustration was palpable, and I tried to focus on the game, but it was hard to ignore the way Kylian's gaze remained fixed on me, his frustration evident.

The atmosphere in the room felt charged, every glance and every word seemed to carry a deeper meaning. As Caleb returned to his spot, I could feel the weight of Kylian's stare, the unspoken words hanging heavily between us.

The game finally came to an end, and I slipped outside to the edge of the pool to catch my breath, my mind replaying the night's events. The cool night air felt refreshing against my flushed cheeks. I was lost in thought when suddenly, someone nudged me from behind. My balance faltered, and my heels, precarious on the slippery ground, betrayed me. I tumbled forward, my feet unable to find solid ground.

The water enveloped me, and I struggled against the weight of my drenched clothes, which seemed to pull me down. Panic set in as I flailed, my attempts to swim only making it harder to stay afloat. My breaths came in ragged gasps, and I felt my strength waning.

A scream of fear escaped my lips, muffled by the water. I was about to lose hope when strong arms wrapped around me, lifting me effortlessly out of the pool. I emerged, gasping for air, my wet hair plastered to my face. I blinked up at Kylian, who had pulled me to safety.

"Thank you," I managed to croak, still trying to regain my composure. My heart was pounding in my chest, a mix of relief and embarrassment flooding over me.

Kylian looked at me with a worried yet amused expression. "I'd say you're quite the catch, but I think you'd prefer to stay out of the water from now on."

I managed a shaky laugh, though I could feel my face burning with embarrassment. "Just put me down, please," I said, my voice trembling slightly. "I'm sorry for—"

Before I could finish, he gently set me down on the edge of the pool. "Don't worry about it," he said softly, a smile tugging at his lips. "I'll always be around if you need a hand."

I nodded, trying to ignore the flutter in my chest at his words. "Thanks, again. I—I need to go."

As I walked away, my heart was still racing, both from the panic of nearly drowning and from the confusing feelings Kylian's presence always stirred in me. I quickly made my way back to the dorm, feeling his gaze on my back, the night's events swirling in my mind.

I took a long, hot shower, trying to wash away the embarrassment and adrenaline from the night. The steam filled the small bathroom, and I leaned against the cool tiles, letting the water cascade over me. I couldn't believe I almost kissed Kylian in that damn closet. The thought made my cheeks flush again, even as the warm water soothed my tense muscles.

Why did he have to be so close, so tempting? And why did I have to feel so conflicted about it? I shook my head, trying to clear my thoughts. It was just a moment, just a game. I needed to focus on something else, anything else, to distract myself from the confusing emotions that seemed to swirl around him.

The next morning, I rushed to get ready for class, the alarm clock's relentless beeping reminding me of how late I was. In my scramble, I couldn't find any hair ties, so I resigned myself to a messy hair day. I pulled on my sweater, only to notice Kylian's jacket draped over a chair. I still hadn't returned it.

I sighed, thinking it might be colder today than I anticipated. I shrugged off the idea of returning it now and slipped into his jacket. It was warm and surprisingly comforting. I bundled up with my coat and scarf and hurried out the door to find Regina waiting for me at the corner.

"Wow, you're really embracing the 'fashionably late' look today," Regina teased as we walked toward campus. "And is that Kylian's jacket you're wearing? I thought you said you weren't interested in him."

"Not for him, just because it's cold," I muttered, trying to ignore the warmth of the jacket and the way it smelled faintly like him.

Regina raised an eyebrow, a mischievous grin spreading across her face. "Sure, sure. So, what happened in that closet? I heard some things and—"

I rolled my eyes dramatically. "Oh, Regina, it's not what you think. We just talked. And, um, almost kissed. But I stopped it."

Regina's eyes widened with interest. "Almost kissed? That's more than talking. Was he being all intense and brooding, or did he manage to crack a joke about it?"

I chuckled, remembering the awkward yet electrifying moment in the closet. "He was being his usual charming self, trying to flirt and tease me. But you know how he is, always pushing my buttons."

"And what about Caleb? Did he get the wrong idea?" Regina pressed, nudging me playfully.

"Caleb was just caught up in the game," I said, shrugging. "And honestly, I was just as confused as anyone. Now can we focus on making it to class on time?"

Regina laughed, her eyes sparkling with curiosity. "Alright, alright. But you owe me the full story later. Deal?"

"Deal," I agreed, rolling my eyes again but unable to hide my smile. "Let's just get to class before we're even more late."

As we walked, I couldn't help but notice how snug and oddly comforting Kylian's jacket felt. Even if I was just borrowing it, it seemed to fit just right, and I tried not to let my thoughts wander too much.

As I entered the classroom, I spotted Caleb seated near the back, his gaze lingering on me as I made my way to my seat. His eyes fell on the jacket I was wearing, which, despite my attempts to ignore it, felt oddly comforting.

Caleb raised an eyebrow, a playful smirk on his lips. "I didn't know you were on the swim team. Nice jacket—looks pretty official."

I glanced down at the jacket, suddenly aware of how snug and warm it was. It was a deep navy blue, with the team's logo embroidered on the left chest, and it seemed to carry a faint scent of chlorine and Kylian's cologne. I hadn't realized just how much it stood out until now.

"Oh, this?" I said, trying to sound nonchalant, though my cheeks were already warming up. "I'm, uh, just borrowing it from a friend. It's really cold today, and I guess I didn't want to freeze."

Caleb chuckled, his eyes twinkling with curiosity. "A friend, huh? Must be a really generous friend. Or maybe a really good friend?"

I laughed awkwardly, feeling the heat rise to my face. "Yeah, something like that. Anyway, how was your night?"

He shifted in his seat, clearly enjoying my discomfort. "Not bad. Just the usual. But enough about me. Are you going to be at the swim meet this weekend? You seem pretty cozy in that jacket."

I nodded, trying to shake off the lingering thoughts of Kylian. "Yeah, I'll be there. Just, you know, trying to stay warm until then."

As the class started, I found it nearly impossible to focus. My mind kept drifting back to the night in the closet, Kylian's teasing, and his touch. I tried to concentrate on the lecture, but the warmth of the jacket and the memory of Kylian's presence made it hard to stay engaged.

As the class ended, I walked through the corridors, pulling up the hood of the oversized jacket. My hair was a complete mess, sticking out in all directions, and the hood was a desperate attempt to hide it. My hands were snug in the jacket's pockets, and despite its size, I felt oddly comfortable wrapped in its warmth.

The faint scent of Kylian's cologne lingered, enveloping me like a hug—ugh, stop thinking about that, Kathleen.

I turned a corner and spotted Kylian with his friends. He glanced up, and his eyes lit up when he saw me. A curious, almost amused expression crossed his face as he made his way toward me.

"Hey, Kathleen," he greeted, his smile broadening. "Nice to see you rocking the swim team's jacket. You're really giving off that 'team spirit' vibe today."

I tried to maintain a casual tone, even though my cheeks were flushed. "Yeah, just borrowed it. It's freezing outside, and I didn't have a chance to do my hair."

Kylian's eyes twinkled with mischief. "Looks like you've made yourself at home in my jacket. Don't tell me you're trying to get extra credit for wearing it."

I rolled my eyes playfully. "Very funny. I just needed something warm."

He chuckled, stepping closer. "Well, I must say, you're pulling it off. But seriously, don't get too used to it. It's not like you're auditioning for the swim team or anything."

Before I could retort, he reached out and ruffled my hair gently, a teasing grin still plastered on his face. His hand lingered on my head for a moment, and I felt a jolt of warmth from his touch, despite the teasing.

"Alright, I've got to run," he said, pulling his hand away. "Don't get too comfortable with my jacket. I might need it back."

As he walked away with his friends, I couldn't help but smile, feeling a flutter of something in my chest. I tugged the jacket tighter around me, trying to ignore the warmth that seemed to grow every time I thought of Kylian.

At the end of the day, I grabbed my coat and scarf, pulled up my hood, and started walking toward the exit. Passing by the pool, I hesitated for a moment, then decided to go in. The sound of splashing and the sight of swimmers in action were oddly calming. I found a quiet spot in the bleachers, set up my laptop, and started working on my homework while the athletes trained.

I was lost in my work when I noticed Kylian approaching, a focused look on his face. He sat down next to me, making a little more noise than necessary as he plopped onto the bench.

"Hey, Kathleen," he said casually, though his eyes were already drawn to the pool. "I didn't expect to find you here. Busy studying, huh?"

I quickly removed my hood, not wanting him to think I was lounging in his jacket. I closed my laptop and turned to him, trying to seem nonchalant. "Yeah, just trying to get some work done. It's quieter here."

Kylian looked over at me, still watching the swimmers with a mixture of admiration and concentration. "You know, I didn't think I'd see you here. I mean, it's not exactly the most popular study spot."

I laughed softly. "Well, it's not like I planned it. Just needed a change of scenery, I guess."

He grinned, his gaze still fixed on the pool. "Fair enough. And here I was thinking you had some secret affinity for swimming. I mean, borrowing my jacket, showing up at the pool—could it be you're secretly plotting to join the team?"

I chuckled, shaking my head. "Definitely not plotting anything. Just here for a bit of peace and quiet."

Kylian shifted closer, his arm brushing against mine. "You know, it's kind of nice to see you here, actually. Makes me think you're not just all work and no play."

I felt a warm flush on my cheeks. "I guess I'm a bit of both. And you? Always so dedicated to your training?"

He shrugged, his eyes still on the swimmers. "Yeah, I guess you could say that. I just really enjoy it. Watching people push their limits, strive for more... It's inspiring."

I looked at him, admiring the way his eyes sparkled with passion. "It's really impressive. You're not just in it for yourself."

He turned his head slightly to look at me, a soft smile playing on his lips. "Thanks. I guess it's something I can't help. What about you? Any hidden talents or passions I should know about?"

I smiled, feeling a bit shy under his gaze. "Not really. Just trying to figure things out as I go."

He leaned in a little closer, his voice dropping to a more intimate tone. "Well, if you ever need a partner for anything—whether it's studying or maybe something more fun—just let me know."

I met his eyes, feeling a flutter of something in my chest. "I might take you up on that offer."

As we both turned our attention back to the pool, the conversation lingered between us like a gentle, unspoken promise. Kylian's presence was unexpectedly comforting, and I found myself enjoying the quiet companionship, even if I still had plenty of homework to finish.

As I pulled my hood up again, trying to shield myself from the chill, I noticed Kylian's eyes crinkling with a playful smile. He seemed to find my attempt at warmth amusing.

"Cold, are we?" he asked, his tone light and teasing. "I'd offer to lend you my jacket, but I see you're already making good use of it."

I laughed softly, feeling my cheeks flush a little. "Yeah, it's definitely cooler in here than I expected. I might just freeze if I'm not careful."

Kylian shifted closer, his arm brushing against mine. "You know, if you're cold, you could always come a little closer. I've been told I'm pretty good at keeping people warm."

I felt a flutter in my chest as he draped his arm around me, pulling me gently into his side. His touch was surprisingly warm, and his proximity made me acutely aware of how close we were. I tried to shift away slightly, but his hold remained firm, as if he didn't want to let go.

"Hey," I said, trying to sound casual, though my voice came out a bit breathy. "You really don't have to—"

Kylian interrupted with a soft chuckle. "Oh, but I do. It's practically my duty as a friend to make sure you're comfortable."

I felt my heart race as I settled against him, unable to ignore the pleasant warmth radiating from his body. "You're quite the gentleman, then."

He gave a playful nudge, his arm tightening slightly around me. "I try my best. Besides, I'd hate to see you shivering while I'm right here. It's kind of nice having you close."

The closeness of his body against mine was both comforting and distracting. I could feel the steady rhythm of his breathing, and the scent of his cologne was oddly soothing. I tried to focus on the pool, but it was hard with Kylian so close, his presence enveloping me like a cozy blanket.

"Ugh, you're impossible," I said, rolling my eyes though a smile tugged at the corners of my lips. "But thanks."

Kylian grinned, his face just inches from mine. "Anytime. And who knows, maybe you'll need me to keep you warm again soon."

I felt a shiver, but not from the cold. His arm around me felt like a gentle promise, and despite my attempts to stay cool and composed, I couldn't help but enjoy the comforting, if confusing, closeness.

As Jared and Scott approached, Kylian and I quickly pulled apart, the sudden distance feeling oddly empty. Jared shot us a knowing look while Scott grinned mischievously.

"Well, well, well," Jared began with a smirk, "looks like someone's found a cozy spot."

Scott leaned in closer, his eyes twinkling with amusement. "Didn't expect to see you two sharing warmth. Should we be worried about you two getting too close?"

I shifted uncomfortably, my face heating up. "We were just—"

Kylian cut in smoothly, "Just trying to keep Kathleen warm, that's all. Didn't realize it'd make us the subject of a roasting session."

Scott chuckled. "Keeping warm, huh? Seems like you've got quite the 'responsibility' there. So, Kathleen, how's it feel to be under Kylian's protection?"

I shot Kylian a sidelong glance, but he only raised an eyebrow, as if challenging me to answer.

"It's not as dramatic as it sounds," I said, trying to sound casual but feeling the heat rise in my cheeks. "Just working on my homework and trying to stay warm."

Jared leaned back, crossing his arms with a playful grin. "Homework, huh? That's what they're calling it these days?"

Scott added with a wink, "Well, if you ever need help with 'keeping warm' or anything else, you know where to find us."

I tried to hide my embarrassment, focusing on the pool and the athletes. "I'm good, thanks. I can manage."

Kylian, sensing my discomfort, chimed in with a casual tone. "Alright, alright, we get it. We're just here to enjoy some downtime before practice."

Jared and Scott exchanged a glance, their smiles widening. "Sure thing. Just don't let us catch you getting too 'cozy' without us," Jared said.

As we all four watched the pool, I felt Kylian subtly place his arm around my waist. The warmth of his touch was both unexpected and electrifying. My heart started to beat faster, and I could feel my pulse quicken as I tried to stay composed.

Jared and Scott were engrossed in their conversation, oblivious to the shift in atmosphere. I glanced at Kylian, trying to gauge his intentions, but his expression was relaxed and casual. He seemed completely at ease, as if his arm around me was the most natural thing in the world.

I attempted to focus on the swimmers, but the gentle pressure of Kylian's arm made it hard to concentrate. Each time he adjusted his hold, I could feel his warmth seep through the layers of my clothing. My breath hitched slightly, and I fought to keep my composure.

Trying to play it cool, I leaned a bit into him, though I wasn't sure if it was a conscious choice or if I was just pulled by the comfort of his touch. I could hear the faint sound of his breathing, steady and calm, which seemed to match the rhythmic splashes of the pool.

"So, what's the verdict?" Kylian's voice broke through my thoughts, his tone casual but with an undertone of something I couldn't quite place. "Enjoying the view?"

I forced a smile, still trying to steady my racing heart. "Yeah, it's nice. Just a bit cold, that's all."

Kylian's arm tightened around me slightly, his warmth counteracting the chill. "I guess you could say I'm here to keep you warm, then."

His playful remark, combined with the closeness of his embrace, made my cheeks flush. I looked over at him, catching his gaze. There was something in his eyes—an unreadable mix of mischief and sincerity.

Before I could respond, Jared and Scott turned their attention back to us, breaking the moment. "Alright, you two," Jared said with a grin, "we've got to get ready for practice. Don't have too much fun without us."

Kylian gave a light chuckle and removed his arm, though his hand lingered briefly on my back before retreating. "Don't worry," he said, "we'll be here when you get back."

As they walked away, I took a deep breath, trying to calm the rapid beating of my heart. Kylian's touch had left me feeling both exhilarated and unsettled, and I was left with a mix of emotions that I wasn't quite sure how to handle.

Chapter 20

The weekend arrived, and I found myself standing in front of my desk, buried under a mountain of homework. I was supposed to be focusing on my assignments, but instead, my thoughts kept drifting to Kylian and the swim competition that was about to take place. I'd promised myself I'd only go because he'd pleaded with me the night before, despite the pile of work that needed my attention.

As I was in the midst of wrestling with a particularly stubborn essay, there was a knock at my door. I sighed, expecting it to be another distraction, and opened it to find Regina standing there with a mischievous grin on her face.

"Hey, Kathleen!" she chirped, holding out a neatly folded t-shirt. "I brought you something!"

I eyed the shirt warily. It was a bright blue with the school's logo prominently displayed, and across the back, in bold white letters, was Kylian's last name. "Oh no, Regina, I don't think I can wear that," I said, backing away slightly.

Regina's eyes widened, and she gave me a pleading look. "Come on, Kathleen. It's just for today. You're going to the competition, and it would mean a lot to Kylian if you wore it."

I shook my head. "I have so much work to do. I don't even know if I should go—"

"Please?" Regina cut in, her expression turning serious. "You know how much this means to him. And you're already going, so why not show a little support?"

I hesitated, glancing back at the mess of papers and textbooks on my desk. The truth was, I did want to be there for Kylian, despite my mountain of work. I sighed, resigning myself to the fact that I'd have to balance both. "Fine," I said, taking the shirt from Regina's hands. "I'll wear it. But only because you asked so nicely."

Regina's face lit up with a triumphant smile. "Thank you! I knew you'd come through." She gave me a quick hug before turning to leave. "I'll see you at the competition!"

As she walked away, I looked at the shirt in my hands. It was a simple piece of school spirit wear, but somehow, it felt like it carried a lot of significance. I knew I'd be a little self-conscious wearing it, but seeing Kylian's name on my back would also remind me of the support I was giving him.

I quickly changed into the shirt, paired with jeans and a jacket to stay warm. Despite my initial reluctance, I felt a small spark of excitement. I grabbed my bag, threw in a couple of textbooks for any spare moments between the event, and headed out the door.

As I walked toward the venue, I hoped that this small gesture would mean something to Kylian and that maybe, just maybe, it would help me feel more connected to him, even amid the chaos of my academic life.

When I arrived at the competition venue, I was taken aback by its grandeur. The arena was sprawling, with high ceilings that seemed to touch the sky and walls adorned with banners and flags representing various swim teams from around the country. The bright lights illuminated the vast swimming pool, which was flanked by rows of seating that were quickly filling up with spectators, coaches, and athletes. The air buzzed with excitement and anticipation, a palpable energy that made my heart race just a little faster.

I scanned the scene, taking in the rows of competitive swimmers stretching and warming up, their coaches offering last-minute advice and encouragement. This was where they selected athletes for the Olympic Games—a high-stakes environment where every stroke and turn mattered.

As I made my way to the seating area, I spotted Regina waving excitedly from our designated spot. I was the only one wearing the bright blue team shirt with Kylian's last name on the back. My face flushed with a mix of embarrassment and determination. I approached Regina, who was grinning from ear to ear.

"Look at you, standing out in the crowd," she teased, her eyes twinkling with mischief. "I knew you'd make an impression."

I shot her a withering glance but couldn't suppress a reluctant smile. "I'm the only one wearing this shirt, Regina. I feel like a walking billboard."

She chuckled, giving me a playful nudge. "It's all part of the support! And trust me, Kylian will appreciate it."

I rolled my eyes and took a seat next to her, trying to ignore the self-consciousness creeping up on me. The competition was about to begin, and I hoped with all my might that Kylian would perform well and secure a spot for the Olympics. As the swimmers lined up and the announcer's voice filled the arena, I focused on the pool, hoping that this experience would be a memorable one for Kylian—and maybe, just maybe, that it would be a good omen for what was to come.

I reached into my bag for my book, hoping to distract myself during the downtime between races. However, Regina swiftly snatched it away with a mischievous grin.

"No distractions!" she insisted, giving me a wink. "We need to stay focused and cheer for Kylian!"

I sighed but relented, watching the action unfold with renewed attention. The competition began in earnest, and the energy in the arena was electric. Regina and I threw ourselves into cheering for Kylian with every ounce of enthusiasm we had.

Every time he took a turn or pushed off the wall with impressive speed, we were on our feet, screaming and clapping wildly. Our voices merged with the rest of the crowd's cheers, creating a cacophony of support. Each time Kylian touched the wall and looked up at the scoreboard, Regina and I leaped into each other's arms, celebrating each victory as if it were our own.

The tension built as the final results were posted. The arena fell silent, the anticipation almost unbearable. My heart pounded in my chest as I waited to see how Kylian had fared.

Finally, the results were displayed, and Kylian's name was proudly listed in third place. A rush of relief and excitement surged through me. Regina and I hugged tightly, our cheers filling the air. We jumped up and down, our faces flushed with exhilaration and pride.

As Kylian walked out of the pool area, drenched but triumphant, I caught his eye. He flashed a grin that lit up his entire face. I waved frantically, feeling a swell of pride and happiness for him. Regina and I cheered one last time, our voices hoarse but full of joy.

It had been an incredible day, filled with nail-biting moments and overwhelming support. I felt a deep sense of satisfaction, not just for Kylian's achievement, but also for the unspoken connection we had shared through this shared experience.

The competition wrapped up, and the excitement of the day was beginning to settle into a comfortable exhaustion. Regina and I gathered our things, ready to head out, but my attention was caught by Kylian, who remained seated by the edge of the pool, lost in thought.

Regina nudged me gently. "Go talk to him. He's been waiting all day to find out how he did. He could use some company."

With a nod, I walked over to where Kylian sat, his gaze fixed on the still water. The sound of footsteps was almost muffled by the quiet of the emptying arena. As I approached, he turned to look at me, his expression a mix of exhaustion and contemplation.

"Hey," I said softly, trying to keep my voice calm despite the buzz of anticipation I felt. "Great job out there today. You really gave it your all."

Kylian's lips curved into a grateful smile. "Thanks. I'm just... waiting to see if all this hard work paid off. It's a bit overwhelming."

I sat down beside him, glancing at the pool where he had spent so many hours training. "I'm sure it did. You looked amazing out there. No matter what the results are, you've got nothing to be disappointed about."

He sighed, leaning back on his hands. "I hope so. It's just... I've worked so hard for this. It feels like everything's riding on these next few days."

I could feel the tension radiating off him, and without thinking, I leaned my head onto his shoulder. The gesture was gentle, almost instinctive. It felt comforting to be close to him in that moment of uncertainty.

Kylian looked down at me, a little surprised but clearly touched. "Thanks for being here. It means a lot."

I smiled up at him, feeling the warmth of his shoulder beneath my cheek. "Of course. I wouldn't miss it for the world. Besides, it's kind of nice to be able to sit here and share this with you."

He chuckled softly, his fingers brushing against mine briefly. "I guess you're right. It's a lot easier to handle with someone by your side."

We sat in comfortable silence for a few moments, just enjoying the quiet and the closeness. As the last of the spectators filed out and the lights dimmed, the arena felt smaller, more intimate.

Eventually, Kylian broke the silence. "You know, no matter what happens, I'm glad you came. It's been a long day, but having you here makes it better."

I lifted my head, meeting his eyes with a soft smile. "I'm glad I could be here for you. And I'll be here for whatever comes next."

He returned my smile, a mix of gratitude and something deeper flickering in his gaze. "Thanks, Kathleen. I really mean it."

As we both stood up, ready to leave, there was a shared sense of anticipation and hope between us. It was clear that whatever the future held, this moment would be one we'd remember fondly.

As we lingered by the poolside, the quiet of the arena enveloped us. Kylian's gaze held a depth that made my heart race with an unspoken tension. He looked at me with an intensity that made my breath hitch.

His voice was barely more than a whisper, yet it carried a weight of longing. "Kathleen... I can't keep pretending anymore."

Before I could process his words, he closed the distance between us. His hand gently cupped my cheek, his thumb brushing lightly against my skin. My pulse quickened as his lips hovered close to mine. The air between us crackled with electricity, and then, as if unable to resist any longer, he pressed his lips against mine.

The kiss was sudden, intense. I was caught off guard, my mind racing as I felt his warmth, his urgency. It was a moment that felt both overwhelming and exhilarating, a collision of emotions that left me breathless.

When he finally pulled away, his expression was a mixture of relief and regret. "I... I'm sorry, Kathleen. I need to go."

He turned and walked away, leaving me stunned and disoriented. My thoughts tumbled over each other as I tried to comprehend what had just happened. I stood there, my lips still tingling from his touch, trying to form coherent words but finding only stammered sounds escaping my lips.

"Wait... Kylian, I—" My voice faltered, the words failing to come out as I watched him walk away, his silhouette disappearing into the distance.

The arena was now eerily quiet, the echo of our kiss lingering in the stillness. I was left standing there, feeling a mix of shock and confusion. The Kylian I knew had just been replaced by someone new, someone whose emotions were raw and unfiltered. And as for me, I wasn't the same Kathleen who had come here earlier. The kiss had altered something fundamental within me, leaving me questioning everything I thought I knew about us.

As I finally turned to leave, I realized that whatever had just transpired had irrevocably changed the dynamic between us. The echoes of that unexpected kiss were now intertwined with my thoughts, and I knew that nothing would ever be quite the same.

As I stepped outside, the rain poured down in relentless sheets, drenching me almost instantly. The chill of the rain contrasted sharply with the lingering warmth of Kylian's kiss on my lips. I trudged through the downpour, my mind a chaotic swirl of thoughts and emotions.

Regina was waiting for me by the entrance, her umbrella struggling against the gusts of wind. She looked up as I approached, her expression turning to one of concern as she took in my disheveled appearance.

"Kathleen, are you okay? You look like you've seen a ghost," she said, her voice rising above the roar of the rain.

I opened my mouth to respond, but all that came out was a stammered, "I—uh... I..."

Regina's concern deepened. "What happened? You're shaking."

Taking a deep breath, I tried to steady my voice, though it still wavered. "Kylian... he—he kissed me. Just now. At the pool. And then he just... walked away."

Regina's eyes widened in shock, the rain creating a curtain of droplets around us. "Wait, what? He kissed you? And just left?"

I nodded, trying to keep my voice steady despite the rush of emotions. "Yeah, he said he couldn't keep pretending, then... he kissed me. And then he just left. I don't even know what to think anymore."

Regina took a step closer, her expression softening with sympathy. "Oh, Kathleen... I'm so sorry. That must have been really overwhelming."

I nodded again, feeling the weight of the situation settle heavily on my shoulders. "It was. I don't even know how to process it. Everything feels... different now."

Regina placed a comforting hand on my arm, her presence a small relief amidst the storm. "Look, let's get out of the rain and talk this through. We'll figure it out together."

We hurried to the safety of her car, escaping the downpour. As we settled inside, Regina started the engine and turned to me with a supportive smile. "Tell me everything. I'm here for you."

I took a deep breath, trying to gather my thoughts as we began to drive away from the competition. The rain continued to fall, but inside the car, a sense of warmth and support enveloped me. And as I began to recount the evening's events, I felt a small measure of relief, knowing that Regina was there to help me navigate this unexpected and confusing turn in my life.

As I stumbled into my room, the rain-soaked clothes clinging to me, my mind was a whirlwind of confusion and conflicting emotions. I threw my bag onto the floor and sank onto my bed, feeling the weight of the day's events pressing heavily on my chest.

I tried to remember why I had disliked Kylian so intensely at the beginning. The irritation and frustration seemed like distant memories now, obscured by the intensity of what had just happened. Back then, his actions had seemed thoughtless and disruptive, but now, in the aftermath of that kiss, those feelings felt like they belonged to another lifetime.

Lying there in the dim light of my room, I couldn't help but replay the scene over and over in my mind. His lips against mine—tender, urgent, and undeniably electric. The way he had looked at me, as if he was trying to convey something profound, something he couldn't quite put into words.

Was it possible that I had developed feelings for him? The thought seemed both exhilarating and terrifying. Kylian had always been a source of irritation, a challenge, and now he was a source of heart-pounding confusion. The lines between animosity and attraction had blurred, leaving me unsure of where I stood.

And what about him? Did he really feel the same way? Or was it a fleeting impulse, a moment of weakness? He had seemed so intense, so sure of himself when he kissed me. But now, in the quiet of my room, I was left to wonder if his feelings were as genuine as mine might be.

Things had changed so much since we had come to this place. The everyday interactions that once seemed trivial had taken on a new meaning. The spark of our rivalry had shifted, evolving into something more complex and intimate. Was it the new environment that had changed us, or was it something deeper?

I sat up, running a hand through my damp hair, trying to make sense of it all. The questions swirled in my mind, each one as perplexing as the last. I needed answers, but for now, all I had were the echoes of that kiss and the lingering confusion of what it meant for us moving forward.

It was clear that things were different now. The walls I had built around my emotions were beginning to crumble, and with them, a new and uncertain reality was taking shape. As I stared at the ceiling, I knew that the only way to find clarity was to confront these feelings head-on and to discover whether Kylian was truly a part of this evolving story.

Chapter 21

It's been a week since that confusing kiss, and things have gotten awkwardly complicated. You'd think after a dramatic, impromptu lip-lock, we'd either be all over each other or shouting at the top of our lungs. But no, instead, we've settled into a masterclass in avoidance.

It's like we've become experts in the fine art of not making eye contact. I avoid the pool like it's a haunted house and Kylian's lurking inside. I've even started taking longer routes to avoid passing by the pool area, as if a few extra laps around campus will magically erase my chance of seeing him. Meanwhile, Kylian has developed this uncanny ability to be wherever I'm not. If I'm in the dorm, he's mysteriously absent. If I pop by the dining hall, he's apparently got an urgent meeting with a library book or something equally plausible.

The situation is almost comical. There's this dance we're doing, each of us pretending to be deeply engrossed in our own lives while we sneak glances at each other from behind various convenient obstructions. I find myself muttering, "Oh look, a bird! Isn't that fascinating?" while I desperately try to avoid

Kylian's gaze. And Kylian? He's apparently developed a sudden fascination with studying the intricacies of the floor tiles in the common areas.

It's reached the point where even Regina has noticed. "So, you and Kylian still in that dramatic avoidance phase?" she asked, her eyebrows raised in mock innocence. "You two are like an old married couple who've decided to sleep in separate beds."

"I'm not avoiding him," I protested, though it sounded weak even to my own ears. "I just... have other places to be."

"Sure, sure," she said with a grin. "And I'm sure Kylian isn't busy timing how long he can stand in the library without bumping into you. It's like a soap opera around here."

The truth is, avoiding each other has become a full-time job. The hallway becomes a minefield of strategic maneuvers, and the common room? An obstacle course of awkward small talk and stiff smiles. Even our mutual friends seem to have taken sides in this silent tug-of-war.

Every time I do catch a glimpse of Kylian, it's like a scene from a slapstick comedy. There was that time he nearly tripped over his own feet trying to look casual as I walked by, or the way he ducked behind a potted plant when I turned a corner. And me? I've had a few less-than-graceful moments, too—like the time I tried to make a dramatic exit from the library and walked straight into a stack of textbooks.

In the end, it's all become a ridiculous game of cat and mouse. The more we try to avoid each other, the more we end up making fools of ourselves. And the more we do that, the harder it is to face the fact that avoiding each other might be the last thing either of us truly wants.

One evening, just as I was about to leave the dorm, Kylian walked in. Neither of us was paying attention, so we collided right there in the doorway. The impact wasn't hard, but it was enough to knock the breath out of me and force me to look up.

We both froze. His hand was still on the doorknob, mine clutching the strap of my bag. For a moment, we just stood there, staring at each other like two deer caught in headlights. His expression was unreadable, those deep eyes of his locked onto mine as if searching for something I couldn't quite place.

Then he cleared his throat, breaking the silence that hung heavy between us. Without saying a word, he stepped to the side, his gaze shifting to a spot somewhere over my shoulder. His jaw was clenched, his posture stiff, like he was trying to hold back... something.

"Thanks," I mumbled, barely audible, as I moved past him, my shoulder brushing his arm.

He didn't respond, just kept staring straight ahead, his lips pressed into a thin line. I could feel the tension in the air, so thick it was almost suffocating. I didn't dare look back as I walked out, but I heard the soft click of the door closing behind me.

My heart was pounding in my chest, and I couldn't shake the feeling of his presence, the warmth of his body so close to mine. As I stepped into the cool night air, I took a deep breath, trying to calm the storm of emotions swirling inside me. What was happening between us? Why did such a simple encounter feel so charged, so intense?

I kept walking, but my mind stayed stuck in that doorway, replaying the scene over and over, wondering what it all meant and why it felt like a turning point, even though nothing had really happened.

The next day, I went to see Regina, hoping to make sense of everything that had been happening. As soon as I walked into her room, she looked up from her phone, instantly sensing something was up.

"I need to talk to you," I said, my voice laced with frustration and confusion.

She patted the bed next to her, and I sat down, running a hand through my hair. "He's been avoiding me. Like, seriously avoiding me. It's been a week, and every time I look at him, he looks away. And when he does see me, it's like I'm not even there. I don't get it."

Regina tilted her head, her eyes narrowing slightly. "Kylian? He's ignoring you?"

"Completely," I confirmed. "Ever since... well, you know."

She nodded, understanding immediately. "So, what do you think's going on? Maybe he's confused? Or scared?"

"Scared? Of what?" I asked, frowning.

"Of his feelings," she said, shrugging. "It sounds like he's not sure what to do with them. I mean, if you guys kissed and now he's acting weird, it could be because he doesn't know how to handle it. Maybe he's worried about how you feel."

I sighed, rubbing my temples. "But why ignore me? It's like he's pretending nothing happened. And I don't know... it's just—" I broke off as the door to Kylian's room suddenly swung open.

My heart skipped a beat as he walked out, looking as composed as ever. My words died in my throat, and I quickly clamped my mouth shut.

Kylian didn't even glance my way. He greeted Regina with a casual, "Hey," grabbed an apple from the counter, and walked out without a single word to me. Not even a nod.

I stared after him, my chest tightening. Regina shot me a sympathetic look, but it didn't make me feel any better.

"He didn't even say hi," I muttered under my breath, more to myself than to her.

Regina bit her lip, then said softly, "He's clearly struggling with something, Kathleen. But ignoring each other isn't going to solve anything. You need to talk to him, find out what's really going on."

I knew she was right, but it didn't make it any easier. As I sat there, replaying the moment in my head, I couldn't help but feel a strange mix of hurt and anger. How could he just walk past me like that? And why did it bother me so much?

That evening, after classes, I walked into the common area, feeling the usual weight of the day dragging at my shoulders. The sight of Regina and Kylian sitting on the couch caught me off guard. They were watching Pretty Woman, of all things. Regina spotted me lingering at the entrance and gave me a nod, gesturing for me to join them.

I hesitated for a moment, then slowly made my way over, sliding onto the couch next to Kylian. As I did, I noticed his eyes widen slightly before he shifted away from me, putting a little more space between us. The sudden distance made my chest tighten, but I tried to ignore it.

Regina suddenly stood up, stretching dramatically. "I just remembered, I need to grab something from my room," she announced, her voice a bit too cheerful. Before I could respond, she was already halfway out the door, leaving Kylian and me alone.

The room seemed to grow smaller, the silence between us thick and awkward. I stole a quick glance at him, only to find him staring intently at the screen, as if the movie had suddenly become the most fascinating thing in the world.

I cleared my throat, hoping to break the tension. "Uh, so... Pretty Woman, huh?" I said, my voice coming out more awkward than I intended. "I didn't peg you as a fan of romantic comedies."

He didn't look at me, but I saw the corner of his mouth twitch slightly. "It's not that bad," he replied, his tone casual, though it felt forced. "Regina wanted to watch it."

"Right," I murmured, my fingers fidgeting with the hem of my shirt. "She's into these kinds of movies. Always looking for the happy endings."

Kylian nodded, still not meeting my eyes. "Yeah, she's a sucker for that kind of stuff."

I bit my lip, the silence creeping back in, heavier this time. "So... how was your day?" I asked, grasping for anything to keep the conversation going.

"Fine," he said shortly. "Yours?"

"Same," I replied, feeling more and more like I was talking to a wall. "Just... classes, you know. Nothing exciting."

He hummed in acknowledgment, his eyes never leaving the screen. I could feel the awkwardness settling over us like a thick blanket, and it was suffocating.

Just when I thought I couldn't take it anymore, Regina returned. She glanced between the two of us, clearly sensing the tension. Kylian wasted no time in motioning for her to sit between us, and she obliged without question, settling in with a small smile.

That hurt. More than I wanted to admit. I felt like I'd just been pushed out, replaced by a buffer to avoid whatever uncomfortable feelings were brewing between us.

As the movie continued, I tried to focus on the screen, but all I could think about was how different things were now. How close we used to be, and how far apart we seemed now, even when we were sitting right next to each other.

I could feel the sting of tears beginning to well up in my eyes, blurring my vision. Why was he doing this? I couldn't stand it anymore—the distance, the coldness, the way he seemed determined to push me away. It was like there was an invisible wall between us, one that he had built brick by brick, and I was helpless to tear it down.

"I'm sorry, Regina," I mumbled, my voice trembling as I stood up from the couch. I tried to keep it together, forcing myself not to break down right there in front of them. I didn't want to make a scene. "I just... I need to go."

Regina looked at me, concern flashing in her eyes, but I couldn't bring myself to meet her gaze. I glanced quickly at Kylian, hoping for some kind of sign, anything that would tell me he cared. But all I saw was him turning his eyes toward me, his expression unreadable.

It was too much. I spun around and hurried to my room, barely holding it together until the door closed behind me. The moment I was alone, the dam broke. I collapsed onto my bed, burying my face in my pillow as the tears finally came, hot and uncontrollable.

Why did everything have to change? Why did he have to pull away just when I realized how much he meant to me? The ache in my chest grew sharper with every sob, the pain of his rejection cutting deeper than I'd ever expected.

This wasn't the Kylian I thought I knew. And maybe I wasn't the Kathleen I used to be either. But what hurt the most was the thought that maybe, just maybe, we were better off when we didn't care so much.

I wiped away the tears with the back of my hand, my resolve hardening with each passing second. If Kylian wanted to play this game, then fine—I could play it too. There was no way I was going to let him see how much he was getting to me.

I took a deep breath, trying to compose myself before heading back to the living room. Regina was still sitting on the couch, the movie playing in the background. I plastered on a smile as I walked over and settled onto the couch next to her, deliberately choosing the spot Kylian had just vacated.

"Regina," I started, keeping my tone light and casual, "did you notice how the male lead in *Pretty Woman* just *can't* seem to get his act together? It's like he's completely clueless about what's right in front of him."

Regina raised an eyebrow, catching the edge in my voice. "Yeah, it's frustrating to watch. He's so oblivious."

"Totally," I agreed, letting out a small, exaggerated sigh. "I mean, you'd think by now he'd have figured out what he really wants, instead of pushing everyone away and pretending like he doesn't care. But I guess some guys are just... hopeless."

Kylian shifted slightly on the couch, but I kept my gaze fixed on Regina, refusing to acknowledge his presence. He was sitting right there, pretending to be absorbed in the movie, but I knew he was listening. The tension in the room was thick enough to cut with a knife.

"You'd think," Regina said, playing along with a knowing smile, "that eventually they'd realize they're only making things harder on themselves."

I nodded, feeling a small sense of satisfaction as I continued. "Exactly. But, you know, some people just love to complicate things. Maybe they're afraid of what would happen if they were actually honest about their feelings."

Out of the corner of my eye, I saw Kylian stiffen, but he didn't say a word. Instead, after a few more seconds of silence, he stood up from the couch. "I, uh... I need to go see a friend," he mumbled, still avoiding my eyes as he addressed Regina.

He turned to leave, and just as he reached the door, he hesitated. For a brief moment, his gaze met mine, a flicker of something unreadable passing between us. But before I could decipher it, he was gone, the door clicking shut behind him.

I stared at the door, my heart pounding. What was his problem? And why, despite everything, did I still care so much?

As soon as the door clicked shut, Regina turned to me, her eyes wide with curiosity. "Did you see how he looked at you just now?" she asked, leaning in closer as if she was afraid of missing something.

I tried to shrug it off, though my heart was still racing. "Yeah, I saw. So what?" I replied, trying to sound nonchalant, but I could tell my voice wavered slightly.

Regina gave me a look that said she wasn't buying it. "So what? Come on, Kathleen, he looked at you like he was trying to figure something out. Like he couldn't decide whether to say something or not."

I rolled my eyes, even though part of me was replaying that moment over and over. "He's just being weird, Regina. One minute he's all distant and the next he's staring at me like that. I don't get him."

Regina smirked, clearly enjoying this more than I was. "Maybe he's trying to figure out how he really feels about you. Or maybe he's just scared."

"Scared?" I echoed, raising an eyebrow.

"Yeah," Regina said, crossing her arms and leaning back against the couch. "Guys like him—they're all confident and cool on the outside, but when it comes to actual feelings, they freak out. They don't know how to deal with it, so they act all hot and cold."

I let out a frustrated sigh. "I just don't understand why he's acting this way. First, he kisses me, and now he's avoiding me like the plague. It's like he's playing some kind of twisted game, and I'm the one stuck trying to figure out the rules."

Regina gave me a sympathetic look. "Maybe he's trying to protect himself. Or maybe he's trying to protect you. Who knows? But one thing's for sure—he's definitely not indifferent to you. You should've seen his face when he left. He looked like he didn't want to go."

I chewed on my bottom lip, unsure of what to say. I didn't want to admit that his confusing behavior was driving me crazy or that his lingering gaze had affected me more than I wanted to admit.

"So, what are you going to do?" Regina asked, her tone softening.

I shrugged, feeling the weight of it all. "I don't know. I guess I'll just... wait and see what he does next. I mean, he's the one who's been acting strange, not me."

Regina nodded, but her expression told me she was thinking something else. "Just be careful, Kathleen. Don't let him mess with your head too much."

I gave her a small, grateful smile. "Yeah, I'll try."

But even as I said it, I knew it wouldn't be that easy. Kylian was already in my head, whether I liked it or not.

Chapter 22

The next morning, I sat across from Regina at the small kitchen table, pushing my cereal around with my spoon. The air between us was thick with unspoken words, both of us caught up in our own thoughts. The awkwardness of the night before still lingered, and neither of us seemed eager to break the silence.

Suddenly, the door to Kylian's room creaked open. He stepped out, looking slightly disheveled, and made his way over to the counter. He grabbed a bowl and box of cereal without saying a word, the sound of the milk carton opening filling the quiet room.

I kept my eyes fixed on my breakfast, trying not to look too obvious in avoiding him. My heart was beating faster than it should've been, considering the circumstances.

As he poured the milk, there was a moment of hesitation, and then he looked up, his eyes meeting mine. "Morning," he said, his voice simple and casual, but it sent a jolt through me.

I forced myself to respond, trying to sound equally casual. "Morning." My voice came out softer than I intended, and I mentally kicked myself for it.

Kylian nodded, then picked up his bowl and headed back to his room, the door closing behind him with a quiet click.

As soon as he was out of sight, I let out a breath I didn't realize I'd been holding. My eyes darted to Regina, who was staring at me with a knowing look.

"You okay?" she asked, her tone laced with curiosity.

I shrugged, trying to downplay the sudden rush of emotions. "Yeah, I'm fine," I said, but the pounding in my chest told a different story.

Later that day, after a week of tense avoidance, I found myself walking past the pool again. I was lost in thought when I spotted Scott by the edge, chatting with a few teammates. I gave him a casual wave, and he waved back, strolling over to me with a friendly grin.

"Hey, Kathleen," Scott said, his tone light. "You're just the person I was hoping to run into."

"Hey, Scott. What's up?" I asked, trying to keep my tone neutral.

He leaned in slightly, lowering his voice as if sharing a secret. "So, Kylian's been talking about you a lot lately."

I raised an eyebrow, genuinely surprised. "Really? Like what kind of stuff?"

Scott shrugged, a playful glint in his eye. "Just that he's been thinking about you. Seems like he can't stop mentioning you during practice. It's kinda weird."

My heart skipped a beat. "Weird? Why?"

He chuckled. "Well, he never really opens up like that. You must have made quite an impression. He's been a bit distracted at practice, and we all know why now."

I frowned, feeling a mix of confusion and frustration. "Why does he keep talking about me if he won't even speak to me directly?"

Scott shrugged again, looking slightly perplexed himself. "That's the million-dollar question. I guess he's just not great with confronting things head-on. But hey, you should come by the pool this afternoon. It'd be a good chance to see what's up."

I hesitated, my mind racing with possibilities. "I'll think about it."

Scott nodded, understanding. "Alright. See you around."

As I walked away, my thoughts were consumed by Scott's words. Why was Kylian bringing me up so much if he couldn't face me? The unanswered questions left me feeling uneasy.

I decided to go to the practice, feeling a mix of curiosity and apprehension. As I arrived at the pool, Jared spotted me and approached with a grin.

"Hey, Kathleen! Want to time the swimmers today? We could use an extra hand."

I hesitated, remembering how awkward this could be with Kylian around. "I don't know, Jared. I'm not sure it's a good idea."

He persisted, giving me a playful nudge. "Come on, it'll be fine! You used to be great at it."

Eventually, I agreed, figuring it might be worth it to get a better understanding of the situation. I headed to the locker room to change into a swimsuit. It had been a while since I put one on, and slipping into it brought a flood of memories—mostly involving Kylian and our time together at the pool.

When I emerged in my swimsuit, I could feel the weight of Kylian's gaze. He looked a bit taken aback, but quickly turned his attention back to the practice. The swimmers were doing laps, and the rhythm of their strokes filled the air with a steady, calming noise. The sun was setting, casting a warm glow over the water, making everything look almost magical.

The practice itself went smoothly. Swimmers dove in, cut through the water with impressive speed, and the coach shouted encouragements and corrections. I did my best to time their laps accurately, jotting down numbers and trying to keep up with the fast-paced environment.

However, the real challenge was Kylian. Every time he swam past, he seemed to deliberately avoid making eye contact. When I called out his times, he barely acknowledged me, focusing intensely on his strokes. It was like I was a ghost, existing only in his peripheral vision.

"How's it going?" Jared asked, noticing my frown.

"Eh, could be better," I replied, trying to keep the frustration out of my voice. "Kylian's acting like I'm invisible."

Jared raised an eyebrow. "Really? That's odd. He usually gets along well with everyone."

I shrugged, feeling a tinge of annoyance. "Well, if you say so."

Throughout the rest of the practice, Kylian's behavior didn't change. He ignored my attempts to communicate and didn't even bother to check his times. It was as if he was putting up a wall between us, and no matter how hard I tried, I couldn't seem to break through.

As the session wound down, I couldn't help but feel a bit disheartened. The evening had been pleasant enough, but Kylian's aloofness had cast a shadow over it. I finished up with Jared, packed up my things, and headed out of the pool area, still wondering what was going on in Kylian's head.

I trudged through the falling snow to the bus stop, feeling the cold seep through my layers. The snowflakes danced gently in the air, creating a soft blanket over everything. I could see my breath puffing out in little clouds, each one reminding me of how cold I was.

When I reached the bus stop, I noticed Kylian sitting at the far end of the bench, engrossed in his phone. He seemed completely absorbed, not even acknowledging my presence. My heart sank as I saw him, and a mix of frustration and hurt bubbled up inside me.

I took a deep breath, trying to steady myself, but my emotions were too raw. With a determined stride, I walked over to him, my frustration boiling over. I stood there, arms crossed, as he continued to stare at his phone, oblivious to the world around him.

"Kylian," I said, my voice trembling with barely contained anger. "Is this how you're going to be now? Acting like I don't exist? It's been a week of this, and I can't even get a simple conversation out of you."

He glanced up briefly, his eyes meeting mine for a fleeting moment before he looked back at his phone. "Kathleen, I—"

"Save it," I cut him off. "I don't want to hear excuses. You're the one who kissed me, who made me believe there was something real between us. And now, you're treating me like I'm invisible. Do you have any idea how that feels? To be so completely ignored by someone you thought cared?"

His mouth opened slightly, as if he wanted to say something, but no words came out. He looked at me with an expression that was a mix of confusion and regret, but he didn't speak.

I shook my head, feeling the sting of tears pricking at the corners of my eyes. "I don't understand why you're doing this. If you didn't want to be with me, you could've just told me. But instead, you choose to act like I'm a ghost. It's cruel and it's confusing."

The silence stretched between us, heavy and uncomfortable. I could feel the tears threatening to fall, my vision blurring with the cold and my emotions. I blinked rapidly, trying to hold back the tears, but it was a losing battle.

Kylian looked like he wanted to reach out, to say something that might make things better, but the words seemed to fail him. I turned away, not trusting myself to speak further. My heart ached with each step as I walked to the end of the bus stop, the snowflakes gently landing on my shoulders.

The bus finally arrived, and I climbed aboard, my heart heavy with the weight of unspoken words and unresolved feelings. As I took a seat, I glanced out the window, watching the snow-covered streets blur by, my tears mingling with the falling snow.

The bus came to a halt, and I quickly descended the steps, trying to escape the chilly air and the even chillier tension between us. I picked up my pace, eager to get away from Kylian and the emotions that seemed too tangled to unravel.

"Kathleen!" His voice pierced through the cold air, making me stop in my tracks. I turned around slowly, feeling the sting of the tears I had tried so hard to hold back. My face must have looked like a mess—red and puffy, with trails of tears still glistening on my cheeks.

Kylian rushed towards me, his expression a mixture of desperation and anguish. "Kathleen, please—wait."

I shook my head, feeling the ache in my chest deepen. "What's the point, Kylian? What's there left to say?"

His face fell, and he took a deep breath, clearly struggling to find the right words. "I... I'm sorry. I've been avoiding you because I didn't know how to face you. I thought it would be easier if I just—"

"Easier for whom, Kylian?" I interrupted, my voice cracking with emotion. "It's been hell for me. You kissed me and then just shut me out. Do you know how much that hurts?"

He seemed to recoil from the force of my words but then stepped closer, his eyes locked onto mine. "Kathleen, I didn't mean to hurt you. I... I've been so confused. I thought that if I distanced myself, it would make things simpler, but it's only made it worse. I... I care about you so much, and I can't stand seeing you hurt because of me."

I looked at him, my heart aching with a mixture of anger and sadness. "Then why have you been acting like this? Why couldn't you just talk to me?"

He looked pained, and for a moment, I saw the vulnerability in his eyes. "I was afraid. Afraid that if I told you how I truly felt, I'd mess everything up even more. But it's killing me to see you like this."

The silence stretched between us, heavy with unspoken words and raw emotions. I opened my mouth to respond, but nothing came out. I was too overwhelmed, too hurt to find the right words. My chest tightened, and the lump in my throat made it hard to speak.

In frustration and sadness, I simply shook my head. "I... I don't know what to say."

I turned on my heel, my heart pounding as I walked away. Kylian's voice called out to me, raw and pleading, but I couldn't turn back. I felt the tears welling up again as I walked into the building, the door closing behind me with a final, decisive thud. I entered without another word, the emotional weight of the day feeling like it was pressing down on my very soul.

As I shut the door to my room, the dam finally broke. The tears I had been fighting back since our encounter came rushing down in uncontrollable streams. I sank onto my bed, feeling the weight of my emotions pressing down on me like a heavy, suffocating blanket.

Why couldn't he have just told me how he felt from the start? Why did he have to make me suffer through this confusion and pain? My mind raced with questions, each one more painful than the last. I buried my face in my hands, trying to muffle my sobs as the memories of our recent interactions played on a loop in my mind.

The way he had avoided me, the cold distance he put between us—it all felt like a cruel game. Did he really think that shutting me out would be easier for either of us? Every moment we had spent avoiding each other, every silent treatment, every unspoken word seemed to have only deepened the wound.

I thought about his confession on the bus. The vulnerability in his eyes, the way he struggled to express his feelings—it was clear he was conflicted and hurting too. But why did it have to come to this? Why did he let it get so out of hand? The idea that he cared about me was bittersweet. It was comforting to know that he felt something, but it also made the pain of his absence even more acute.

The questions spun around in my mind like a storm, leaving me feeling lost and raw. I couldn't understand why he had chosen to hurt me this way when all I wanted was honesty and clarity. His actions had left me feeling like I was drifting in a sea of uncertainty, and the emotional turmoil was overwhelming.

As the tears finally began to slow, I lay down on my bed, feeling drained and emotionally spent. I knew I needed to sort through my feelings and find a way to heal from this. But for now, all I could do was let the tears flow and try to make sense of the tangled mess of emotions swirling inside me.

Chapter 23

The next morning, I found myself at the pool, seeking solace in the calming embrace of the water. I had come here not just to escape but to find a moment of peace amid the chaos of my thoughts. As I floated on my back, I spread my arms and legs out like a starfish, letting the water support my body and cradle me gently.

The pool was serene, its surface reflecting the early morning light in a shimmering dance of blues and silvers. The water felt cool and refreshing against my skin, a stark contrast to the storm of emotions I had been grappling with. Each slow, deliberate breath I took was a soothing balm to my frayed nerves, the rhythmic rise and fall of my chest matching the gentle lapping of the water around me.

I gazed up at the clear, open sky, feeling the weight of my worries lift slightly with each breath. The simple act of floating, suspended between earth and sky, provided a rare sense of calm. My mind, for a brief moment, was free from the relentless whirl of doubts and sadness. The water's buoyancy was like a silent partner in my quest for tranquility, offering a temporary escape from the emotional strain.

The slight ripples created by my movements made small waves that caressed my skin, adding a sense of gentle motion to the stillness. I let my thoughts drift as I focused on the rhythmic patterns of the water and the soft sounds of my breathing. The isolation of the pool and the soothing nature of the exercise provided a much-needed reprieve, allowing me to center myself and regain some semblance of calm.

In that quiet, suspended moment, it felt as though the world outside had paused, giving me a precious chance to recharge and reflect. The peaceful solitude of the water offered a brief respite from the tangled emotions that had been consuming me.

As I floated in the pool, lost in my thoughts, I suddenly heard a familiar voice call out my name. My heart skipped a beat, and I slowly straightened up in the water, only to see Kylian standing at the edge of the pool. I didn't want to talk, not now, not after everything. "I don't want to talk right now," I said firmly, hoping he would get the message.

But he didn't. Instead, he stepped into the pool, wading through the water until he was right in front of me. His presence was overwhelming, but I held my ground, trying to keep the distance between us.

"Kathleen, please," he started, his voice thick with emotion. "I can't keep this inside anymore. I've been acting like a complete idiot, and I know it. I've been so scared of what I'm feeling for you... that I've been pushing you away, but it's only made things worse."

I stayed silent, just watching him, my heart pounding in my chest. His words were everything I had wanted to hear, but I didn't know how to respond. It felt like the walls I had built around my heart were crumbling, leaving me vulnerable and exposed.

"I tried to ignore it, to pretend that what I feel for you isn't real, but every time I see you, it's like I'm drawn to you all over again. I'm done pretending, Kathleen. I'm done running away from this."

He reached out, gently taking my hand in his. I tried to pull away, but his grip was firm yet tender. Before I could say anything, he pulled me closer, his eyes searching mine for any sign of hesitation. Then, without another word, he leaned in and kissed me. It was soft, hesitant at first, but then it deepened, and I felt everything he had been holding back pour into that kiss.

When he finally pulled back, he looked at me with a tenderness that made my heart ache. "You're all I think about," he whispered, his voice full of sincerity. "I don't want to lose you, Kathleen. I'm sorry for everything, but I can't imagine not having you in my life."

I stared at him, my thoughts a tangled mess. "I... I..." I stammered, trying to find the right words, but nothing came out. Overwhelmed, I turned and started to walk away, needing a moment to process everything. But before I could get too far, he caught my hand again.

"Please don't go," he murmured, his voice almost pleading. "Stay with me."

His words, so simple yet so full of meaning, made my heart clench. I looked back at him, seeing the vulnerability in his eyes, and I knew he was being completely honest. But I couldn't handle it all at once. I gently pulled my hand from his grip and left the pool, not daring to look back, my mind and heart in turmoil.

As I walked into the locker room, my mind was a whirlwind of emotions. Why was I so scared to trust him? If I felt the same way about him, why couldn't I just let myself believe that he meant every word? I shook my head, trying to push those thoughts away as I began to change out of my swimsuit.

Just then, I overheard a group of girls chatting nearby. Their voices were hushed, but I could still make out what they were saying. I froze, listening intently.

"Did you see Kylian earlier?" one of them giggled. "He's been flirting with everyone lately. I swear, he was all over that new girl last week."

"Yeah, right? He's such a player," another girl chimed in. "He thinks he can just flash that smile and get away with anything."

"Honestly, I wouldn't be surprised if he's seeing someone else on the side. He's got that 'bad boy' vibe, and you know how those types are," the first girl added with a smirk.

I felt a surge of anger rise within me. So, this was who Kylian really was? Despite everything he'd said, despite the way he'd kissed me and told me I was all he thought about, he was still the same flirtatious guy who couldn't be trusted. I clenched my fists, my heart pounding with a mix of fury and disappointment.

Was he just playing me this whole time? Making me believe that I was special when, in reality, he was still entertaining other girls? I couldn't believe how foolish I'd been to think that maybe, just maybe, he'd changed.

Furious, I slammed my locker shut, the noise startling the girls who quickly fell silent. I stormed out of the locker room, my mind set. Kylian might have claimed that I was important to him, but if he thought he could keep playing games, he was sorely mistaken. This was a side of him I had no intention of dealing with again.

As I walked into the locker room, my mind was a whirlwind of emotions. Why was I so scared to trust him? If I felt the same way about him, why couldn't I just let myself believe that he meant every word? I shook my head, trying to push those thoughts away as I began to change out of my swimsuit.

Just then, I overheard a group of girls chatting nearby. Their voices were hushed, but I could still make out what they were saying. I froze, listening intently.

"Did you see Kylian earlier?" one of them giggled. "He's been flirting with everyone lately. I swear, he was all over that new girl last week."

"Yeah, right? He's such a player," another girl chimed in. "He thinks he can just flash that smile and get away with anything."

"Honestly, I wouldn't be surprised if he's seeing someone else on the side. He's got that 'bad boy' vibe, and you know how those types are," the first girl added with a smirk.

I felt a surge of anger rise within me. So, this was who Kylian really was? Despite everything he'd said, despite the way he'd kissed me and told me I was all he thought about, he was still the same flirtatious guy who couldn't be trusted. I clenched my fists, my heart pounding with a mix of fury and disappointment.

Was he just playing me this whole time? Making me believe that I was special when, in reality, he was still entertaining other girls? I couldn't believe how foolish I'd been to think that maybe, just maybe, he'd changed.

Furious, I slammed my locker shut, the noise startling the girls who quickly fell silent. I stormed out of the locker room, my mind set. Kylian might have claimed that I was important to him, but if he thought he could keep playing games, he was sorely mistaken. This was a side of him I had no intention of dealing with again.

As I stormed out of the locker room, trying to keep my emotions in check, I felt a presence beside me. I turned to see one of the girls from earlier walking up to me. Her expression was a mix of concern and curiosity.

"Hey, are you okay?" she asked, her voice soft, almost hesitant.

I didn't answer, too focused on keeping the tears from spilling over. My throat felt tight, and I couldn't trust myself to speak without breaking down.

She shifted awkwardly, as if trying to decide whether to say something more. Finally, she took a deep breath and confessed, "I just wanted to let you know... at the Halloween party... I, um, I spent the night with Kylian. We've been kind of close ever since, and I really like him."

Her words hit me like a punch to the gut. The tears I had been fighting back were now threatening to spill over, but I swallowed hard, determined not to break down in front of her. I couldn't believe what I was hearing. So, it wasn't just rumors—Kylian had actually been with someone else, despite everything he had said to me.

I forced a smile, though it felt like my heart was shattering into a million pieces. "That's great," I managed to say, my voice barely above a whisper. "We were just friends, so... the way is all clear for you."

Her face lit up with excitement, completely oblivious to the turmoil I was experiencing inside. "Really? Oh my gosh, that's such a relief! Thanks, Kathleen!" she exclaimed, her eyes sparkling with happiness.

I nodded, barely able to keep my composure. She smiled brightly and quickly walked away, probably eager to share the news with her friends. As soon as she was out of sight, I couldn't hold back any longer. The tears I had been holding in finally spilled over, hot and heavy, as I leaned against the wall, my heart aching with betrayal and loss.

I had told her she was free to pursue Kylian, but the truth was, I felt anything but free.

As I stormed out of the locker room, trying to keep my emotions in check, I felt a presence beside me. I turned to see one of the girls from earlier walking up to me. Her expression was a mix of concern and curiosity.

"Hey, are you okay?" she asked, her voice soft, almost hesitant.

I didn't answer, too focused on keeping the tears from spilling over. My throat felt tight, and I couldn't trust myself to speak without breaking down.

She shifted awkwardly, as if trying to decide whether to say something more. Finally, she took a deep breath and confessed, "I just wanted to let you know... at the Halloween party... I, um, I spent the night with Kylian. We've been kind of close ever since, and I really like him."

Her words hit me like a punch to the gut. The tears I had been fighting back were now threatening to spill over, but

I swallowed hard, determined not to break down in front of her. I couldn't believe what I was hearing. So, it wasn't just rumors—Kylian had actually been with someone else, despite everything he had said to me.

I forced a smile, though it felt like my heart was shattering into a million pieces. "That's great," I managed to say, my voice barely above a whisper. "We were just friends, so... the way is all clear for you."

Her face lit up with excitement, completely oblivious to the turmoil I was experiencing inside. "Really? Oh my gosh, that's such a relief! Thanks, Kathleen!" she exclaimed, her eyes sparkling with happiness.

I nodded, barely able to keep my composure. She smiled brightly and quickly walked away, probably eager to share the news with her friends. As soon as she was out of sight, I couldn't hold back any longer. The tears I had been holding in finally spilled over, hot and heavy, as I leaned against the wall, my heart aching with betrayal and loss.

I had told her she was free to pursue Kylian, but the truth was, I felt anything but free.

I grabbed my phone with shaky hands, scrolling through my contacts until I found Caleb's name. My heart was still pounding from the conversation in the locker room, but I needed a distraction—someone who could help me clear my mind, even if just for a little while. Caleb had always been a good friend, someone I could rely on when things got tough.

I pressed the call button, and after a few rings, he picked up. "Hey, Kathleen! What's up?" His voice was warm and familiar, instantly soothing some of the tension in my chest.

"Hi, Caleb," I replied, trying to steady my voice. "I was just wondering... are you free right now? I could really use some company."

There was a brief pause on the other end, and I could hear him shuffling around, likely checking his schedule. "Yeah, I'm free. What's going on? You sound a bit off."

I hesitated, not wanting to get into the details over the phone. "It's... it's just been a rough day. I don't really want to be alone right now."

He didn't press for more information, which I appreciated. Caleb had always known when to give me space. "I get it. I'll head over to your dorm, okay? We can hang out, talk, or just do nothing if that's what you need."

A small smile tugged at my lips. "That sounds perfect. Thanks, Caleb. I really appreciate it."

"Hey, don't mention it. I'll be there in a few minutes," he reassured me. "Just hang in there, okay?"

"Okay," I whispered, feeling a bit of relief. "See you soon."

We hung up, and I took a deep breath, trying to push away the lingering hurt from earlier. Caleb's coming over would at least help me get through this evening. I put my phone away and started heading back to the dorm, hoping that seeing him would help me find some clarity amidst the confusion and pain.

As soon as I pushed the door open to the dorm, I noticed Kylian sitting on the edge of the couch, his face a mix of frustration and determination. My heart skipped a beat, but I quickly pushed the feeling down. I wasn't ready for this—whatever this was.

"Kathleen, we need to talk," he said, standing up as soon as he saw me.

I shook my head, walking past him towards my room. "There's nothing to talk about, Kylian."

He followed, his voice pleading. "Please, just hear me out. I know things have been messed up, but—"

"Messed up?" I interrupted, turning to face him with a bitter laugh. "That's an understatement."

He looked at me, his eyes searching mine as if trying to find something that had already been lost. "Kathleen, I—"

"No, Kylian," I cut him off, my voice sharp. "Let's stop pretending like any of this mattered. It didn't. I was never interested in you, okay? Whatever you thought this was, you were wrong."

The words tasted bitter as they left my mouth, and I could see the shock register on his face. He took a step back, as if I had physically hit him. The hurt in his eyes was undeniable, but I forced myself to hold my ground, even though every part of me wanted to take it all back.

"I'm sorry... I didn't realize you felt that way," he muttered, his voice barely audible. He looked down at the floor, the defeat in his posture clear.

"Yeah, well, now you do," I said coldly, though my heart ached seeing him like this. "So let's just move on, okay? This whole thing was a mistake."

Kylian's jaw tightened, and for a moment, he didn't say anything. The silence between us grew heavy, the weight of unsaid words hanging in the air. He opened his mouth as if to say something, but nothing came out. It was like he couldn't find the words—or maybe he realized there was nothing left to say.

I took a deep breath, trying to steady myself. "You're such a... such a jerk, Kylian," I added, my voice trembling with the effort to keep my composure. "I can't believe I ever thought you were different."

Just as I was about to turn away, Regina appeared from her room, her eyes wide with concern. "What's going on here?" she asked, stepping between us.

Before I could respond, there was a knock at the door. I glanced at Kylian one last time, seeing the pain etched on his face, and a part of me almost faltered. But then I remembered everything—everything he'd put me through—and I pushed it aside.

Regina moved to answer the door, and I knew who it would be before she even opened it. Caleb stood there, smiling warmly as soon as he saw me.

"Hey," I greeted him, forcing a smile onto my face. "Perfect timing."

Kylian's expression shattered as he realized who was at the door. I could see the devastation in his eyes, but I ignored it, focusing on Caleb instead.

"We should go," I said, linking my arm with Caleb's. "I need some fresh air."

"Sure thing," Caleb replied, oblivious to the tension in the room.

As we walked towards the door, I glanced back one last time. Kylian was standing there, his expression a mixture of heartbreak and regret. His shoulders were slumped, and it was clear that my words had cut deeper than I'd intended.

For a moment, our eyes met, and I almost stopped in my tracks. But then I reminded myself of everything that had happened, everything I'd heard, and I forced myself to keep going. Without another word, I turned away, walking out the door with Caleb, leaving Kylian behind.

Chapter 24

Caleb and I walked through the chilly November evening, the cold biting at our cheeks as we made our way to a small café he mentioned earlier. The warm glow of the streetlights cast long shadows as we moved, the sound of our footsteps muffled by the freshly fallen leaves.

He glanced over at me, his breath visible in the cold air. "You seem a little off tonight. Want to talk about it?"

I hesitated, not wanting to dive into the tangled mess that was my mind right now. "It's nothing serious," I said, forcing a smile. "Just a bit of school stress, you know how it is."

Caleb chuckled softly. "Yeah, I get it. But you know, you don't have to pretend with me, Kathleen. I'm here if you ever need to vent."

His words were genuine, and I couldn't help but feel a warmth spread through my chest that had nothing to do with the café we were approaching. Caleb had always been kind, attentive, and easy to talk to. It made me wonder why I had been so hung up on Kylian in the first place.

"Thanks, Caleb. That means a lot," I replied, my voice soft as we stepped inside the cozy café. The warmth hit us immediately, along with the comforting aroma of freshly brewed coffee and pastries.

We found a small table by the window, and I took off my coat, settling into the comfy chair. Caleb ordered us two hot chocolates with extra whipped cream—something he knew I loved—and I couldn't help but smile at how thoughtful he was.

As we waited, Caleb leaned in slightly, his blue eyes locking onto mine. "So, really... What's going on? You've been quieter than usual."

I sighed, looking down at the table as I tried to come up with an answer that didn't involve Kylian. "It's just... things have been weird lately. I'm trying to figure out some stuff, that's all."

Caleb nodded, his expression understanding. "Life can be messy sometimes, huh? But you don't have to go through it alone. I'm always here if you need someone to talk to—or just to hang out."

His sincerity made my heart ache in a different way. Why was I still thinking about Kylian when Caleb was right here, being the kind of person I knew I deserved?

"I appreciate that, Caleb," I said, my voice barely above a whisper. I looked up at him, our eyes meeting, and for a moment, I wondered if this was how things were supposed to feel—simple, warm, and safe.

He reached across the table, his fingers brushing against mine. "I've always enjoyed spending time with you, Kathleen. You make everything feel... easier, I guess."

I smiled, my heart fluttering at his words. "I feel the same way."

The hot chocolates arrived, and we both took a sip, the warmth spreading through us. Caleb's smile was contagious, and I found myself laughing at his jokes and stories, feeling a sense of lightness I hadn't felt in days.

But as we talked, as easy as it was to be with Caleb, I couldn't stop the thoughts of Kylian from creeping back into my mind. His hurt expression when I'd left with Caleb, the way he had looked at me before I turned away—it was all still there, lingering in the back of my thoughts.

Why was it so hard to let go of him? Caleb was right here, everything I could ask for, yet a part of me was still stuck on Kylian, on the pain and confusion that came with him.

As we walked back towards the dorms, Caleb's hand occasionally brushed against mine, and I wondered why I couldn't just let myself be happy with him. He was sweet, caring, and made me feel good about myself. But deep down, no matter how hard I tried, I couldn't shake the feelings I still had for Kylian.

"You seem lost in thought again," Caleb said, nudging me playfully as we stopped in front of my dorm.

"Yeah," I admitted with a small laugh, "just a lot on my mind."

He smiled softly, brushing a strand of hair from my face. "Whatever it is, I hope you figure it out soon. You deserve to be happy, Kathleen."

"Thanks, Caleb. That means a lot," I whispered, my heart heavy with the confusion of it all.

As he leaned in to give me a gentle hug, I couldn't help but wonder why my heart still yearned for something—or someone—that seemed so out of reach.

As I walked into the dorm, the sight that greeted me made my heart sink. Kylian was there, laughing and chatting with a girl I didn't recognize. They seemed to be having a great time, and my heart twisted painfully as I saw him lean in to give her a kiss.

My breath caught in my throat, and I froze for a moment. I wanted to turn away, but my feet carried me toward my room, each step feeling heavier than the last. The image of him with her burned into my mind, intensifying the ache in my chest.

When I reached my room, Regina was sitting on my bed, her face serious. She glanced up at me, her eyes filled with a mix of frustration and concern.

"Kathleen, can we talk?" she asked, her voice firm.

I nodded, too exhausted to say anything. I slumped onto my bed, feeling the weight of the day bearing down on me.

Regina sat up straight, her eyes locking onto mine. "You know, you really messed things up with Kylian."

I looked at her, confusion and hurt mingling in my expression. "What do you mean?"

"He's been a mess since that night. You know, the one when you walked out on him?" Regina said, her voice tinged with frustration. "He's been acting out, hanging out with anyone who'll pay him attention. It's like he's trying to distract himself from what happened."

I swallowed hard, feeling the sting of her words. "I didn't mean to hurt him. I just... I didn't know what to do."

Regina's expression softened a bit, but her tone remained serious. "Kathleen, I know you're confused. But you can't just ignore the way you've impacted him. He's not the same since you started avoiding him. He actually cared about you, and now he's trying to numb that pain."

I felt a lump in my throat as I tried to process her words. "I didn't think it would be this complicated. I was just trying to deal with my own feelings."

Regina sighed, her frustration evident. "Well, it's complicated because you're not the only one involved. He's been trying to move on, but every time he sees you, it's like he's reminded of what he lost. You need to figure out what you want and communicate it clearly, or things are just going to keep getting worse."

I bit my lip, struggling to hold back the tears. "I don't know what to say to him. I'm just so confused about everything."

Regina stood up, giving me a sympathetic look. "Sometimes, you have to take a step back and really think about what's best for everyone involved. I know it's hard, but it's the only way to resolve this."

She left me alone with my thoughts, the silence in the room feeling like a heavy weight pressing down on me. I lay back on my bed, staring at the ceiling, trying to make sense of everything that had happened. The image of Kylian with that girl, combined with Regina's words, left me feeling more lost than ever.

Why had things become so tangled? Why did my heart still ache for someone who seemed to be moving on so easily? The questions swirled in my mind, unanswered and heavy, as I tried to navigate the storm of my emotions.

I stared at the medal hanging on the corner of my wardrobe, the one Kylian had given me. Its gleam seemed almost to mock the turmoil inside me, a symbol of something I had once cherished but now only reminded me of my mistakes.

A faint, sad smile tugged at my lips as I thought about how I had let fear and confusion drive me to lie to him. Why did I say I didn't share the same feelings when, deep down, I knew it wasn't true? Why did I let my insecurities and doubts push me to be so cruel? The memory of his broken expression, the pain in his eyes as he stood there, helpless and vulnerable, cut through me like a knife.

I felt a pang of guilt, wondering how I had managed to hurt him so deeply. Why did I allow myself to act out of anger and fear instead of confronting my feelings honestly? The weight of my actions pressed down on me, making it hard to breathe.

I thought about how he must have felt—alone and rejected, and how I had contributed to his pain. I regretted the harsh words, the lies, and the distance I had put between us. It was as if I had taken a beautiful, delicate thing and smashed it to pieces without a second thought.

Lying there, my eyes fixed on the medal, I realized the depth of my mistake. I wished I could go back and undo the hurt I had caused, but I knew that wasn't possible. All I could do now was confront my own feelings and try to find a way to make things right, if that was even possible. The journey ahead seemed daunting, but I knew I had to start somewhere, and it began with acknowledging the pain I had caused and facing my own heart's true desires.

In the days that followed, Kylian seemed to move on with a new woman every week. It was as if he was drowning out his feelings with fleeting relationships, and his dedication to swimming, once so intense, appeared to wane. Each time I saw him, he was with someone new, his laughter and easy demeanor masking the pain I knew he must be feeling.

Every time I tried to approach him, he shut me out with a coldness that stung more than I expected. It was as if he had built an impenetrable wall around himself, refusing to let me in or acknowledge the history we shared. It was clear that both of us were suffering, each in our own way. I could see the hurt in his eyes, even as he tried to put on a brave face, and it mirrored the ache I felt inside.

I attempted to bridge the gap between us, to talk things out and find some form of resolution, but each effort was met with a firm rejection. It felt as though every time I reached out, I was met with the same, unyielding silence. The distance between us grew wider, leaving a chasm filled with unspoken words and unresolved emotions.

The sight of him with someone else was like a fresh wound, constantly reopening the pain of my own mistakes. It hurt to see him trying to move on, to see him so distracted by new relationships that his passion for swimming seemed to fade. It was as if he was desperately searching for something to fill the void left by our broken connection, and it only made the situation more painful for both of us.

I knew that both of us were suffering, but neither of us seemed ready to confront it. We were both lost in our own ways, trying to navigate through the mess of emotions and regrets we had created. The silence between us spoke volumes, but the hurt remained unaddressed, a constant reminder of the love we had and the pain of losing it.

As the days passed, I found myself spending more and more time with Caleb. He was a steady presence in my life, someone who listened without judgment and offered comfort during the turbulent times. We spent hours talking, sharing laughs, and finding solace in each other's company. Caleb's support was a balm for my aching heart, and his kindness helped distract me from the relentless thoughts of Kylian.

Caleb and I grew closer, and though part of me wondered if I was just using him as a means to forget Kylian, there was genuine affection between us. He made me feel valued and appreciated, something that had been sorely missing lately. We found small joys in simple activities, like grabbing coffee or watching movies together, which helped to fill the void left by Kylian's absence.

On the other hand, Kylian seemed to immerse himself in a series of new relationships. It was as if he was attempting to fill the gap left by our breakup with fleeting encounters and superficial connections. He appeared to be on a quest for distraction, with each new woman becoming a temporary escape from his own emotions. I could see him trying to move on, but it seemed like he was just as lost as I was, seeking solace in others while struggling to confront his own feelings.

It was painful to see him with someone new each week, as if he was desperately trying to prove something to himself or to me. His relationships were brief and seemingly superficial, a stark contrast to the depth of what we once had. While he was out trying to forget me with someone else, I was grappling with my own regrets and attempts to move on with Caleb's support.

In our separate ways, we were both trying to navigate the aftermath of our breakup, each of us seeking solace and distraction while struggling to deal with the emotions we had left unresolved. The pain of seeing Kylian move on, combined with my own efforts to find closure and healing, created a complex emotional landscape that we were both trying to manage.

The snow fell gently, covering the streets in a soft, white blanket. I sprinted to the bus stop, my breath visible in the cold air. As I reached the shelter, I spotted Kylian standing at the other end of the bench, his eyes fixed on the falling snow. Despite the cold, I could feel the heat of my emotions rising. I hesitated, unsure whether to approach him or let him remain in his solitude.

We waited in silence, the only sounds being the occasional gust of wind and the soft crunch of snow underfoot. I stole glances at him, watching as he stood with his hands stuffed in his coat pockets. His face was partially obscured by the collar of his jacket, but I could see the tense set of his jaw and the furrow of his brow. He seemed lost in thought, his gaze distant and contemplative.

After a few moments of internal struggle, I broke the silence, my voice tentative and fragile. "Kylian... can we talk?"

He looked at me, his eyes betraying a mix of pain and resignation. "I don't think there's much to say," he replied quietly. "You've made it clear that you're not interested in me. I thought I was moving on, but seeing you here, I just... I don't know anymore."

His words stung, each one like a small cut that reopened the old wounds. I took a deep breath, trying to steady my voice. "I didn't mean to hurt you. I just... I didn't know how to handle everything that was happening. I was scared, and I didn't know what I wanted."

Kylian's gaze softened momentarily, but then he shook his head, a hint of sadness in his eyes. "I understand. But right now, I need some space. I need to figure things out on my own."

He took a few steps away from me, his movements slow and deliberate. As he walked toward the street, the snowflakes gathered on his shoulders, adding to the melancholy of the scene. I watched him go, feeling a pang of regret and heartache.

The bus arrived, but I remained where I was, unable to move or take my eyes off Kylian's retreating figure. He was walking away, and though I wanted to call out to him, to tell him how sorry I was and how much he meant to me, the words caught in my throat.

As Kylian disappeared into the distance, I felt a deep, aching emptiness. The snow continued to fall, each flake a reminder of the distance that had grown between us. I climbed onto the bus with a heavy heart, the reality of our fractured relationship sinking in with each passing moment. The silence of the bus ride was filled with the echo of our unresolved feelings and the unspoken words that lingered between us.

As I sat on the bus, staring out at the snow-covered streets, the weight of my regret settled heavily on my shoulders. I felt the cold, biting through my coat, but it was nothing compared to the chill of my realization. I had been so consumed by fear and uncertainty that I hadn't told Kylian the truth—how I truly felt about him.

I had let my fears and insecurities dictate my actions, pushing him away when all I really wanted was to be close to him. The truth was, despite everything that had happened, I loved him. I loved him deeply, and it hurt to think that he might never know just how much he meant to me.

The snow outside blurred into a white haze, mirroring the confusion and regret swirling in my mind. I replayed our conversation in my head, wishing I could go back and say the words I had kept hidden for so long. Words that could have changed everything.

The realization hit me like a ton of bricks—Kylian had been right there, so close, and I had pushed him away because I was too scared to face my own feelings. I had thought I was protecting myself, but all I did was build a wall between us.

As the bus rumbled forward, I made a silent promise to myself. If I ever got another chance, I would tell him how I felt. I would be honest, even if it meant risking more heartache. I had to, because living with the regret of never having said those words was far worse than any fear I had about opening up.

The snow continued to fall, each flake a reminder of the love I had neglected to express. I stared out at the passing landscape, hoping for another chance to make things right with Kylian.

Epilogue

As I walked out of school, the chill of the late afternoon seeped through my coat. I pulled my scarf tighter around my neck and rubbed my hands together, trying to fend off the cold. My heart was pounding, not just from the brisk air but from the weight of my resolve.

When I reached the bus stop, I spotted Kylian standing a few feet away. He looked lost in thought, his face set in a contemplative expression. I felt a rush of determination, mingled with fear, as I sprinted towards him. My boots slipped on the icy pavement, and I stumbled but caught myself, determined not to let this chance slip away.

"Kylian!" I called out, my voice catching in my throat as I finally reached him.

He turned, surprise and something softer—maybe concern—flashing in his eyes. "Kathleen? What's wrong?"

Tears pricked at the corners of my eyes, and I struggled to find the right words. "I—I need to talk to you. I'm so sorry for everything. I've been an idiot, and I've been trying to pretend like my feelings don't matter, but they do. I love you, Kylian. I've been so scared to admit it, but it's true."

His expression softened, and I saw a flicker of hope in his eyes. He took a step towards me, his gaze locked on mine. "Kathleen, I—"

Before he could say more, a girl approached, her hand slipping into the crook of Kylian's arm. She smiled at him and then turned to me with a look of concern. "Is everything okay?"

I looked from Kylian to her, my heart breaking. He looked between us, and I saw the internal struggle in his eyes. He was torn, but I could no longer stand the pain of watching him be with someone else.

Without another word, I turned on my heel and walked away. My heart felt like it was shattering with every step, and the tears I had been holding back streamed freely down my face. I heard Kylian call out to me, but I didn't stop. The cold wind stung my cheeks, but it was nothing compared to the ache in my chest.

As I reached the bus stop, I tried to steady my breathing, my hands trembling as I wiped away my tears. The snow began to fall again, each flake a cold reminder of the moment I had let slip through my fingers. The bus pulled up, and I climbed on, feeling as though I was leaving a piece of my heart behind in the snow.

The snow had started falling more heavily by the time I reached the lake, and the cold air seemed to seep right through my clothes. The lake, partially frozen, lay before me like a giant, shimmering mirror, reflecting the overcast sky. I walked carefully across the icy path, my boots crunching softly with each step. I reached a spot by the water's edge, where the ice was thin and the snow hadn't settled, and sat down with a heavy sigh.

The stillness of the lake was almost unbearable, mirroring the turmoil within me. I felt an overwhelming sense of despair, and the tears I'd been holding back fell freely now. I couldn't stay at home, not with everything feeling so heavy and painful. I needed to be here, where Kylian and I had shared one of the few truly peaceful moments we'd had together.

I closed my eyes, letting the memories wash over me. I remembered the first time I met Kylian Rivera. It was at a school event, a friendly gathering that I had approached with a mix of hope and apprehension. Kylian had been there with his usual confident demeanor, surrounded by friends and chatting effortlessly. But what struck me most was the way he seemed to glide through the crowd with an air of arrogance.

I had heard stories about him, stories that painted him as a classic rich kid—entitled, out of touch, and disdainful of those not in his social circle. When I finally had to interact with him, my instincts confirmed my initial thoughts. He'd been charming but superficial, and there was an air of condescension in his smile that had instantly put me off. I had written him off as someone I wanted nothing to do with, convinced that our worlds were too different, our values too misaligned.

But now, as I sat by the lake, I thought about how dramatically things had changed. All those initial judgments had crumbled, replaced by feelings I hadn't anticipated. Kylian had come to mean so much to me, despite the rocky start. His genuine moments of kindness, the way he had opened up to me, and how he had managed to break through my tough exterior—all of it had led to a deep connection I couldn't deny.

Yet, despite the love that had blossomed between us, I found myself sitting here alone, crying over the mess we'd become. The irony was almost unbearable. Kylian, who had once seemed so distant and unapproachable, had become the person I wanted most in my life. And now, I was facing the reality that we were both suffering because of my own mistakes and fears.

The four months of this intense, complicated experience were dragging on, each day feeling heavier than the last. All I could think about was how desperately I wanted things to be different, to find a way to mend the rift between us, and to make things right. But for now, all I could do was sit by the lake, lost in my thoughts and the snowy silence, waiting for the storm inside me to pass.

I was lost in my memories, trying to make sense of everything that had happened between us. The lake, with its icy surface and the gentle snowfall, seemed like the perfect backdrop for my turmoil. As I sat there, feeling more isolated than ever, I suddenly felt a presence beside me. I turned to see Kylian sitting down next to me, the familiar scent of his cologne mixing with the crisp winter air.

I blinked in surprise, the tears still fresh on my cheeks. "How did you know I'd be here?" I asked, my voice trembling slightly.

Kylian shrugged, his expression serious. "I didn't know you'd be here. I just felt like coming here. Something about this place... it just felt right."

We sat in silence for a moment, the quiet broken only by the sound of the wind and the occasional crunch of snow underfoot. I glanced at him, trying to gauge his emotions.

"I've been an idiot," he finally said, his voice soft but laden with emotion. "I pushed you away because I didn't want to deal with my feelings. But the truth is, I can't stop thinking about you. I've been trying to distract myself with other people, but it's all just a mess. I realize now that I was wrong."

He looked at me, his eyes searching mine for a reaction. "Kathleen, I'm not good at this—at expressing how I feel. But... I love you. I didn't want to admit it, but it's the truth. I've been trying to avoid facing it, but I can't ignore it any longer."

I was taken aback, unable to find the words. The shock of his confession left me speechless. He sighed deeply, looking away. "I should go," he said quietly, starting to stand up.

Without thinking, I leapt to my feet and dashed after him. My heart raced, and the cold air stung my cheeks, but I didn't care. I caught up with him just as he was about to walk away, grabbing his arm gently.

"Kylian," I said, my voice breaking with emotion, "I'm so sorry for everything. I was scared and didn't know how to handle my feelings. But... I love you too. I always have, even when I didn't want to admit it."

His eyes widened in surprise as he looked at me. Before he could say anything, I leaned in and kissed him, pouring all my emotions into that single, desperate gesture. His lips were warm against mine, a stark contrast to the cold around us.

When we finally pulled away, I could see the relief and hope in his eyes. "I've been waiting for you to say that," he whispered, a smile tugging at his lips.

I smiled through my tears, feeling a wave of warmth and happiness wash over me. "Me too," I said softly, "me too."

As we stood there, the snow continuing to fall around us, everything felt right. The confusion and heartache seemed to melt away, leaving behind a sense of peace. We walked back together, hand in hand, ready to face whatever came next.

As we stood there, the snow gently falling around us, I felt the tears streaming down my cheeks. Kylian noticed and, without a word, took off his gloves. He reached up and carefully wiped the tears from my face with his warm, bare hands.

"You're even more beautiful when you smile," he said softly, his voice filled with sincerity.

His touch was gentle, and the warmth of his hands on my skin made me shiver slightly. I wrapped my arms around him, holding him close, and I felt his arms tighten around my waist, pulling me in even more.

He whispered into my ear, his breath warm against my neck, "I never want to see you sad again, not when I'm here."

I looked up at him, my heart swelling with a mixture of joy and relief. "You're such a sap," I teased, a smile breaking through despite my lingering tears.

Kylian chuckled, his laughter soft and melodious. "Guilty as charged," he replied, his eyes crinkling with amusement.

He pulled back slightly, a mischievous glint in his eyes. "I want to see you smile," he said, his tone playful. When I pretended to pout, he leaned in and placed a tender kiss on my neck, making me giggle uncontrollably.

The sound of my laughter seemed to make him even happier. "There's that beautiful smile," he said, grinning.

We stood there for a moment longer, wrapped up in each other, the world around us fading away. The snow continued to fall, and despite the cold, everything felt warm and perfect.

As we settled down on the snowy edge of the lake, Kylian looked at me with an apologetic expression.

"I'm really sorry for everything," he started, his voice earnest. "I know I messed up and I shouldn't have pushed you away."

I gave him a playful, dramatic frown. "Oh, so now you're sorry? After all that?"

He chuckled, his eyes sparkling with mischief. "Yeah, I guess I should have been better at, I don't know, communicating or something."

I pretended to sulk, crossing my arms over my chest. "Well, it's about time you figured that out. You really have a knack for making things complicated."

Kylian laughed softly, shaking his head. "True, true. I've been told I'm not the best at this whole emotional stuff."

He placed his hand gently on top of my head, but I playfully swatted it away. "Don't try to act all comforting now," I said, trying to keep my tone stern.

With a grin, he quickly moved his arm around my shoulders, pulling me close. "Alright, alright. I promise to work on it. How about a truce?" he asked, his voice warm and sincere.

I looked up at him, my heart fluttering despite my efforts to stay annoyed. "A truce, huh? You're lucky you're so charming."

He smiled and gave me a gentle squeeze. "I guess I have my moments," he said softly. "But seriously, I just want us to be okay."

I leaned into him, feeling the comforting warmth of his embrace. "Yeah, I guess we can work on that. Just don't make a habit of making me cry, okay?"

Kylian nodded, his face close to mine. "Deal. No more tears. Just smiles from now on."

He held me close, and for a moment, everything felt right.

Kylian's fingers gently slid my glasses off, his touch sending a shiver down my spine. He gazed at me with a tender smile. "You know," he said softly, "without your glasses, you're even more stunning. I never realized how much your eyes sparkle."

I chuckled, a bit nervously. "Oh really? And here I was thinking you were just trying to flatter me."

He leaned closer, his voice dropping to a seductive whisper. "Flattering you is just an added bonus. What I really want is to kiss you, but I'm not letting you push me away this time."

Before I could respond, his lips were on mine, warm and insistent. The kiss was deep, filled with a mixture of longing and relief. It was as if he was trying to make up for all the lost time and misunderstandings. My resistance melted away, and I found myself kissing him back, the world narrowing down to just the two of us.

Kylian pulled back slightly, his eyes gleaming with a mix of excitement and nervousness. "I wanted to tell you—I'm going to the Olympics," he said, his voice filled with both pride and hope.

Before I could react, he closed the gap between us, kissing me again with a blend of urgency and affection. I pulled away, laughing softly. "Is this your way of announcing big news? Just kiss me and hope I get the message?"

He grinned, brushing a strand of hair from my face. "Well, I figured it's a lot more fun than just saying it outright. But you're not off the hook yet."

As his lips met mine once more, I couldn't help but laugh, the sound bubbling up from my chest. When we finally pulled apart, I looked at him with a smile that felt like it might never fade. "I'm so proud of you, Kylian. You've worked so hard for this."

He wrapped his arms around me, pulling me close. I felt a warmth and contentment I hadn't experienced in a long time. For the first time, everything felt right, and I knew that no matter what challenges lay ahead, we'd face them together.

Kylian's eyes twinkled with mischief as he looked at me. "So, what do you say? Do you want to spend Christmas with me in the United States?"

I raised an eyebrow playfully. "Only if you promise to let me use the bathroom this time. Remember that flight where you made me wait for two hours?"

He laughed, the sound warm and genuine. "How could I forget? I was just trying to see how you'd handle the 'pressure.'"

I rolled my eyes but couldn't suppress a smile. "Well, if you can guarantee a bathroom break, then I'd love to."

He grinned and reached out, taking my freezing hands in his. Gently, he slipped them into his coat pockets, his hands wrapping around mine to warm them. "Deal. I'll make sure you're comfortable this time."

I felt a rush of warmth from his touch, and as we stood there together, the cold seemed to fade away. His presence made everything feel right, and I couldn't help but look forward to the Christmas we'd share.

Kylian leaned in closer, his breath warm against my ear. He whispered, "You know, no matter where we go, as long as I'm with you, it feels like home."

I chuckled, shaking my head. "That was so cheesy," I teased, looking up at him with a smirk.

He pulled back slightly, feigning a hurt expression. "Hey, I'm serious here!" Then, with a playful glint in his eye, he added, "I love you, Humpty Dumpty."

I burst out laughing, the sound echoing around us as I playfully nudged him. "Humpty Dumpty? Really?"

He grinned, his arms tightening around me. "Yeah, because even if you fall, I'll be there to put you back together."

I couldn't help but smile, the warmth in his words melting away any lingering doubts. As he leaned in to kiss me again, I knew there was no one else I'd rather be with.

And as we stood there, wrapped in each other's embrace, I felt whole—like all the broken pieces had finally come together.